MICHELLE VERNAL LIVES in Christchurch, New Zealand with her husband, two teenage sons and attention seeking tabby cats, Humphrey and Savannah. Before she started writing novels, she had a variety of jobs:

Pharmacy shop assistant, girl who sold dried up chips and sausages at a hot food stand in a British pub, girl who sold nuts (for 2 hours) on a British market stall, receptionist, P.A...Her favourite job though is the one she has now – writing stories she hopes leave her readers with a satisfied smile on their face.

If you'd like to know when Michelle's next book is coming out you can click here to receive her newsletter http://tiny.cc/0r27az

To say thank you, you'll receive a short New Year's Eve O'Mara family story.

https://www.michellevernalbooks.com/
https://www.facebook.com/michellevernalnovelist/
https://www.bookbub.com/authors/michelle-vernal

Also by Michelle Vernal
The Cooking School on the Bay
Second-hand Jane
Staying at Eleni's
The Traveller's Daughter
Sweet Home Summer
When We Say Goodbye
The Promise
And...
Introducing: The Guesthouse on the Green
Book 1 - O'Mara's
Book 2 – Moira Lisa Smile
Book 3- What Goes on Tour
Book 4 – Rosi's Regrets
Book 5 – Christmas at O'Mara's
Book 6 - A Wedding at O'Mara's
Book 7 – Maureen's Song
Book 8 –The O'Mara's in LaLa Land
Coming soon...
The Autumn Posy, Liverpool Brides series
All Available on Amazon

The
Dancer
Michelle Vernal

For Dad

THIS BOOK IS WRITTEN from the heart and dedicated to my beautiful Dad. The best kind of Dad, the kind who never let me down and always made me feel I had a safety net. He pushed swings for hours, mended my broken hearts, ferried me around, advised but never dictated and always listened, encouraged and was there if things didn't work out as planned. He was patient and thoughtful. He was kind and he made us laugh, a lot. He walked me down the aisle, became a great friend to my husband and had grandchildren who adored him, we all did. I love him, my dad. xxx

Chapter 1
Veronica

VERONICA PLUNGED HER fork into the fat wedge of triple layered mud cake and popped it in her mouth. She knew before her taste buds had time to acknowledge what they were being served up that no matter how sweet its taste it would still be bittersweet. Today, March the tenth was Isabel's birthday. She'd be turning twenty-seven and it was this knowledge that yet another year had ticked by that would turn the chocolate ganache slightly bitter.

She was eating the decadent dessert not because she'd had a craving for cake but because it was tradition. Her tradition. It was a tradition that involved unearthing the shoebox from the shelf in her wardrobe first thing in the morning too. It was tucked in behind the pile of sweaters she'd folded up hoping not to have need of them again until next winter. She'd pushed them aside and slid the box out before carrying it over to her unmade bed. Perching on the edge of the mattress, she'd taken the lid off casting it aside to allow her fingers to touch the precious bits and pieces contained inside. A small photograph, a plastic identity bracelet, paperwork and Isabel's blanket. She'd sat for an age remembering and wondering, a tear sliding down her cheek.

She'd only moved when Haydn bellowed, 'Mum! Hurry up. We'll be late.' It was an about-turn given it was usually her shouting the sentiment and, brushing the tear away, she'd put the box back from where she'd gotten it. She wouldn't look at it again for another year. She'd learned a long time ago that some memories were too painful to touch and she had the boys to think of, she couldn't wallow. It wouldn't be fair but she was allowed to today, on Bel's birthday.

Her morning ritual with the memory box and this cake ceremony of sorts had been her way of marking Isabel's birthday for the last twenty-seven years and she wasn't about to stop now even if she was supposed to be watching her calorie intake.

An attractive young woman with mid-brown hair who reminded her of her younger self minced into the café shaking off the chill of early spring. Her hair was pulled back in a low ponytail and she was dressed in a high-necked leopard spot blouse with a pencil skirt and black, heeled ankle boots. She stood eyeing the cabinet of food and Veronica wondered what she did for a job. Her confident air and clothes suggested something high-powered and, realising she was staring, she forced herself to look away before she got caught out. She'd be around the same age as Bel and the tug of loss came keenly.

Chapter 2
Isabel

HER BIRTH MOTHER'S name was Veronica Kelly or it had been twenty-seven years ago. She was married now, separated according to her Facebook page, and her name was Veronica Stanley. She was forty-four years old with twin sons who were fourteen. Isabel had worked their age out from the last post on Veronica's social media feed, two years ago; it was of their twelfth birthdays. Her birth mother had let social media slide after that with only one other entry to say Veronica Stanley was at Sunny Days Caravan Park in Devon. Isabel stared greedily at the screen scrolling through the pictures of Veronica and her boys, Haydn and Hunter. She was sitting at their dining table the laptop open in front of her.

She tried to imagine herself tacked into the middle of their tableau. Where would she slot in? Would they even want her to? Then the familiar churning as to how even thinking those thoughts would make her parents feel revved up. She should be happy with what she had because she was far luckier than some, most even, but still there was a tug, a need to spend time with these people on the screen in front of her.

How would it make Veronica feel to know she was, at that this moment in time, scouring her Facebook posts? She scanned the boys faces and Veronica's for physical similarities deciding she had the same eyes as her birth mother and, although the boys' eyes were darker, they were shaped like almonds as were hers. They didn't share the small bump in their noses she had in common with Veronica though, lucky them, and where she and Veronica had a smattering of freckles and pale skin that burned easily the boys had the sort that would tan to a mahogany in summer. Twins! Didn't they run down family lines? She couldn't imagine one baby at the moment let alone two. Not that she didn't want children because she did, but not just yet.

She touched her finger to the screen in wonder. This lady had given birth to her. It was strange to think of it and that nineties movies her mum had on DVD sprang to mind, *Sliding Doors*. If different choices had been made, she could have had a completely different life. She'd never thought she'd have siblings but she did and there, frozen in time on the screen in front of her, was the proof. Two beautiful brothers. Were they outgoing or shy? It was hard to tell from photographs although she fancied she could see a cheeky glint in both their eyes. Was Veronica a nice person? The sort of person who'd check in on an elderly neighbour to make sure they were okay or was she self-centred and all about herself and her boys? She felt Rhodri's breath on her neck as he leaned over her shoulder to see what she was up to.

'Put yourself out of your misery, Isabel, and write to her.'

'But I don't know what to say or what I even want from her.'

'Tell her about yourself,' he said, planting his hands on her shoulders. 'And tell her you'd like the opportunity to meet her. Baby steps. Don't overthink it.'

Isabel was the queen of overthinking and she'd been doing plenty of it. A part of her was frightened of reaching out only to be rebuffed. There was no guarantee Veronica would be pleased to hear from her. There were no guarantees if they did meet up that they'd like one another. It was all so very uncertain and Isabel didn't like uncertainty. For all she knew, Veronica might have closed the page permanently on the chapter of her life in which Isabel had been born and not want reminding of it.

'It just feels—'

'Disloyal, I know, you've said, but it doesn't change how you feel about your mum and dad. You've a right to be curious and for all you know, Veronica might be desperate for you to get in touch.'

Veronica couldn't access Isabel's adoption records, contact had to be initiated by her. This was something Isabel had been grateful for growing up, insomuch as she didn't know how she would have felt if her birth mother had suddenly appeared on the scene. It would have dented the security of growing up Isabel Stark, the daughter of Babs and Gazzer who were a bit mad but whom she loved wholeheartedly. They were solid and could be counted on and that's what good parents were all about.

It hadn't been easy asking her parents if she could have her adoption records. She'd seen the hurt flash in her mum's eyes and understood it was hard for her. She was frightened of losing her daughter, something Isabel had told her emphatically would never happen. She hadn't done anything initially with the information Babs had presented in a plain manilla folder but she had it and when the time had felt right, she'd begun to try to find Veronica. Now she had, she didn't know what to do.

'I've bought you a present,' Rhodri said, moving over to the sideboard and opening the top drawer.

'What is it?'

'Close your eyes.'

Isabel did so, feeling a soft breeze as something thumped down on the table in front of her.

'Okay, open them.'

It was a pen, along with a pretty writing set.

'Write to her, Isabel,' Rhodri said before planting a kiss on top of her forehead. 'You've no excuse not to now.'

'No excuse not to,' she echoed.

Chapter 3
Veronica

AT FORTY-FOUR AND THREE-quarter years of age, Veronica Stanley had officially become an invisible woman. Oh, she hadn't donned her cloak, Harry Potter style and vanished as such but she had just been blanked. The Patels' oldest lad who worked at the family newsagents come the university holidays had looked right through her. He'd flicked back his greasy fringe to ring up a bag of crisps instead of the chocolate bar she was first in the line waiting to buy. The salt and vinegar flavoured Walkers were in the hand of a girl with hair down to her waist, crayoned in eyebrows and sprayed on jeans. Veronica knew all this because she'd unconsciously scanned the teenager's face. *Was Bel like that at that age?*

The girl was all of sixteen if she was a day and if Veronica's nose served her right and it usually did, given her job, she'd drenched herself, like a sheep being dipped, in Vera Wang's Princess perfume. She shot the girl a look that said queue-jumper and then, eyes flitting from her to him, she tapped her foot while love's young dream embarked on the youthful version of flirtatious banter.

'Me and my squad are going to the Minstrel tonight.' The girl flicked her hair back and nearly took Veronica's eye out.

'That club's supposed to be lit but I'm trying to save my cheddar.' Greasy fringe flick.

'Yolo.' Eyelash bat.

Veronica rolled her eyes; it was like listening to a foreign language and given she was the mother of two teenage sons she should be up with the play. But come on, whatever happened to would you like to go out with me sometime?

'Yeah, you're right. Me and my bruv might check it out.' Eyebrow raise of acknowledgement.

'Dope.' Lip-glossed half smile.

She'd been tempted at that point to slam the chocolate bar down on the counter and march out of the shop. The only thing stopping her was she knew she'd regret a rashly made decision come her morning tea break at work. It was her Saturday morning treat. Having said that, what she should be having as a mid-morning snack was carrots and hummus sticks but sadly they were nowhere near as creamy or satisfying as a Galaxy bar. That was another thing about being forty-four and three-quarters, her metabolism had decided to grind to a halt. This was something Abi her younger sister was keen to point out happened to women approaching their mid-forties. In the end it was two things that swayed her decision in the chocolate bar's favour and saw her stand her ground. The first being chocolate and coffee were a partnership made in heaven and the second being it wouldn't be fair to breathe garlic hummus breath all over her customers.

The gruesome twosome eyed one another and Veronica cleared her throat excessively. The girl took the hint and with one last hair flick wiggled her bum out of the shop.

It wasn't only the Patel boy, Veronica mused, the buzzer sounding as she left the shop, Galaxy bar in her hot little hand. It was little things like the way people's eyes would move past her as she walked down the street. It was as though she wasn't there. A ghost. Granted, the uniform she wore five days a week and on Saturday mornings wasn't exactly eye-popping. A navy blouse tucked into black trousers, or navy, or black tights under a knee length skirt. Her footwear, Hush Puppies black, slip-on shoes.

She'd never thought the day would come when comfortable footwear was a priority. The Hush Puppies weren't uniform and they were a far cry from the dainty ballet slippers she'd once spent her time in, but when you were on your feet all day there was a lot to be said for sensible footwear. Sometimes, when she closed her eyes, she'd conjure that salty smell of passion mingling with hairspray and sweat and she was back there once more behind the curtains, adrenalin beginning to course.

She also liked to imagine what Heidi, her line manager, would do if she broke rank and wore fishnet stockings under her navy skirt, or impossibly high red strappy sandals. Her old pal, Saskia, had been on holiday to Cuba last year and she said that was how the women working at the airport in

Havana dressed. Go girls, she'd thought, hearing this and had wound up with that old Eurythmics hit Aretha Franklin had joined in on, *Sisters Are Doin' It for Themselves*, stuck in her head all day.

It rankled being talked down to by Heidi, a girl barely out of school, especially given her long service to Blakeley's department store. She'd worked on the perfume counter there since the boys had been old enough to attend nursery. She loved her job too, the stories behind the different perfumes learned at the various training schools she'd been sent to over the years caught and fired her imagination. Like dance had once upon a time. It was what made her a good salesperson. It was also was why Heidi wouldn't give the Saturday shift she resented having to work to young Sophie who did the late-night Thursday for her.

'You've had the training, Veronica, and Saturday is the busiest day of the week in the parfumerie,' Heidi would say in that snippy little upstart manner of hers. What she wouldn't say but what hung heavily in the air between them was that Blakeley's had paid for Veronica to attend the various perfume training schools and as such they intended to get their pound of flesh. Heidi didn't believe in work-life balance. She was also the sort of person who managed to look busy even when they weren't doing much of anything. She'd perfected the art and would often be heard as she marched around the shop floor, sighing over how busy she was. Busy my arse, Veronica would think.

At twenty-six the line manager had no dependents and still lived at home with her mum who probably cooked her dinners and did her washing for her. What she wouldn't give to get off the treadmill and not spend her free time catching up on the one hundred and one things she hadn't managed to get around to in the week. How lovely it would be to spend some time with her boys that didn't involve nagging at them to get their lazy backsides into gear and help her.

Veronica aimed her keys at the red Ford Fiesta, shivering in the chilled morning air. The colour made her feel like she was driving a sports car. It made her feel young and carefree. The boys said the car was cringey. It was their new catchphrase and apparently their mother was 'cringe' full stop. Come to that everything in the boys' world where adults were concerned was an embarrassment these days. To be fair though, they'd gotten so tall of late they did look funny sitting in it with their hair grazing the roof. Unlocking it she settled herself in behind the wheel.

She picked up the banana she'd tossed on the passenger seat for breakfast and peeling it, a long-ago incident sprang to mind. She couldn't help but smile as she took a bite before buckling in. She'd not long left school, and back then was working in Miss Selfridge. It wasn't her dream job but she had the best wardrobe along with an enormous shop bill. There she'd been on her lunch break, making the most of the glorious day and trying to get a spot of colour on her lily-white legs in the parklike grounds of the old abbey.

She'd peeled the skin back from a banana and had been about to take a bite when she'd spotted the chap, old enough to be her dad had he stuck around and not gone and gotten himself killed, sitting on a nearby bench. He had a newspaper open in front of him, not that he was reading it. He was too busy staring over the top of it, mesmerised by her mouth and the banana. It dawned on her as she looked at the phallic shape she was holding that he wasn't thinking about how much he liked bananas and so she took a vicious, teeth bared chomp from it. It had been satisfying to see him grimace and cross his legs tightly before burying his nose in his paper.

Veronica turned the ignition and sighed all the way from the tip of her shoes. It was ironic given as a woman barely out of her teens she'd once bemoaned the attention she'd gotten from the opposite sex. 'All men are perverts,' she'd declared with passion to Saskia, who'd nodded, equally emphatic in her agreement. Nowadays she could dance around the park bloody naked and nobody would notice. Okay, she was exaggerating but it had been over a year since she'd had a wolf whistle and it didn't count given it was from a flipping bird. The only bonus being she'd dined out on the story of her having donned her Lycra activewear before striding off on a power walk in an attempt to gee up her metabolism. She'd stood straighter, had even done a hair flick of her own when she'd heard the whistle, glancing around to see who the culprit was, just in case he was cute. You never knew your luck; only she should have known her luck.

It had taken her a moment to pinpoint him, he was swinging on his perch inside his cage which hung in the doorway of number 19. George the cockatoo. She used to stop and say 'Who's a pretty boy then,' making kissy noises at him back in the days when Haydn and Hunter had still wanted her to walk them to school. George was getting payback.

Veronica indicated and pulled out in the gap in the traffic, taking another bite of the fruit. It should stave off any rumblings until morning tea.

A FIRM BELIEVER IN stock rotation, both at work and in her own kitchen cupboards, Veronica was placing the order of cellophane wrapped boxes she'd ignored yesterday in an orderly row behind the sole remaining box already on the shelf. A man moved into her peripheral vision and, glad of something to distract her on what was proving to be an unusually slow Saturday morning, she paused her task to give him a sneaky once-over instead. His suit had to be bespoke she concluded eyeing the soft, wool fabric in a jacquard grey check managing to resist the urge to stroke the luxury material. It fitted his lanky, definitely not skinny frame too well not to be.

She waited impatiently for him to look her way and give an indication of requiring assistance but the manner in which he was scanning the men's fragrance shelf told her he knew what he wanted and was best left to it. The seconds ticked on and fed up with waiting she was about to say 'hello', the first rule of sales was to always approach the customer with an open greeting, when he plucked a rectangular box from the shelf. He scanned the text on the back.

It was as she'd thought, he was a man who knew what he wanted and at that moment she fell a teeny bit in love with him as she spied his chosen aftershave. Tom Ford's latest men's fragrance, Beau De Jour. It was a scent she could imagine on the pillow next to hers at night and the thought made her shiver. The cologne was pitched as classic, sharp, and maverick for the perfectly groomed gentleman and she'd always had a soft spot for gentlemen.

Her dad had been a gentleman and it might seem old-fashioned but she'd loved the way he always walked on the roadside of her mother and held doors open. Okay, so upping and leaving not just his wife but his children too, for a younger model, hadn't been very gentlemanlike but nobody deserved the sort of karma he'd gotten. He'd died in a car accident not long after he moved away and Veronica and Abi had been told by their mother, he wouldn't be coming back so they needed to put him from their minds. She never spoke of him again. It was as if he'd been chalk on a blackboard and she'd wiped him off in one swipe.

She also knew in marrying Jason with his good-looks and easy charm, she'd married a version of her lost father. It was what daughters did. It was why Abi had lurched from relationship to relationship and her mother had refused to trust in another man beyond a few casual dates too. Thinking of Jason sent an instant spike of irritation through her because her ex was sporting a lovely tan at the moment. He'd just spent a week in Ibiza despite him giving her constant earache about what he had to pay in maintenance.

She wouldn't mind a holiday. What bliss to flop poolside while the boys grazed the all-day buffet and she devoured a good book and, since she was daydreaming, she might as well throw in a handsome Spaniard who couldn't take his eyes off her. A holiday wasn't on the cards though, not with a mortgage and said boys, teenage twins, who despite their lean builds put away enough food on a daily basis to feed a small village. Jason was good with the boys when it suited him but the way he carried on about opening his wallet to help out with all the extras having two strapping sons brought, you'd think he'd had nothing to do with the actual conception of them.

She'd married Jason or the Useless Git as she called him when the mood took her in her early twenties and they'd been separated for five years now. He was an electrician who'd plugged another woman's socket. Neither of them had gotten around to doing the proper divorce bit. It was on her never ending to-do list. Despite the length of time they'd been apart she was still his first port of call for advice and help but then he'd always been needy. She'd love to muster up the courage to tell him to fuck off when he showed up to see if there was a spare plate going for dinner, or if she could sew a button back on his shirt but, truth be told, she was frightened if she did, he would. It wouldn't be her that would bear the consequences if she said her piece, it would be the boys.

To be fair to her fickle ex, he was a man who needed to feel he was the centre of her attention and it must have been hard to love a woman who wasn't whole. She'd always held a part of herself back from everyone because that part belonged to Bel. It was a part he knew he'd never be able to fill.

Jason hadn't coped with taking second place when she'd been trying to cope with two babies, thank God for her mum! But they'd gotten through that and come out the other side or, so she'd thought. They'd plodded along happily enough, no marriage was perfect after all. When her mum got sick though, her time was once more consumed elsewhere. The boys were ten when he announced he was moving to greener pastures.

The anger that still lurked over his leaving her when she'd needed him most smacked her in the face. Twin boys, a mother who'd been diagnosed with early-onset Alzheimer's, a sister who flitted in and out of their lives when she saw fit, and he'd gone and left her for a younger woman. As soon as Greta, his girlfriend had made noises about wanting a baby he'd been out of there and these days he was a lad about town. A long-in-the-tooth lad she thought, shoving her ex aside because Suit-man as she'd decided to nickname him was about to place his purchase down on the counter. She straightened the row of pretty pink Miss Dior boxes and turned around with a smile.

His hand was thrust in his pocket, searching for his wallet presumably, and she watched as it moved on from his trouser pocket to patting down his jacket. She bit her lip so as not to smile, noticing the coffee stain on his tie. There was no wedding band or telltale white ring mark where one had recently been on his finger either.

'Ah, there it is.' He pulled the errant wallet from the inside pocket of his jacket looking at her for the first time with a sheepish, almost shy grin. 'Sorry about that.'

His hair was salt and pepper brown and in need of a trim and his eyes were deep, the colour of dark-washed denim. His jawline, which once would have been chiselled making him almost too handsome, was showing the softening of middle age and was stubbled which gave him a slightly unkempt air. It was decidedly sexy, Veronica thought, but it was his smile that caught and held her in its embrace making her knees feel trembly.

Her knees hadn't felt that way, apart from when she'd attempted the power walking, since Jason had first pinned her in his line of sight. His grey eyes had sparkled with the promise of things to come. This man smiled with his whole face in a way that told her he was without guile and she found herself beaming back at him. Crumbs, how fortuitous she'd gone for the Galaxy bar because this was definitely not a hummus breath moment.

'Lavender, moss and amber, classic aromatic accords; you've made a good choice,' she said taking the Beau De Jour and holding it up as though posing for an advertisement. She cringed as the words popped forth from her mouth.

Suit-man looked taken aback she saw with a quick glance up at him before she slid the aftershave into a Blakeley's bag.

'Good to know, thanks.' He grinned.

Cringe, cringe, cringe as her boys would say.

She completed the sales transaction, all fingers and thumbs, conscious of him watching her. She held his gaze a tad too long and he took the bag from her with a lazy smile and thank you. A feeling of dissatisfaction that the transaction was complete stole over her as she watched him go but a split second later her breath snagged. Instead of striding out of her life he'd walked straight into the MAC lipstick stand causing young Tyrone to startle, his hand fluttering to his chest as Suit-man apologised profusely, casting a flustered, red-faced glance back at her. She liked him all the more for being human.

Chapter 4
Isabel

ISABEL STARK
Pier View House (upstairs flat, above the Leap of Faith Art Gallery)
The Esplanade
Ryde
Isle of Wight
Dear Veronica,

I hope this letter doesn't come as too much of a shock and if it is a shock then I hope it is a good one. My name's Isabel Stark and I'm your birth daughter. I decided to reach out to you now because recent experiences made me think about things differently. I suppose they made me look at my adoption from your perspective not just my own and I hope that doesn't make me sound terribly selfish. The saying goes there's two sides to every story but where adoption's concerned, there's three. I want to tell you my story.

I'm an only child but I don't think I've been spoiled as a result. I never went without anything but there wasn't lots of money to go round in our house either. I'd have liked a sibling but it wasn't to be and in the end that was okay because it's what I know. I had a wonderfully, ordinary childhood with my parents, Barbara and Gary who everyone calls Babs and Gaz. They are salt of the earth people.

I grew up in Southampton and there's not a lot to tell you about that. I did okay at school but was hardly the brain of Britain. I wasn't sporty. I was too much of a dreamer for that. I think I could have done better at school if I'd known what I wanted to do with myself once I'd left. Actually, I did know what I wanted to do and that was the problem. I wanted to sing. I spent my time in class and on the sports field or in the gym dreaming about that instead of paying attention to what I was supposed to be doing.

I've always loved to sing and I have a good voice but to be professional you need more than that and I never had the confidence to perform in front of others. I only ever sang in the shower or bath and the thought of stepping out onto a stage on my own was terrifying so I did nothing about it and just drifted along instead.

I worked a few dead-end jobs in the ensuing years and was in a relationship I thought was going to be long-term until he cheated on me with my friend. It was humiliating to say the least but at least it spurred me into action. I took off travelling to put some distance between myself and what happened and I wound up having the best time. There's such an amazing sense of freedom when you're in a new country with no responsibilities to anyone other than yourself and the opportunity is there to be whomever you want to be.

I spent my time abroad working, exploring, and having fun in Australia and didn't want to go home without jumping the ditch as the Aussies and Kiwis call visiting one another's country. It was when I was in New Zealand that something happened. It changed the course of, well, everything.

I was road-tripping in a camper van with my friend when we came across an accident in the middle of nowhere. There was only one car involved with a single occupant, the driver who was an elderly woman. She wasn't in a good way but was still conscious and I held her hand until she passed away. She told me in those last minutes she'd wanted to go back to the Isle of Wight, that she was wrong and she should never have left. Before the light went out of her eyes she made me promise I'd tell Constance she was sorry. Of course, I had no idea who Constance was or why she was sorry but I did know I had to keep the promise I'd made her.

It's a long story and it began when I went to the woman's funeral. Her name was Virginia or Ginny as everyone called her. Her son Teddy and his wife and daughter had flown in for the funeral from Hong Kong where they live. I learned Ginny hailed from Southampton originally but had ties to Ryde on the Isle of Wight. Hearing this was a goosebumps moment, it was too coincidental but then my whole journey through to now has been full of coincidences. So much so, I half believe Ginny's been looking down on me orchestrating everything, trying to put things right. I felt like it was fate that I was the one who held her hand when she died and I couldn't get her or the promise I'd made out of my head.

I arrived back in Southampton shortly after this and found myself a fish out of water. It's strange when you've been away because you come home expecting things to be the same as they were when you left, only time doesn't stand still. Oh, Mum, Dad and our corgi, Prince Charles (Mum's a staunch royalist) were the same, they don't change thank goodness but my old friends had moved on. I didn't know where I fit and with nothing keeping me there, I set off on a quest of sorts to the Isle of Wight to find Constance. It sounds completely mad, I know, but it all worked out.

I got a job the day I arrived on the island, behind the bar in a local pub called The Rum Den, here in Ryde where I live. The landlady put me up for the night and then the next day I set off to door knock at various rest homes in the area. I was walking down the Esplanade which if you've never been to Ryde, straddles the sea when I spotted a sign advertising a room to let in the window of an art gallery. The gallery was called A Leap of Faith and the owner was a rather good-looking Welshman called Rhodri who lived in the two-bed (the third's a study) flat above his gallery. He was looking for someone to rent the spare room and split the household bills. I thought the flat with its views out over the water was lovely and moved in straight away, pleased to have found both work and somewhere to live so quickly while I looked for Constance.

I didn't have to look for long because when I confided in Rhodri what I was up to, he told me he'd bought the building, Pier View House from a woman called Constance Downer. He said she was one of the island's more colourful characters. A firm believer in the healing powers of herbs, she'd run Constance's Cure-alls, from what's now his gallery, selling natural remedies for years. Her shop had been an island institution with some of the locals whispering she was a witch but this only added to her allure and brought the curious customers flocking in.

I went to Sea Vistas the care home she was residing in to find out if she was the woman I was looking for. She was, and by now you'll understand what I meant about coincidences. Meeting Constance changed my life, and hers too, though neither of us knew it would the first time we met.

Ginny, I found out was Constance's sister-in-law. Constance lost her brother, Ginny's husband during the war and poor Ginny suffered a stillbirth not long after. Constance, who was sixteen at the time met and fell in love with a Canadian air force man stationed on the island and he was killed in a bombing in the building where she now lives, Sea Vistas. Back in the war it served as a convalescent home for servicemen. She was devastated and she was also pregnant. It was decided Ginny would adopt Constance's baby and bring the child up alongside the family in Pier View House. Instead, she disappeared with the baby, a boy, as soon as the papers were signed and the first Constance knew of what had happened to her son was when I came to pass on Ginny's last words to her.

So many wonderful things have happened since then. Constance's story was a sad one but it has a happy ending. I helped her reconnect with her son, Teddy. She's become a big part of my life. It was Constance who opened my eyes to the power of natural healing and it's down to her encouragement that I'm on my way to qualifying as a Naturopath. She's also a driving force behind my decision to reach out to you.

I work at The Natural Way and for the first time in my life have a job I love. It's a herbal health store around the corner from where I live and Delwyn, my friend who owns it, has asked me to go into business with her. I'm pretty excited about that. Delwyn's partner is a drop-dead gorgeous potter called Nico and when I first met her I thought she had designs on Rhodri. He was taking pottery lessons from Nico at the time and I got it in my head she was offering lessons with benefits. Turned out it wasn't him she was interested in at all. I hadn't a clue she was gay! It worked out well for me that she was destined to be with Delwyn because I wound up with my lovely Rhodri and he makes me smile every day.

I'm singing too and not just in the shower. I finally got up on the stage. I joined an acapella group called The Angels of Wight. It's lots of fun being part of something so much bigger than just myself and it's given me confidence. Hmm, what else? I can't cook to save myself but fortunately Rhodri is a whizz in the kitchen. He's chief cook and I'm the bottle washer. I love classical music too. I always have which is weird given Mum and Dad are rockers of old who love nothing better than cranking up a bit of Springsteen. They fancy themselves Southampton's answer to Bruce and Patti lip-syncing and playing air guitar along to the Boss's music. It has to be seen to be believed! Oh, and I have a secret crush. Andréa Bocelli, I adore him and my dream is to one day see him perform at Teatro del Silenzio in Tuscany. I'll get there one of these days.

So, there you have it, that's me. I've wondered about you a lot over the years, Veronica, and would love to meet you and your sons. I'd like to talk to you about who my father is too. You can write to me at the address on the envelope or if you'd rather ring or email, these are my details:

isabelstark@thenaturalway.co.uk

07716 434391

I hope we can connect and I hope this letter hasn't brought up unhappy memories.

xxx Isabel

ISABEL PUT THE PEN down on the table and flexed her fingers. She'd debated with herself over how to sign off for the longest time but yours faithfully or yours sincerely were too formal and to use the word love didn't seem right. Love was earned. It grew. It wasn't automatic.

A briny breeze was drifting in through the open window and she could hear the familiar thrum of early afternoon activity on the street below. Saturday's were always busy on the island as visitors and locals alike ventured out and about. It had been her turn to work the morning shift at The Natural Way with Delwyn relieving her at midday. She'd come straight home to write the letter knowing she'd not be able to settle at anything else until she'd got everything she wanted to say down on paper.

She folded it and placed it in an envelope leaving it unsealed. A plate with the crumbs of the sandwich she'd slapped together for a quick lunch decorating it sat next to her cup of tea. It would have a skin on it by now she thought. She'd been so absorbed in what she was writing she'd forgotten to drink it. Pushing her chair back she got up and stretched before carrying them over to the sink. She tipped the cold tea down the drain and rinsed the cup and plate.

She'd lost count of how many times she'd written versions of this letter only to screw them up and toss them in the bin. There were only two sheaves of paper left in the set Rhodri had bought her. Was she giving too much of herself away? Did she sound like a crackpot? Maybe she'd be better getting straight to the point of why she was writing and leave it there. The questions butted for attention making her feel anxious and she made up her mind she'd go and see Constance next chance she got and ask her opinion on this latest effort.

She left the dishes to drain and rolling her shoulders tried to ease the knots in them. It didn't help so she decided to try her luck downstairs because if the gallery was quiet, Rhodri might just give her a shoulder rub. He'd be pleased she'd finally gotten the words down and in an envelope.

SHE FOUND HIM SITTING behind the counter reading a letter of his own. The gallery, she saw with a quick glance around the shop floor, was quiet. There was a pile of half-opened mail scattered next to him. Bills mostly by the look of it. Rhodri's gaze flicked up at her, his usually toffee coloured skin, a throwback to his Celtic heritage, pale.

'Are you okay?' Isabel asked.

He shook the paper he was holding. 'It's from Sally.'

Chapter 5

Veronica

ST REBUS'S CENTRE IN the old Tudor market town a hop, skip and a jump from London where Veronica had lived all her life was teeming with shoppers. None of whom she'd have to serve now Blakeley's was closed for the afternoon. She'd rue the day the department store ever decided to extend their Saturday opening hours past one o'clock like their high street counterparts had done. A young woman with more carrier bags than was sensible nudged her as she strode past. Her lack of apology dropped Veronica right back into her invisible woman rhetoric of earlier that morning.

She'd left her car where she always left it on a Saturday, tucked away down Eason Lane, a cobbled, narrow, one-way side street where she could more often than not nab a spot for the morning. There was no employee parking at Blakeley's. The bag she'd tossed on the backseat that morning was still there. It had been hard to resist the temptation not to lose herself in memories as she opened the plastic container full of her old dance costumes and other accoutrements earlier that morning, but there'd been no time for that and she'd rifled through the layers of tulle and satin until she'd found the leotard she was after.

The traffic was light given the time of day and it wasn't long before she'd edged away from the town centre into the suburbs. It was only a matter of minutes before the rows of houses had given way to a smattering of posh converted barns, on acreage of the sort you'd see on those home renovation programmes. She angled off to the right and bounced down the lane that would take her to Holly Grange House; now there was nothing but fields and livestock either side of her. Her mood lifted as she spied the bright yellow bobbing heads of daffodils. Spring was her favourite time of year. Nobody could be miserable in spring, well not for long anyway, she thought, keeping her finger to herself as a farmer's vehicle nosed out of the hedgerow too quickly for her liking.

She'd only managed to listen to three songs off her playlist when the gates to the house loomed in front of her. She left the car idling to get out and enter her passcode; it was easier than hanging halfway out the window. The iron palings began to groan their way apart and she slid back behind the wheel in time to nip through them, her car crunching over the gravel.

'Sorry, Elton,' she muttered as she nosed in between two cars and switched him off mid flow. She reached over into the back seat and grabbed the bag before getting out of the car. She stood there staring up at the two-storey Victorian, red-brick home with its sturdy chimney stacks and gabled windows.

It still took her by surprise each time she visited that this rather grand old house that had once been presided over by a lord and lady of the manor was now her mum's home. She didn't know if she'd ever get used to it. The Virginia creeper that covered the entrance was beginning to green up once more. It had been splendid last autumn when her mum had first moved in with its fiery hues.

A carer she didn't recognise, her hair pulled back in a ponytail, attired in the pale blue tunic top with its band of pink flowers and blue pants the staff wore, appeared in the entrance and Veronica gathered herself. She couldn't stand here gawping at the building all afternoon. Taking a deep breath, she told herself to pretend she was about to dance out from behind the red velvet curtains and with her smile firmly in place she breezed in, greeting the receptionist before putting her hand to the scanner box. Hearing it click she pushed the door to her mother's wing open, ensuring her smile was still intact. Being greeted by the sight of her long face would not do her mum or any of the other residents any good. A long face wouldn't do her any good for that matter. If you smiled long enough and hard enough, eventually you forgot all about the daily grind. She knew this from experience although some days it was harder than others to keep her teeth gritted and grin in place.

Whenever she entered the spacious, light-filled living area she fancied she could be boarding a cruise ship minus a buffet. It was the furnishings that did it, they were luxurious but somewhat impersonal. An interior designer had waved his or her magic wand over the place with stylish groupings of ornaments, always in threes, on artfully placed corner tables and an array of beautifully framed paintings of landscapes and bowls of fruit adorned the walls. Only, instead of being one of those themed cruises for nineties music fiends, or ballroom dancers, it was a cruise for those afflicted by the memory thief.

She caught a whiff of something and pinpointed it as a roast meat that must have been served at lunchtime. At least she couldn't smell cabbage. Her friend Saskia's horrified face when she'd told her her mother had gone into care floated to mind. 'Please don't tell me the place smells of cabbage and piss.'

'Of course it doesn't, not for what it's bloody costing,' she'd replied, grateful for her mother's squirrelled away nest egg which had been plumped up considerably by an unexpected and large sum of money a great aunt, whom none of them had ever met, had bequeathed her. She and her mum had visited Holly Grange when she was well enough to absorb that this was where she'd one day live and, while not happy about the prospect, she'd said, 'If I have to live in a care home then I'll jolly well make it a posh one.'

'Where'd you get that idea from?' she'd asked Saskia, affronted at the very idea.

'My nana was in a place like that, I used to dread having to visit her of a Sunday. It was ridiculous when I think about it because Mum always made me and Rona put on our Sunday best. Holly Hobby ankle socks, the works, to go see her. Nana couldn't have given a toss what we were wearing or whether we were there or not.'

'You don't know that. The aging brain's still a mystery and there's not so much of a sniff of cabbage or the other at Mum's place, thanks very much,' Veronica had said, her guilt at no longer being able to care for her mother herself making her defensive. It would have been easier if she could have shared the load with her younger sister, Abigail. Abi had her head well and truly buried in the sand where their mother was concerned though and so it had fallen to Veronica to sort it all out as per usual.

'She's not going to get better,' Veronica had told her one afternoon, fed up with her bleating on about how she didn't think Holly Grange was a good idea. 'And do you plan on taking over her care? Because it's not easy Abi and I can't imagine Brandon taking too kindly to having her about the place. If I can't manage, I don't know how you think you're going to. She needs full-time care now because if she goes wandering anything could happen. Besides it's what Mum wanted, you know that. She didn't want either of us giving up our jobs to become full-time caregivers. She said we're her daughters not her carers and it should stay that way. I've got the boys to think of too.' Things had escalated from there, with Abi resorting to her usual taunt of 'Saint Veronica.' She knew how much it annoyed her big sister.

Making the decision that the time had come for her mum to go had been the second hardest thing she'd ever had to do. She'd gotten to the point where she could no longer be left on her own in the day and was needing more and more help with everything from toileting, showering and dressing to eating. She'd bundled her off to Holly Grange with her suitcase full of labelled clothes, as per the instruction sheet she'd been given, and kept a cheery façade up right up until it was time for her to go. Her mother had sat on the bed in her new room with her hands clasped on her lap, the tears rolling down her cheeks utterly bewildered as to why she was there. It had broken Veronica's heart and she'd sobbed all the way home just as she had on the twins' first day of school. At least her mum hadn't bitten any of the carer's hands like Hunter had done when the teacher had tried to detach him from her leg.

Now as she wandered into the space where the residents whiled away their days, she could feel the carpet plush beneath her feet, no sound of Nurse Ratched's, from *One Flew Over the Cuckoo's Nest*, shoes clipping down echoing corridors at cosy Holly Grange. Veronica waved hello to Helen. The carer was leading a sing-song, valiantly clapping her hands trying to gee-up the semi-circle of residents seated around her. A quick scan of the disinterested faces revealed her mother wasn't amongst them. She could hear music being played and moved over to the alcove where the armchairs were positioned around the large flat screen TV on the wall. André Rieu filled the screen along with his vibrant waltz playing orchestra. Her mother was ensconced in a striped chair, almost dwarfed by the plump cushions. She'd always been small. A dainty, attractive woman, born to sing and dance who never got the chance and so had lived her dream vicariously for a short time through her eldest daughter. Lately she seemed shrunken.

Margo was mesmerised by the dancing pastel shades in front of her. Her hands were mimicking the conductor's as she sat lost in the music. Veronica held back for a moment watching her. Her hair, once the same colour as her own, was now silver and thanks to the regular six-weekly trips to a local hair salon, cut into an easy to manage short style. It seemed pointless to keep dying it for her. Her pretty face was beginning to droop with gravity's pull which seemed to have tugged harder since she'd gotten ill.

Her mother had always loved music, and her face lost the haunted look she'd worn these last few years when she listened to it. Her hands would unknit themselves and move to the rhythm almost of their own accord. Andréa Bocelli was her favourite in those last few months when things had been going pear-shaped and Veronica had done her best to look after her. The only thing that would settle her when she got upset by her encroaching illness was the Italian opera singer. It had been her mother's dream to see him play on his home ground of Tuscany but it had never happened. She'd had lots of dreams, her mother.

She had a beautiful singing voice too. She could have sung professionally, Veronica always thought but her life had been devoted to raising her and Abi. She'd not had an easy time of it.

Veronica moved into her line of sight and Margo looked at her daughter, her expression blank momentarily as she grasped to place her and when she did her face broke into a smile. It was wide and childlike which was an anomaly with the pink lipstick she was wearing.

'You're still in there, aren't you, Mum,' Veronica said, smiling back before taking hold of her hand. 'It's lovely to see you.' She pulled a chair up alongside Margo who was blinking at her expectantly not sure what was expected of her. Veronica breathed in the scent of L'Air du Temps perfume. It was Margo's favourite. French perfume was a luxury not afforded to her mother after their dad left as she'd grimly tried to meet the bills each week. As such, she'd made sure her mum always had a bottle once she began work at Blakeley's.

She knew the story of fashion house, Nina Ricci's signature fragrance by heart. It was released at the end of World War Two with the idea of it being a breath of fresh air to celebrate the return to peace and feminine elegance after the war. The original bottle had been a starburst pattern made by Lalique, and then his son, Marc, went on to design the crystal bottle with the famed dove stoppers symbolising peace. Veronica loved the bottle. It was a showpiece in itself.

She was guessing it was Danika, the carer Veronica felt she had a rapport with, who'd helped get her dressed this morning. She knew how much Margo loved the fragrance. It also pleased her that her mother was always well turned out. She was a stylish woman who'd taken pride in her appearance albeit on a budget and it was things like this that made Holly Grange worth every penny because what price could you put on dignity?

'What are you doing here?'

'I've come to see you, Mum.'

'Am I going out?'

'No, not today. I thought we could have a cup of tea here.'

'Where are...?' she frowned. 'Where are—'

'Hunter and Haydn are playing football this afternoon, Mum. They'll come and see you on Thursday.'

Margo nodded and then leaned forward to whisper conspiratorially. 'There's some very strange people in here.'

'Is there, Mum?'

'There is, look around you. Quite mad some of them. I don't know what I'm doing here.' She pointed to a docile woman sitting near the doors to the garden, her eyes half closed as she dozed in the land between sleep and wakefulness. 'She shouts you know.' Margo pleated the hem of her sweater, her eyes wide. 'I'll go home with you today, I think. I shouldn't really be here.' Tears threatened.

Please don't cry, Mum. The tears were the hardest to take. Veronica had heard this lament before from her mother who some days took it in her stride that this was where she now lived and on others looked around her with fresh eyes unsure as to what had brought her here. Veronica looked back over her shoulder to where an elderly gent, who looked dapper in his shirt and suit trousers, was clutching a walker as he shuffled forth. It buoyed her to see him looking so smart and well cared for but as she listened to him ask no one in particular if they'd seen his wife, Nora, a wave of sadness filled her. It was how he spent his days, looking for his wife. She only came to see him on a Sunday at afternoon tea time. Danika had told her this.

She caught sight of another gentleman standing in the doorway of the corridor to where the bedrooms were. He had a shirt and socks on and underpants in between. A pair of trousers were slung over his arm. One of the carers, Gloria, excused herself from the table where she'd been helping a woman do a puzzle to take him by the arm. She steered him gently back down the hall to his room. They were such a special lot the people who worked here, made of sterner stuff than she was, she thought, watching her go before turning her attention to the bag she'd brought with her.

'Ah well, never mind. I've something to show you.' She was doing something different today. She usually brought in a photo album on Saturday afternoons, to sit and flick through with her. Shared memories of when the boys were small, outings to the beach or park, the holiday they'd gone on to Cornwall when Jason was still under the same roof. Happy memories before the hated memory thief happened along.

Thrusting her hand into the bag, she pulled out the tiny blue leotard, shaking it out before passing it to her mother. Veronica knew from experience not to say, 'Do you remember this, Mum?' To do so would cause her mother's eyes to grow dull as she worried at her memories trying to remember, wanting to please. They'd begin to glint with sparks of anger and frustration as she tried to place the item. So, instead Veronica said, 'This is the first ballet leotard you bought me, Mum.'

'Was it? I don't remember that.'

'It was. It's so small, isn't it?'

Margo nodded and stroked the fabric, a look of wonder on her face.

'Shall I tell you a story, Mum?'

Margo's expression was distant. She was lost in her own world holding the leotard to her cheek as Veronica began to talk.

Chapter 6
Isabel

ISABEL WAS ON THE RECEIVING end of a lone wolf-whistle as she hurried down the Esplanade toward Sea Vistas. Its source was a lad hanging out a car window, sunglasses pushed up on top of his head as he and his pals cruised down the waterfront for something to do on a Saturday afternoon. 'Hey, Katy.' He called referencing Katy Perry on account of her pink hair. She wasn't in the mood for that sort of carry-on, she thought, primly keeping her gaze focused on the footpath in front of her. Her mind was churning like the sea she was walking alongside, and had been since Rhodri had handed her Sally's letter to read. She was desperate to talk over what his ex-fiancée had said in it with Constance.

She kept up her almost trotting pace until Sea Vistas, with its grand stone façade and soaring chimneys loomed into her line of sight. Risking a telling off from one of the gardeners, she cut across the sweep of manicured lawn, the grass soft and spongy beneath her feet, to the entrance. The automatic doors to the retirement home slid open and she strode through them, passing by Kristin the young receptionist with a wave and a hello. She'd normally pause for a quick chat and to marvel at how much makeup Kristin, a YouTube makeup tutorial devotee, could actually apply to her face. Today though she headed straight for the lift. It obliged by opening to reveal its empty chamber before she'd even pushed the button and, stepping in, she pressed her finger on number one.

A few seconds later, Isabel alighted into the familiar corridor and walking the few short steps to Constance's door she tapped lightly on it. 'Yes?' bounced back at her from within and she turned the handle, opening the door a crack to call through it.

'Constance, it's me, can I come in?'

'I hope you've got my Cyclax,' came by way of reply.

Isabel pushed the door open and stepped inside the plush room. Constance was sitting by the window with the rich, rose drapes either side of it framing her. She was a colourful vision in pink and Isabel recognised the outfit as one she'd helped her choose from their favourite boutique in the Royal Victoria Arcade. They always did well there on their shopping trips. Constance trusted the judgement of young Tara who worked there. Nurse Jill, who was the only staff member at Sea Vistas Constance would allow to help her dress of a morning, always did her proud too, ensuring she was well turned out.

'Of course I have. I wouldn't dare show my face otherwise.' She'd been under strict instructions from Constance to pick her up a bottle of Cyclax from Boots to bring with her the next time she popped into Sea Vistas. Constance had declared her face would be like a leather handbag if she were to run out of her favourite moisturising lotion. She swore by it, saying if it was good enough for Queen Elizabeth it was good enough for Constance Downer.

Constance made a humphing sound as Isabel placed her bag down on the bed. She searched through it and retrieved the bottle of moisturiser.

'I'll put it on your dressing table, shall I?'

Constance gave a nod. 'How much do I owe you?'

'Don't be silly it's an early going away present.' Isabel deposited the bottle down and caught a glimpse of herself in the mirror. She looked windblown but couldn't be bothered attempting to smooth her hair down. There were bigger things than the state of her hair to be worrying about.

'You'd think I was emigrating the way you're carrying on wanting to hold a going-away party and whatnot. Are you trying to see me off for good?'

Isabel laughed and turned away, looking at her dear friend. 'It's all organised; there's no getting out of it. Six weeks is a long time and Canada is a long way away, Constance. I'll miss you.'

'Not when you get to my age, it flies by in a flash you'll see. Anyway, I haven't gone yet.'

'Your hair looks lovely by the way.' Isabel noticed the gentle white curls dancing around her face becomingly. She pulled out the chair by Constance's bedside so that she could sit opposite her and sat down.

'I had it blow-dried and set yesterday downstairs in the salon.' Constance preened at the compliment, every bit the grand dame presiding from her throne. It was her favourite place to while away time because she could see out to her beloved Solent—the same water vista she'd been gazing at the evening she met Henry. Of course, back then the water had been dotted with navy ships and was a very different scene to the peaceful rolling sea of today with nothing but ferries and white sails dipping up and down on it.

Isabel looked past her to where she could see what looked like a seal but realised it was a surfer being buffeted about on the waves. There was always something going on out there, she thought. Those surfers were hardy souls. It might be a glorious day but the water still held a spring chill.

'Have you written your letter?' Constance demanded, her attention now focused squarely on Isabel.

Isabel didn't need to ask what she meant. Constance had urged her to write to her birth mother, batting away any arguments Isabel brought up, and she'd brought up many, countering back with, 'The best thing that's ever happened to me in all my ninety-one years is having Edward in my life, Isabel, and that wouldn't have happened without your help. I'd be doing you a disservice if I didn't keep pressing you into at least dipping a toe into the waters to see what she says. As a woman who's been in Veronica's shoes, I know what it is to have a part of yourself missing.'

She asked again. 'Well, have you?' Constance was not, and never had been, a patient woman. She acknowledged this trait by saying that when you got to ninety-one years of age you had every right to be impatient because there was a risk you might not hear the end of the story if you didn't jog people along.

Isabel nodded and, opening her bag for a second time, she retrieved the envelope. 'I wanted to run it by you.' She'd half pulled it from the envelope when Constance waved her hand at her to stop.

'I've never known such a procrastinator, Isabel. You don't need to read it to me because you don't need my opinion you just need to get it in the post. You've got to get over this fear of being rejected. I know you're not one of life's risk takers but in this case you must be. Promise me, you'll send it.'

Isabel slid it back in the envelope and tucked it away in her bag once more. 'I will, I promise.'

Constance gazed at her speculatively. 'Don't think I won't check you've done so.'

'I'll do it on my way home today.'

'Make sure you do.' Constance clapped her hands in a manner suggesting that subject was now closed. She picked up the open packet of Maltesers from the occasional table next to her and shook it in Isabel's direction.

Isabel helped herself to one and popped a chocolate covered malt ball in her mouth, moving it to her cheek before saying, 'Something's happened.'

'Yes? Should I be worried?'

'No, but I am. I've told you Rhodri was engaged before he came to the island?'

'You mentioned it, yes. It wasn't an amicable break up you said.'

'No. Sally, that's his ex, she took up with another man behind Rhodri's back. It was his best friend, Darian, which was a double blow and when it all came out Sally and Darian moved away and Rhodri came here wanting to put it all behind him. The thing I didn't tell you, because it didn't seem relevant at the time, was Sally was pregnant when she and Darian left. Rhodri understandably had no further contact with either them but he heard through mutual friends she'd had a son. He was never sure if the baby was his or Darian's but Darian had taken on the role of father which was the likeliest scenario anyway or so he thought. So far as he was concerned stomping in demanding to know whether the child was his wouldn't have been in anyone's best interest especially not the baby, Austin's. It was easier to leave things be.'

Constance stayed silent, letting what Isabel was telling her settle in, she knew first-hand the pain of betrayal.

'A letter came today from Sally. She's broken up with Darian and decided now's the right time to tell Rhodri the truth. He's Austin's biological father.'

'Sounds rather like she's hedging her bets to me,' Constance said.

'Doesn't it, but if you'd seen the photo she enclosed with the letter, Constance, you'd know Austin's Rhodri's. He's the spit of him.' Isabel had teared up upon seeing the miniature version of the man she loved; she couldn't even begin to imagine how it had made Rhodri feel. He'd closed the gallery early as she skimmed the letter and then when she'd finished he'd taken it from her along with the photograph and gone upstairs. She'd made to follow him but he'd asked if she minded him having a little time alone to absorb what he'd just learned. Part of her had desperately wanted to stay with him, a part of her that on some level understood things were about to change in their life together. Another part recognised his need for space inside his own head so she'd headed here to Constance. Her port of call in a storm.

'It makes my blood boil that she's decided to come clean now that things haven't worked out for her. What's that going to do to Austin's sense of place in the world? I mean one day he has a father the next day he's gone and by all accounts severed contact with him. Then the poor kid's told he has a new daddy.' She looked at Constance who reached over and patted her hand.

'It does seem selfish, I agree. What is it she's wanting?'

Isabel blinked back the hot tears that had sprung up at the gesture. 'She says their son needs his father and she'd like for Austin and Rhodri to meet one another.' She swallowed hard against the tide of emotion. 'Constance, you'd think he'd have raged about her lying to him but he didn't. He just went quiet. It's going to change things between us.' She thumped her chest. 'I can feel it in here.' She remembered how, when she'd first come to the Isle of Wight, she'd had blue hair. She'd only realised Rhodri, who technically back then was her landlord, had feelings for her when she'd found the painting he'd been working on. It had been of a girl with blue hair whipping about her face as she stood on the pier gazing out at the Solent, it was of her.

The painting hung on the wall of their living area in Pier View House now. It was called The Mermaid and they'd spent an age arguing as to where it should go. Rhodri wanted it nearer the window for the light but Isabel wanted it placed so whenever she looked up from her seat at the table it was there in her line of sight. She'd won.

She'd been unsure how to let him know she felt the same way initially and had gone to Constance for advice. 'Do you remember what you said to me when I asked you how I should let Rhodri know I felt about him?'

'I do. I told you to be brave. I said it's the twenty-first century and you couldn't expect a man to do all the running anymore. I stand by my words, Isabel.'

Isabel mustered a smile. She might be in her tenth decade but she was still sharp as a tack. 'You did and then you told me not to dilly-dally over it all because life's short and when something good comes our way we must grab it with both hands.'

'Grabbing it with both hands sounds rather forward, Isabel, are you sure I said that.'

Isabel gave a small laugh. 'I'm sure.'

'I do recall suggesting you cook a nice meal, set the scene, that sort of thing and to use your imagination.'

'Look how that worked out!' Given Rhodri was the one in charge of cooking in their domestic arrangement she'd decided to surprise him by whipping up something special and setting the scene as Constance had suggested. So, she'd taken herself off to the Ryde Bookshop on High Street and nearly lost herself in the Aladdin's cave of books. She'd taken her time meandering through the ten rooms overflowing with all manner of reading material until eventually she'd found exactly what she was looking for. A Julia Child book called *Mastering the Art of French Cooking*. Hugging the book to her chest with growing excitement she'd taken it to the counter and paid.

She'd poured over the recipes that evening in bed, acutely aware that it was only a wall separating her and Rhodri. She'd decided, as she tried to concentrate on what was in front of her instead of the man sleeping next door, on coq au vin mostly because the dish sounded vaguely familiar. The next day, after she'd left The Natural Way and without breathing a word to Delwyn of her seduction plan, she'd gone firstly to the butchers, then the supermarket to pick up wine before calling in on her old boss Brenda at The Rum Den to beg a quarter cup of cognac from her.

The recipe called for the cognac and she was blowed if she was going to buy a whole bottle for the sake of such a small amount. A deal had been struck in relation to Brenda's ongoing issue with bunions. A packet of the turmeric powder she mixed with water to make a paste to soothe her feet in exchange for the cognac. Isabel had long since stopped telling her to wear flat shoes as it would help her poor feet. The pub landlady wearing flats would be akin to her running a pub that didn't serve beer. Naturally, Brenda had grilled her as to what she was up to but she'd refused to divulge her reasons and they'd had a stand-off for five minutes until Brenda, deciding she wasn't going to crack, had relinquished the alcohol.

Isabel had been pleased upon arriving back at Pier View House to see Rhodri in conversation with a customer and she'd been able to get her supplies up the stairs without him noticing. She'd decided she'd prepare the meal and set the table then go and change out of her customary jeans and T-shirt into her special occasions dress. It wasn't the stuff of femme fatales but she knew the green suited her and its nipped-in waist and full skirt that finished just above her knees was flattering. She wasn't a little black dress and killer heels sort of girl.

Things hadn't gone quite to plan however.

Rhodri had raced up the stairs as the smoke alarm shrilled to find Isabel flapping her hand, ineffectually trying to clear the smoke in the kitchen. She'd gone upstairs to make herself pretty and had come back down half an hour later, opening the oven door to check on her casserole. The acrid smoke had billowed out as Rhodri deduced the oven wasn't on fire and the cause of the drama was whatever she'd been cooking boiling over and smouldering until it ignited briefly on the oven tray. Isabel, whose eyes were watering and stinging had promptly burst into tears and babbled on about how all she'd wanted to do was impress him with a delicious dinner and now it was all ruined. Rhodri had looked at her then, seen her dress and noticed she'd put her hair up and had makeup on, and the penny had dropped it was for his benefit.

He'd wiped her tears away with his thumbs ever so gently and her skin had tingled at his touch. His eyes had furrowed trying to gauge whether he was reading her signs correctly and his hands cupped her face. She'd tilted her head to look at him, suddenly oblivious to the burnt smell as she became aware of the smell of him. It was a curious mix of the oil-based paints he favoured and the coconut shampoo in their bathroom. She'd thought she could smell something else too, something musky, almost earthy, but her breath caught as she'd seen something change in his eyes. Her lips parted slightly willing him to kiss her and he'd leaned down, his lips soft as they'd tentatively brushed hers. Her body relaxed as a feeling of languid bliss overtook her and she'd been grateful for his arms which had encircled her pulling her into him, holding her against his body and—

'Earth to Isabel.' Constance intruded on her reverie.

'Sorry, I was just—'

'Yes, I could tell by the look on your face what you were thinking and it wasn't the fact you nearly burned my old kitchen down.' Mirth twinkled in Constance's wily eyes.

'It was a small oven fire and it all worked out in the end.'

'Exactly, Isabel, and this business with Rhodri and his ex-wife will too, you'll see. It's his son he cares about not her.' Constance shook the Malteser packet at her once more.

Chapter 7
Veronica
1985

'COME ON, RONNIE, I told you not to dawdle today of all days coming out of class. You don't want to be late for your first lesson, and stop scratching for goodness sake.' Margo's voice was laced with impatience as she bumped the stroller along in which Veronica's three-year-old sister, Abigail was perched. She paused to cross herself seeing the Catholic church across the road. Veronica reluctantly let the sleeve of her school blouse drop. Her eczema had flared at the thought of this ballet lesson and it burned the tender skin inside her elbow. She bit her lip, looking at her sister in an effort to distract herself as she plodded up the road.

Veronica was five years older than Abigail and felt very grown up by comparison. Her sister was still such a baby. Look at the way she'd stamp her foot and cry whenever she didn't get her own way. Now her plump legs were crossed like a lady's as she nibbled her way through an apple. She had a lunch box open on her lap, filled with pieces of fruit and crackers, which made Veronica jealous. She was guessing the food was there to keep her sister's mouth occupied while she did her first ballet lesson. It wasn't fair because she was hungry too, starving in fact. But Mummy had said she'd get a stitch if she ate before the class and that she could have a biscuit when they got home.

She eyed Abi's tufts of curly blonde hair. She sometimes wished she had blue eyes and blonde hair too because she might get her own way more often if she had. She didn't though and her pleas to not be made to do this stupid dance class had fallen on deaf ears. She hadn't even been able to get Daddy to take her side this time and he always took her side but lately when she spoke to him it was as if he wasn't there anymore.

Veronica's eyes were a grey-green colour. The colour of the sea her mum said. They were like her beloved daddy's and her hair was brown like his too. He was film-star handsome her dad, not that it made much difference to Mum because so far as she could see he didn't get his own way very often where she was concerned either. She'd tried turning on the tears like Abigail but if she was naughty, she'd still get told off and if she were particularly naughty, she'd feel the sting of her mum's hand across the back of legs. Tears or no tears. Whereas if Abigail was naughty, she looked at her mother with those big blue eyes threatening to brim over and was given a cuddle to ward off the waterworks and told not to do it again. It was most unfair!

When Abigail had first come on the scene, Veronica had been very concerned, not only because she was no longer the centre of her mummy's world but that her baby sister was never going to grow any hair. She was bald as a badger's bum, she'd heard Nana say and Daddy used to call her Kojak, in a nice way, after a bald actor on the television whose show he watched re-runs of. Mummy hadn't liked it when he said that though. It used to make her cross. Sometimes Veronica didn't think her mum had any laughter in her because Dad was the funniest person she knew. If she'd known her sister would wind up with blonde curls and a sneaky streak however, she wouldn't have wasted her energy feeling sorry for her.

Now she propelled her legs forward trying to keep pace with her mother and sister. She wondered if she might fare better at ballet than she had at school sports. At eight years of age she was already acutely aware that she didn't possess any prowess on the netball court, or with a hockey stick—especially not the latter. It wasn't because she was no good at it but rather because it didn't hold her attention. She couldn't see the importance of getting the ball into the net or through the hoop. What did it matter? She'd given Hayley Griffiths an enormous green and blue bruise when she'd accidentally whacked her with her hockey stick though, in her attempts to impress the new girl Megan Holmes.

Would she have to wear a tutu at ballet? she wondered. She'd like to be able to stand on her toes; that would surely impress Megan no end. Megan wanted to be a ballerina when she grew up. It was the one good thing about this lesson she was on her way to, Megan would be there. She might even invite her to her ninth birthday party if she could stand on her toes. Veronica wanted an invitation to this party as much as Charlie had wanted to win the golden ticket. Megan's mummy was going to take the lucky chosen few roller skating in Hemel Hempstead *and* there'd be a McDonald's dinner followed by a sleepover.

She'd even added her wish for an invitation to her nightly prayer:

Hello Dear God, please look after my mummy, daddy, and Abigail. Please could you stop Abigail from being annoying and from playing with my dolls when I'm at school. Also, could you please stop Mummy and Daddy from being horrible to each other so that Mummy stops being angry and looking all sort of pinched in the face. I think things would get better too if you could help Daddy to find a job. Thank you, God. Please, please, please can you make sure Megan gives me an invitation to her birthday party because I've never been roller skating or had a sleepover at a friend's house before and I've only been to McDonald's three times in my whole life. Thank you, God. Goodnight, God Bless, Love Veronica.

Veronica's family weren't church goers even though her mum was a Catholic something she mentioned a lot as if it made her special. Daddy wasn't but his parents were and she'd heard them arguing because Mummy said she didn't feel she could show her face in church unless he came and they put on a united front. Daddy said they were all hippo—it was a big word and it sounded like hippopotamus but she could never remember what it was. It was all very confusing this Catholic business, Veronica thought.

She'd gone with the neighbours, the Simons family next door, to their church a few times to give Mummy a break when Abi was a baby. They went to one belonging to England and it was cold inside because the walls were made of stone and the ceiling was very high. Davey, Mr and Mrs Simons' son was the same age as her and he'd picked his nose while they were supposed to be singing a hymn and wiped it on the back of the wooden seat in front of them. His mum had cuffed him about the ear and gotten a tissue out of her bag to clean up his bogey. She'd enjoyed the Sunday school and she liked saying a prayer each night because it made her feel safe. It was a nice thought to think of a big man up there in the sky who to her mind looked like Father Christmas smiling down at them all.

She'd given up asking God to please let her not be the last one picked for a team at hockey and netball, just as she'd giving up asking him to get

Mummy to change her mind about the ballet classes once she'd heard Megan was going.

Veronica looked up at her mother. She looked pretty today in lavender. She was wearing what was called a boiler suit. The black belt that pulled it in around her middle made her waist look tiny. Her hair was in a high, side ponytail making her seem young and fun and not at all grumpy. She put her hand to her own bunches. She'd have liked a high, side ponytail but it was pigtails for school. She knew the girls at school all thought she was lucky to have such a pretty, fashionable mother.

Megan's mummy had an enormous bottom and wore bumble bee leg warmers over her jeans when she came to pick her up from school. She always had a cigarette in her hand too and her voice was shouty without her actually shouting. It had a funny twang to it which Mummy said was common. Veronica wasn't sure what common meant but she knew from the way her mother's lip curled when she said it that it wasn't a good thing. Veronica didn't care if Megan's mother was common, she still wanted to go to the birthday party. Megan, she'd thought, when she'd managed to land a prime spot at her table during painting, might have been the prettiest girl at school but her hair smelt of cigarettes. Veronica was glad her mother didn't smoke. She always smelt of flowers and it was a special treat for her to be allowed a spray on the inside of her wrists from the pretty glass bottle with the bird-shaped stopper.

Mummy had been behaving strangely ever since she'd spotted the ad for these stupid ballet classes on the wall at the supermarket where Daddy sometimes looked for jobs. She'd gotten very excited and had talked about nothing else since. Her voice got all funny and fast whenever she mentioned how much Veronica was going to love it. She said it in a way that told Veronica she didn't have any choice but to love it. Mummy also kept saying she couldn't believe their luck in having a former prima ballerina no less, teaching here in St Rebus. Veronica didn't know what a prima ballerina was but knew it must be a very good thing indeed because Mummy was so excited, she'd forgotten to be angry at Daddy.

It was odd and annoying though because Veronica would much rather join the Brownies. She wanted to go on camps and make dampers she could slather jam on like the girls in her storybook annual did. Or, failing that she'd quite like to be left to her own devices so as she could solve mysteries in the neighbourhood after school like Nancy Drew. She'd like to know why the man who lived at the end of their terraced row kept his curtains shut even in the daytime.

As if sensing her daughter's reticence, Margo glanced down at her and mustered up a smile. She was full of nervous tension which she knew was ridiculous but she couldn't help herself. 'It's not far, Ronnie, we've only got to walk to the traffic lights and then turn at the corner, and we'll be there. You're going to love it.'

There she'd said it again! Veronica, didn't think that was likely but she knew better than to say so. She looked around her, taking in the familiar sights of their town. It was busy at this time of the day. The double-decker bus rumbling slowly up the road with the conductor who always waved out; she waved back to him. In the distance she could see the towers of the abbey where Mum would take them sometimes to sit and listen to the choir practice. When Abigail was a baby, Mum said listening to the choir singing like angels was the only thing that would get her off to sleep of an afternoon.

Veronica would sneak looks at her mother as she sat on one of the pews inside the old building. It was cold and made of stone like the church she'd gone to with the Simons family. The abbey was much fancier though with decorated ceilings and windows that would light up with all the different colours when the sun was on them. Veronica didn't like the pictures in those windows, the people's faces looked miserable like they'd hurt themselves and it always made her feel sad looking at them. Mum would sit there with a strange look on her face her eyes closed and it had taken Veronica a long time to work out that she was lost in the sound of all those voices soaring as high as the ceiling.

They passed Zara-Lee's, the boutique Mum would normally pause outside in order to sigh over whatever dress was displayed in the window before muttering, chance would be a fine thing and carrying on. Today she didn't falter in her step even though the mannequin had on a navy-blue dress with white spots and a red belt. It was pretty, Veronica thought, glancing back over her shoulder. She'd like to wear a dress like that one day. Mummy would look very pretty in it.

The next shop worthy of attention was Thomas Cooks, the travel agents. Normally Veronica would stop and gaze at the picture of the castle in the window. It was white and it looked like the one in her story book at home. The only thing missing was a princess. She'd like to go there one day. Mum said it was in Germany. Perhaps she could even be the princess. She liked the beach pictures too with their swaying palms and turquoise waters.

They'd gone on a holiday two summers ago that she could remember bits and pieces of. They'd stayed on an island with a beach where the water was warm like a bath and there were flowers, lots of bright flowers everywhere. It had been a good holiday. Mostly what she remembered was her parents had been nice to each other the whole time. They'd even held hands when they walked down the beach. There was no time for gazing in windows today though, and she could tell by the way Mummy was marching up the street that she wasn't going to be allowed to linger outside her favourite shop in the whole wide world either, the chocolate shop.

Her mouth filled with longing as they approached it and she fancied she could smell hot chocolate like the kind they used to have on special occasions at the coffee shop that Mummy said made lovely scones. She nearly tripped over, trying to keep walking while she soaked up the different shades of sweet, creamy brown and white treats on display. Mummy had told her they were very expensive. They came all the way from another country beginning with S and on her last birthday when she turned eight, she'd been allowed to choose two chocolates from the display in the window and she didn't even have to share with Abigail. It had been the hardest decision of her life and she'd taken forever to decide, terrified of not choosing the most delicious ones. Now as she was told to hurry up once more, she sniffed the unmistakable sugary promise of treats wistfully before running to catch her up.

At last they reached the corner where Blakeley's department store was. The dresses on display in the window had sequins, they were shimmery with enormous shoulders on them. She wondered what sort of mummy would wear those. They'd have to be going to a very special sort of party. The sliding door opened as they walked past and a girl with a white top that said Choose Life and showed her tummy off like Madonna walked out. Veronica would have liked to have gone inside Blakeley's too to have a look. She liked riding the escalator. It always felt risky as though if she didn't get off fast enough when it got to the top it might swallow her toes. The perfume counter was her favourite, though.

She liked to look at the pretty bottles behind the counter. She'd seen the one Mummy had at home on the shelves. There were so many different colours and shapes all locked away like the crown jewels were, or so Daddy had told her, in a glass cabinet. The lady who worked behind the counter always smelt different but in a nice way. Her hair was big and all brushed forward onto her face and her skin was the colour of chocolate. She reminded Veronica of Whitney Houston. She'd like to be able to sing like Whitney Houston when she grew up. Her favourite song of all time was the one about saving my love because Mummy always turned the radio up when it came on and she'd sing along. She was as good as Whitney and hearing her mummy sing made her feel happy which was much nicer than that squirmy feeling she got in her tummy when her parents talked in loud hissing voices or when Mummy accidentally on purpose forgot to give Daddy a kiss goodbye in the morning.

The St Rebus community centre where Tippy Toes Dance Academy was officially in residence from three fifteen pm until five o'clock on Tuesday and Thursday afternoons loomed. Veronica stopped dead in her tracks at the bottom of the stairs leading to the entrance. The unknown always filled her with dread and made her want to bite her nails but if she did that Mummy would put the horrible tasting stuff on them again.

'Come on, Ronnie.' Annoyance was definitely filtering through her mother's voice now. 'I told you, this is costing us good money we can't afford. There's no time for dawdling.'

It was a mystery why, if they couldn't afford it, she was being made to do it. 'Mum, I feel sick. I'd rather learn piano like Lara is.' She scuffed at the ground with the toe of her black Mary Jane.

'Veronica, we don't have a piano and,' she left the stroller and came to crouch in front of her oldest daughter, her face an unreadable expression. 'You don't know how lucky you are being able to have ballet lessons. I would have loved to when I was your age. I'd have given anything to have the opportunity to sing and dance.'

Veronica didn't feel lucky though and she thought an unkind thought about her mother. Her mother straightened and flung an ultimatum, 'I don't know why it's even up for discussion, Veronica. You're going.' There was steel in her tone as she uttered that last sentence and Veronica knew better than to argue. Abigail twisted around in her stroller to look at her sister with those big blue eyes of hers, unsure as to what was going on. Veronica stuck her tongue out at her wishing she were the one in the stroller and that it was Abigail who had to go and do a stupid ballet class. She put one foot in front of the other and followed her mother's lead, up the steps and into the community centre.

Now

VERONICA BLINKED AS she swam back from her memories. For so long she and Margo hadn't spoken of the past and time was running out to be able to revisit it with her. She needed to explain the choices she'd made twenty-seven years ago.

'My daughter was a beautiful dancer,' Margo said holding the leotard to her cheek.

Veronica wondered what memory she was lost in.

Chapter 8
Isabel

ISABEL GAVE RHODRI a wave and closed the gallery door behind her. She paused for a moment to gaze up at the cloudless, cornflower blue sky before setting off. The air smacked of baked salt a promise of the summer to come. It clung to the warm breeze blowing her hair back from her face as she set off. The sea air was something she'd grown used to. It was good for the soul and she didn't like to be away from it, or Rhodri for long.

She'd not shed a tear packing her bags and leaving behind her Finsbury flatmates for the last time. Larissa of the greasy hair and reluctance to pitch in when it came to the housework would not be missed. Nor would Clara who couldn't switch off a light to save herself. It had been a shock to Isabel to realise all those years of her dad trailing around after her switching off lights and muttering about how things would be different if she paid the leccy bill had actually registered in her brain. Clara was payback for not having listened to him. She'd managed to stop herself stomping her foot and saying, 'It's like the flaming Blackpool illuminations in here,' but only just!

Isabel had taken a year out to study naturopathy at the London School of Natural Medicine coming back to the Isle of Wight to see Rhodri, Constance and their friends whenever she could. She'd finish the rest of the course via online correspondence over the next couple of years and in the meantime was putting the knowledge she'd stockpiled during her time in London into practice at The Natural Way.

She was on her way there now to take over from Delwyn. It was her turn to man the fort for the Saturday afternoon shift and she was hoping it would be busy because she didn't want to give the spectre of Sally a chance to raise her head. She'd been popping up uninvited all week. Rhodri too had been distracted ever since the letter had arrived, not that she blamed him. It had been a bombshell. She didn't know what his next move would be. He'd call

Sally she supposed as she'd suggested he do in her letter. He hadn't done so yet and she hadn't pushed him on it either. Still waters ran deep with Rhodri and she could tell by his quietness he was mulling over the news of Austin being his. He'd be trying to process the hurt at having been lied to again by Sally but there'd be anger simmering away too. She supposed he wanted to give that time to cool down before he made the call.

She turned the corner onto Union Street and narrowly missed colliding with a woman.

'Whoa.' It was Nico holding her hand up in a stop gesture.

Isabel grinned her apology to the pretty blonde woman in her flowing boho dress and brown sandals. She saw she had a loaf of fresh bread in a basket, a bottle of red wine and, was that the cheddar she adored from the farmer's market? She always pretended she'd never tried it before in order to taste test a sliver but she fancied the cheesemonger was well and truly on to her. It was hard to be incognito when your hair was magenta coloured. She'd fancied a change from the blue.

'Sorry, I was miles away. I'm on my way to relieve your other half now.' She halted, moving out of the way of a young couple with a squalling baby in a pram, on a mission to get to wherever they were off to. 'Are you and Delwyn off picnicking then?' She looked at the cheese with a watering mouth. Her gaze returned to Nico. She could have stepped off the cover of one of the annuals her mum had kept from her teenage years. All she needed was a daisy chain around her hair.

Isabel used to love looking through those old books, laughing at the hairstyles and outfits much to her mum's chagrin. 'There is absolutely nothing funny about Rockin Rod, or David Cassidy,' Babs Stark would tut before getting a silly look on her face as she pointed to some fellow called Donny Osmond. 'Your father had the look of Donny in his younger days.' Given Donny's all-American pearly-white smile and her dad's middle-aged, British gnashers, Isabel found this a stretch. She also knew her father fancying himself as he did to be Southampton's answer to The Boss would be affronted at the wholesome Osmond comparison. Bruce Springsteen however he was not, and it was embarrassing how he'd tie a bandana around his head when he mowed their tiny stretch of grass out the front of the house where Isabel had grown up.

'No.' Nico drew her attention back and Isabel watched as a gust blew her long hair around her face. She tucked it behind her ears with her free hand. 'Not today, although it would be a good day for it.' She looked wistfully at the Solent. 'It's too hot to be in the studio but I've a pottery exhibition there, organised ages ago from one until two this afternoon. This,' she held the basket up, 'is part of my cunning plan to ply anyone who walks through the door with red wine and a token piece of bread and cheese. Hopefully it will put them in the buying mood.'

'A cunning plan indeed.'

The women said their goodbyes and Isabel picked up her pace, reaching the shop just as the door opened. She smiled at the exiting customer clutching one of their bags before heading inside.

'Hi,' she called out a greeting over the jangling door and, stepping inside she caught a whiff of that curious mix of dried herbs and something else she'd never been able to pinpoint but which she'd grown to love.

'Hi, yourself. It's been mad busy today,' Delwyn said, looking up from behind the counter. Her pretty, round face was framed by a pixie cut which was too short to hide the fact she was frazzled. She was busy changing the till roll and she was wearing the yellow T-shirt with the white dove Isabel coveted. There was one customer in the shop, a rather wan looking woman browsing the vitamin shelves; she made a note to ask her if she'd like some help once she'd got rid of her bag.

'Sod of a thing this is,' Delwyn said finishing her task and clipping the plastic back into place.

'Thanks for not leaving it for me to change.'

'That would be mean. I did leave you this carton to unpack and put away though. Sorry, I haven't had a chance to see to it. I think it's the chlorella supplements we ordered. Here, pass me your bag, I'll pop it out back.'

Isabel did so. 'No problem, thanks. It's a glorious day out there.'

'Good, I'm looking forward to a few hours in the sun with a good book and snacks, plenty of snacks.' Delwyn called over her shoulder before disappearing into the storeroom.

Isabel smiled, pulling off the hairband she had on her wrist and tying her hair back. 'That sounds like bliss, an afternoon lolling about in the sun,' she said when Delwyn reappeared with her bag slung over her shoulder ready for the off. 'But I thought you'd be helping Nico with the exhibition? I just bumped into her on my way here. She had a basket of goodies including red wine and that cheese I like from the farmer's market.'

'Bugger, I'd forgotten about that. Oh well, at least there'll be a glass of red in it for me. Full of antioxidants and all that.' Delwyn grinned. 'Have fun.'

'Will do.' Isabel waited until she'd left before making her way over to the customer who was reading the back of a bottle. 'Good afternoon, how are you today?' she said brightly.

'I'm fine, thanks,' the woman replied with no hint of enthusiasm.

'Was there something in particular you were after?'

'I'm not sure really. I've had a virus and it's left me feeling washed-out. I'm wondering if there's a tonic or something I could take? My old mum was a believer in eating spinach to put the iron back into you after an illness but there's only so much spinach a girl can take.'

'I hear you.' Isabel smiled. The poor woman did look washed-out. 'Sometimes we all need a little extra boost. I've something in mind that will help but first things first, do you have high blood pressure?'

'No, if anything it errs on the low side.'

'Well then, ginseng's very good.' She scanned the shelf for the particular product she was after glancing up as the door jangled. A man too old to be wearing a cap back to front mooched in. She smiled in his direction and then retrieved the container of Korean ginseng she was looking for.

By the time the woman had made her mind up to give the supplement a try the shop had a half a dozen customers browsing its wares and Isabel was halfway through ringing the transaction up when the door sounded yet again. Business was booming today with the good weather bringing people out in their droves. Beverley Barret who'd recently opened a gift shop a few doors down from A Leap of Faith popped her head around the door.

'I'm not stopping, Isabel,' she called out. 'My daughter's minding the shop while I nip out to get us a bite of lunch. I just wanted to call in and tell you I'm feeling much better, thanks.'

'That's good, Bev.' Isabel called back popping the ginseng into a bag and taking the woman's card to pay.

'It's down to you, Isabel,' she boomed and if her customers had looked startled by this loud woman yelling from the entrance it was nothing to the expression on their faces when Beverley added. 'That cranberry powder's just the ticket for a urinary infection. Cleared it up lickety-split. Ta very much. Oh, and before I go, don't forget you promised to make me a brew of rosemary tea.' She'd waggled her fingers in a ta-rah and closed the door.

Isabel smiled to herself as she slid the card through the machine, Bev was one of those larger than life personalities whose voice was loud no matter whatever level she pitched it at. She'd do well here on the island. She also had an impressive pot of rosemary on her balcony and had been most interested when Isabel had told her of its wonderous healing powers.

The afternoon flew by and before she knew it she'd hung the closed sign in the window and was locking up. She glanced across the road at the post box, a red beacon reminding her of the letter which was still in her bag, despite her promise to Constance. She made a step toward the kerb but something pulled her back, she couldn't do it, not today, and turning on her heel she walked down the street.

Chapter 9

Veronica

HAYDN AND HUNTER CAME with Veronica on Thursdays when she finished work at three thirty. The boys met her at Blakeley's straight from school. She had a sneaking suspicion they had crushes on Sophie who came in after school to take over from her for the late night. She was a pretty girl with a sheet of blonde hair which she pulled back into a ponytail as per Heidi's instructions. 'Customers need to talk to your face not your hair,' she'd bossed the schoolgirl. The boys always arrived five minutes early and loitered around the counter, watching Sophie as she settled in for her shift. They certainly didn't have any interest in male fragrance. Veronica had to remind them each morning as they made a bid for freedom out the front door to get back up the stairs and put deodorant on as it was. Neanderthals the pair of them but they were her Neanderthals and she loved them.

She'd pick up her bag, wish Sophie a good night and, with her drooling sons trailing behind her, the three of them would tootle over to Holly Grange. She had to remind herself at times that the way Margo was, was equally hard on them too. They were close to their nana. She'd been hands on with them buzzing in out of their home helping out from the minute Veronica brought them home from the hospital. Her help and presence had helped re-establish a bond that had been frayed between mother and daughter. Jason though had found Margo an annoyance while Veronica didn't know what she would have done without her in those early years. She still didn't know what she'd do without her but the choice was being taken away from her by the dementia.

Each week when the boys sloped in, Margo would exclaim as to the size of them as though she hadn't seen them since they were toddlers. 'When did they get so big?' she'd ask Veronica who would smile indulgently, 'Well I do feed them, Mum.' The boys, bless them, would smile back at their nana. She wondered how they'd cope when she no longer knew them. She'd have to find the strength to cope somehow because it's what mothers do.

The Thursday visit was a tricky one because she'd learned there were windows of time with her mum. Sometimes she'd be better than others. Her mood would dip after four o'clock, sundowning it was called when the confusion would settle over her like a suffocating blanket. It was similar to when the boys were toddlers. There'd always been a pocket in the day she'd thought of as the witching hour when they'd get agitated and refuse to settle at anything. So too was it for her mother.

Saturday afternoon, though, was her and Margo's special time, theirs alone, and so Veronica retrieved the costume she'd decided to bring with her for this week's visit.

'I wore this when I danced to *Coppélia*, Mum. You did such a wonderful job making it.' She held the lacy, pale blue costume, fashioned after a doll's dress, up to show her. Margo stopped worrying her hands and looked up.

'Look at the detail in the bodice. You put so much time and effort into this.' She blinked back the tears beginning to gather. Her mum, unable to afford the costumes she'd needed as time had gone on and her roles had become more elaborate, had gone to night classes, run at the local college, to learn to sew. She'd bought a second-hand machine and had sat up late in the night to make this and many others for her. Veronica had lain in bed hearing the odd choice word and the monotonous hum of the old Singer through the floorboards. She'd pictured her mum, a cold cup of tea on the table next to her as she sat hunched over the machine with pins in her mouth and a frown on her face, her foot pressing the treadle.

Margo held her hands out to take the costume and Veronica handed it to her, watching for a moment as she pored over it with an expression of wonder as Veronica began to talk.

1985

A WOMAN WITH HOLLOWS where her cheeks should be and hair almost the same colour as a fire engine was flitting about the hall, pausing to talk to the mothers clustered near the stacked chairs pressed up against the far wall. Their daughters had presumably disappeared off to the toilets in order to get changed out of their uniforms and into their ballet leotards. Veronica couldn't take her eyes off the woman who had to be the instructor, and not just because of her hair. There was something in the way she moved. It was almost as though she were floating on air. She was wearing a black leotard with a grey skirt that finished where her fluffy pink leg warmers began; ballet slippers peeked out from the bottom of them. She was, Veronica decided, like a fairy but she wasn't sure as yet whether she was a good one or a bad one.

A fair-haired boy all trussed up in a fancy school uniform was looking around the hall seeking out a friendly face while his mother talked to the fairy teacher. Veronica smiled and he stared at her for half a second before returning the smile, albeit shyly. He looked to be about the same age as she was and she decided he must be here under duress while his sister had her lesson. His mum was pretty, like hers, but she looked like she'd stepped out of the pages of one of the magazines her mum liked to read. Veronica had to blink to make sure she wasn't imagining it because she was wearing the dress from Zara-Lee's. The blue one with the spots and the red belt she'd seen in the shop window. She even had shoes and a handbag to match.

'Go and get changed, Veronica.' Her mother intruded on her inventory as she thrust the bag containing the leotard, tights and slippers at her. Abigail, she saw, had moved on to her crackers now and her chubby legs were no longer crossed. It wouldn't be long before she'd be straining at the straps wanting to get out of her seat to run around. She took the bag from her mum and moseyed slowly across the hall, breathing in the peculiar mix of sweaty socks and egg sandwiches permeating the space, to where the Ladies was. She heard her mum call after her, 'Chop, chop, Ronnie, your legs aren't painted on.' She poked her tongue out knowing she couldn't be seen. The boy had seen her rebellious act though and he was grinning at her in complicit understanding. She flashed him a return smile before pushing her way into the bathroom.

Megan and Hayley were giggling as they did the laces of their slippers up. They were already in their leotards. Their hair pulled back from their faces with Alice bands.

'Hello.' Veronica was shy even though she saw the two girls every day at school. It was strange seeing them here in a different context but it was also a stroke of luck. At least it was where Megan was concerned. She wished Hayley wasn't here. She couldn't help but be awkward around her. It was as if her limbs suddenly became odd sizes and she'd find herself wishing her hair would curl under prettily at the bottom, like Hayley's did instead of hanging straight. She began to undress.

'Hi, Ronnie,' Megan said, looking up and smiling. It reached her eyes, unlike Hayley's which managed to be superior and instantly made Veronica feel as though she didn't quite fit into her own body.

'Isn't it great?' Megan had feverish red spots on her cheeks. 'I've always wanted to be a ballet dancer. I was so excited when Mum said I could come.'

Veronica hadn't seen Megan's mum in the gathering outside. She'd probably been allowed to come on her own. Megan was allowed to do loads of stuff she'd never be allowed to do. Like go to McDonald's after school. Maybe she'd gotten a lift with Hayley's mum. Hayley's mum never walked anywhere not even to the corner shop. Veronica wished her mum would learn to drive but she said what was the point, it wasn't as if they could afford a second car anyway and Dad needed his to go to job interviews.

'Yes, it's great. Me too.' Veronica injected enthusiasm into the blatant lies skipping off her tongue as, slipping out of her blouse, she thought about birthday parties, McDonald's and roller skating.

'Yuck, what's that on your arm?' Hayley stared at the angry red patch Veronica had been worrying at on the walk there.

Veronica felt dirty as Hayley's nose screwed up in distaste. She couldn't very well hide the patch she'd scratched raw either. 'It's eczema.'

'Is it catchy?' Hayley took a step back and Veronica wished she had a hockey stick in her hand because she'd give her another bruise.

'No, it's not.' She could feel other eyes around the changing room on her.

'Does it hurt?' Megan asked.

'A little. It burns and it gets awfully itchy.' She was grateful for the sympathetic tone. 'I have a cream to put on it that helps a little.'

'Did you see the boy out there?' Hayley piped up in a change of subject, bored with the topic of Veronica's arm.

Veronica nodded, pulling her skirt down and kicking her Mary Jane's off. She tugged at her rumpled ankle socks and looking around at the eight or so other girls, all in varying stages of undress, wondered which one was his sister.

'He's doing lessons.' Hayley had that look on her face. The same one she'd wear when she knew the answer to whatever question their teacher, Mrs Bliss, was asking.

Veronica, who'd been about to begin rolling her tights on looked at her. 'For real?' She pulled the tights up lickety-split not wanting the other girls to notice the dry, pink patches behind her knees.

'Yes.' She was satisfied she was in the know and the other two weren't because Megan was looking at her curiously too. 'I overheard his mum talking to Miss Laverne. She was saying he had a natural attitude or something like that for music and she wanted him to have the opportunity to learn to dance because it's in his blood.'

Well that was a turn-up, Veronica thought, saying hello to Ruby and Charlotte, two girls from her class who never gave anyone else a look-in on their friendship. They'd linked arms and had matching hair ties holding back their ponytails, which were swinging as they skipped in full ballet mode out of the bathroom. She wondered if his mum had made him come like hers had. She felt a pang of kinship. She must have, she decided, tugging her leotard on because there was no way he'd have come of his own accord. He was a boy and boys didn't do ballet she was certain of that, as she plucked the leotard out from where it was riding up her bottom cheek.

Now

MARGO WAS HUMMING A tune Veronica realised, her throat dry from talking. It took her a moment to recognise it was the music from *Coppélia*. She and Gabe had performed a pas de deux that had given them a standing ovation to that music when they were sixteen. She was tempted to conjure up the emotions dancing in front of an audience had invoked. There was nothing else like them but she'd spent enough time tripping down memory lane. Time was marching on, she saw, glancing over at the clock on the wall with its bold black hands. She should be getting home to see what those lads of hers were up to. 'I'll pop that away now, Mum.' She took the costume gently from her and put it back in the bag. 'It's time for me to go home and see what Haydn and Hunter are up to, Mum.' A lump rose in her throat as Margo swung her gaze toward her.

'What do I do?'

'You stay here, Mum. You're well looked after and it'll be time for your tea soon. It smells delicious too, whatever it is. I'll be back on Thursday.'

'I live with my daughter though.' Her face was pinched as if she'd sucked her cheeks in, her eyes wide, pupils dilated. 'Why's she left me here?'

She was frightened and Veronica didn't know which was harder, the fear or the sorrow. *Oh God, this was so bloody hard and so BLOODY unfair.* 'I'm your daughter, Mum. It's okay.'

A tear rolled down her mother's cheek and Veronica's throat tightened. She picked up her hand and holding it in hers gave it a squeeze. 'Mum, you'll be okay.'

'I don't know why I have to stay. I want to be with my family. Who's going to look after me?'

She did that, drifted in and out of knowing who she was and where she was. The moments where she wasn't certain her mother knew who she was, only that she was someone who loved her, were happening more often. 'Danika will look after you, Mum, and you're here because you're safe and

59

cared for. Shall we sing a song?' Singing was balm for Margo's soul. Veronica would have to lead her into it and she began to croon the opening lines for *Memory*. Her mother loved the West End shows and despite only having seen *Cats* and *Les Mis* live, she knew all the songs from many of the musicals by heart. Margo's voice lilted into the song, quiet at first and then growing in strength. Several heads turned their way but Margo was on a stage all of her own.

Danika moved over to them. 'She's the loveliest of voices, your mum.'

Veronica nodded her agreement. 'She does. It seems incredible she can remember all the words to so many songs but she can't recall what she did five minutes ago.'

'I know. The human brain is a mystery.'

It was a cliché but it was true.

Chapter 10

Isabel

THE TIDE WAS OUT, ISABEL saw, reaching the bottom of the street as she made her way home. She pushed her guilt at yet again not having posted the letter aside and turned her attention to the scene in front of her. A cluster of children with buckets and spades in hand were playing on the stretch of sand lying between the road's end and water that matched the sky. The ferry was plying its way across the Solent and a larger ship idled farther out to sea. This was a vista she never tired of or took for granted even though these days it was one she was treated to everyday. Why then was she looking for something more?

She didn't hang around to ponder it pushing open the door of a Leap of Faith a few minutes later and smiling her greeting over at Rhodri. He was sitting in front of his easel at the back of the gallery. He waggled his paint brush at her by way of greeting as he always did and she found the normality of his greeting comforting. Things would be okay, they had to be, because she couldn't imagine her world without Rhodri in it.

There were two customers standing in front of the wall of local art for sale. It was a colourful mix of both Rhodri's work and that of other artists living on the island.

In another life, his Sally life, Rhodri had been an art dealer living in a fast-paced world but the low-key rhythm of the island had been balm for his wounds and he loved to paint the ever-changing vistas around him. The customers, a man and woman in their early sixties who were wearing the quick-dry gear of travellers both looked up, hearing the jangle of the door. She smiled over at them. 'Hello, there.'

Isabel received a smile back. They were appraising one of her favourite paintings. 'Have you visited Quarr?' she asked, moving closer and gesturing toward the bold and colourful oil on canvas. She was in awe of Rhodri's ability to recreate what he was saw in front of him. Looking at it, she could imagine stepping into the painting and being there in that moment, forever frozen in time.

This was the second painting he'd done of the abbey with its regal towers and unusual sunset coloured bricks. The woodland setting surrounding the imposing monastery made for a beautiful backdrop. Constance had been gifted his first painting but this one she was looking up at now was extra special so far as Isabel was concerned. She'd been there in the grounds with him and Constance when he'd begun work on it. It was the day Constance had confided her story and changed the course her life had been on forever.

'We have.' The woman replied. 'We're Catholic. I found it a very special place.'

The man, her husband presumably, was rubbing the stubble on his chin as he carried on with his studied appraisal of the artwork.

'It is special.' Isabel wasn't Catholic but there was a tranquillity and sense of order about the abbey that always left her feeling as though her equilibrium had been balanced by the time, she left the grounds. Are you Canadian per chance?' She was good at detecting the subtle nuances between the accents from the land of the maple leaf and the Star-Spangled Banner and was pleased when her guess was confirmed as being right.

'Well done, we're Vancouver born and bred. Have you been there?' This time they both looked at her.

'I'd like to, one of these days. A good friend of mine, Constance, is flying there soon. In fact, we're having a going-away party for her this time next week. She lives down the road at Sea Vistas retirement home. Would you believe it's her first trip abroad and she's ninety-one?'

'Wow! Good for her. Does she have family there?' the woman enquired.

'She does in a round about way and she's an amazing woman. Have you seen Sea Vistas? It's the magnificent old stone building at the end of the Esplanade.'

'No, we haven't walked down that far yet.' This time it was the man who spoke. 'We were making our way down there when we called in here. My wife was taken with the painting in the window but then we saw this one.'

'Well, you should definitely wander down farther and check out Appley Folly along the way. As for Sea Vistas, it wasn't always a retirement home. It started life as a manor house and during World War One troops were billeted there. Then, in the Second World War it was used as a convalescent home for the soldiers. Some of your Canadian troops recuperated there.'

'We'll definitely check them out, thank you,' the woman said.

'You're welcome. Are you in a hurry?'

'No, for the first time in forever our time's our own. Andrew,' she smiled at her husband, 'had his own law practice and he retired this year, hence our trip to England. We've had it planned for a long time.'

'Oh, I hope you're enjoying it.'

'We are, the history and architecture is incredible.'

'We take it for granted when it's on our doorstep,' Isabel said.

'Yes, we tend to do that, we're the same at home,' the woman said, her husband nodding his agreement.

'I could tell you a story about my friend Constance and a young air force man called Henry from your neck of the woods that might make you look at the painting differently, if you've got a minute.'

The Vancouver couple's curiosity was piqued by this young woman with bright pink hair. 'Sounds intriguing. Please do.' They stood with their heads slightly tilted to one side as Isabel began to talk.

'Constance was born and bred here on the island. She was a teenager during World War Two when she met Henry. The grounds by the ruins of the old abbey were their special place. Unfortunately, their story didn't have a happy ending because Henry was killed in a bombing at Sea Vistas, which back then was called Darlinghurst House. The reason he was there was to try and raise the spirits of a young cadet, a fellow countryman. The young man only survived because Henry threw himself on top of him.'

'How sad! Constance must have been heartbroken.' The woman's hand had gone to her chest.

'And proud because he was a hero,' her husband added.

'Yes, she was both of those. She was also pregnant, which back then, given they weren't married would have been scandalous if the news had gotten out.'

'Yes, it would have been.' The woman's prudish expression suggested it should still be so. 'What did she do?'

'Her parents sent her to a mother and baby home on the mainland and the baby was adopted.'

'Did she eventually marry someone else, have more children?' Prudishness was replaced by something more compassionate.

'No, she didn't. Henry was the love of her life.'

'How did she get by?' Two sets of eyes swivelled from the painting to Isabel, waiting to hear the answer.

'She ran the premises here as a herbal cure-all shop. She knows every herb and natural remedy that can be sourced on the island. Herbalism was in her blood because her family, the Downers' were related to the last witch on the Isle of Wight, Molly Downer.' She didn't tell them that Constance had gifted her Molly's very own journal of handwritten herbal remedies. It was the most precious thing Isabel had ever been given.

The woman gasped, her hand going to her neck and toying with the pendant hanging there. It was a gold cross, Isabel noted, informing her quickly, 'That was a term bandied about rather loosely in Molly's day. She was a healer and a recluse which was enough for the locals to point the finger.'

The woman's arm dropped back down to her side.

'And what about the child?' Andrew frowned.

'She had a son. They reconnected two years ago. He's based in in Hong Kong with his wife and child. They're going to meet Constance in Canada.

'So, is her trip to Vancouver a pilgrimage to take her son back to where his father came from?' The woman asked, clearly wanting this to be the case.

'It is.'

'I do like a happy ending.' She clapped her hands together in satisfaction and then her eyes swept over the painting once more.

Isabel had seen that look before and knew she was visualising it hanging over their lounge suite where it would be the first thing to be seen upon walking into the room. It would be a conversation starter. Her pièce de résistance.

'Andrew, we have to have this.'

Isabel shot Rhodri a victorious look and after platitudes about it being lovely to have chatted with them she left him to handle the rest of the transaction.

'NOT JUST A FABULOUS sales woman but an absolute stunner too. I'm a lucky man, Isabel Stark,'

Rhodri said appearing at the top of the stairs as she waited for the kettle to boil.

'We should go for a drink at The Rum Den to celebrate. Tea?'

'We should. As for the tea, I'd rather have a kiss.'

'A kiss? Is that all I get after the sale I just netted you?'

'It's lucky I just closed the gallery then isn't it. Upstairs with you, woman,' he growled.

She giggled, doing as she was told, forgetting all about the tea.

Chapter 11

Veronica

'HELLO, MUM.' VERONICA leaned down and kissed her mother's soft cheek, breathing in her familiar flowery scent. Margo reached up and Veronica took her hand giving it a gentle squeeze. 'You look lovely today.'

'I'll have a hug.' It was Winnie. She beamed at Veronica and waited beside her walking frame having stopped midway through to wherever she was intent on going.

'How are you, Winnie?' Veronica straightened and gave the old woman a hug, her wool cardigan scratchy to the touch.

'I'd be better if they'd get to work on time. I don't know what they're playing at.'

'No, it's not good enough, is it?'

'It isn't and I best go and see how the land lies.' She shuffled off and Veronica watched her for a moment, wondering what part of her life she was reliving. That was the thing, she thought, her gaze expanding to take in the other residents, some engaging in activities, others in conversation, and some staring blankly. All these people had had lives. They'd no doubt been productive, contributing members of society outside Holly Grange's upmarket brick façade. It was important to remember that, she thought, turning her attention back to her mum.

Today she was sitting in the lounge area with the activity of others going on around her. She'd a book open on her lap but it was a token gesture. A remembered pleasure of old to sit and read. 'Shall we go and sit somewhere quieter, Mum? I've brought something in to show you.'

Margo looked up at her. 'We'll have to take my book back to the... the...' her face crumpled as she lost the words.

'The library, Mum, and no, we don't want a late fine. Give it to me and I'll sort it for you.'

Margo's face relaxed and she obliged, allowing Veronica to take the book. 'I'll be back soon.' She headed around to the television alcove and put the book on the shelf there, returning to find her mother unmoved. She held out her hand, 'All done. Come on, Mum.'

Margo smiled and took her hand. 'I'm glad we're going out and about today, Veronica. It's such a beautiful day.'

'Yes, it's lovely although that wind's cool, Mum. We might be best to sit over here for a while.' She led her over to two twin armchairs set back from the others and settled her into the plump seat. Sitting down next to her she opened the bag she'd been carrying and felt the rawness of the tulle beneath her fingers. She pulled the sugary pink costume from the bag. 'This is the first tutu you made for me, Mum. I felt like a princess dancing in this.'

1985

'I'M VERONICA BUT MY mum and everyone else calls me Ronnie. Ronnie Kelly.' Veronica had one hand on the bar as she emulated the movements of Miss Laverne. This was their fifth lesson and it was the first time she'd found herself next to the only boy in their class.

She already knew his name from Miss Laverne having said, 'Gabriel, sink deeper into your plie.' Hayley had giggled loudly hearing this and Veronica had overheard her say, 'No wonder he does ballet, he's got a girl's name.'

She'd have liked to have been the kind of girl who said what she thought because if she was, she'd have told Hayley to shut up and mind her own beeswax, nobody cared what she thought. She wouldn't do that, though, not now the birthday invitation was within sight. So, she'd stayed quiet, letting Miss Laverne tap the cane she used to count the beat in irritation as she told Hayley not to talk in the middle of a lesson.

'Everybody calls me Gabe, apart from Miss Laverne,' Gabriel said, looking back over his shoulder. His brown eyes reminded Veronica of Bambi and they were wide as if he was surprised, she'd spoken to him.

She eyed Miss Laverne but she was too busy correcting Ruby's posture to notice she was chatting and not, as per her instructions, extending her leg, knees straight, toes alone touching the ground in a position she'd called tendu. This ballet business was all very strange, she thought, each time she heard a new exercise called out. 'I think Gabe suits you.'

A slow smile spread across his face and Veronica was pleased with herself. She turned her attention back to Miss Laverne who was now instructing them to move their legs out to the side.

Something unexpected had happened during that first class. Veronica, despite her best intentions, had enjoyed herself. She'd loved watching Miss Laverne's fluid movements, and wanted desperately to be able to appear as graceful as she did, like the swan she'd seen floating down the River Hawthorne on her way to school. Best of all though, she had what Miss

Laverne had told her mummy after the fourth class, a natural aptitude. She didn't know what that meant but Mummy had explained that Miss Laverne meant was she was good at it.

It seemed the girl who never paid attention during hockey and netball, who was always the last to be picked for the sports teams at school, could dance, and nobody was more surprised by this than Veronica. Mummy hadn't been surprised though, she'd said she was her mother's daughter and that much was obvious, though Veronica didn't know what she meant by it but she didn't ask her to explain.

The rest of the lesson flew by with Veronica losing herself in the motions of the elevés as she lifted up on the balls of her feet in each of the five positions. A highlight of their hour and three-quarter class was when Hayley couldn't get the hang of her elevés in fifth position, her arms arched overhead as she wobbled like a tree in the wind. The girl who was good at everything at school, flushed pink with annoyance at not being able to master this basic step. The fact it came easily to gawky Veronica irked Hayley and she'd steered Megan away after class without so much as a glance in her direction.

Veronica tried not to let the snub hurt as she took herself off to get changed back into her uniform in the Ladies. The other girls and Gabe didn't bother, they jumped in their mum's cars and went home in their leotards. Not that Gabe wore a leotard; he'd look silly if he did. He wore a white T-shirt, black shorts, and black ballet shoes with white socks. He was very lucky in her opinion not to have to wear a leotard that crept up his bottom. She pulled her tunic over her head. She couldn't very well walk home in her leotard with ballet slippers on her feet and she'd feel stupid with her clumpy T-bar shoes on her feet. The excited chatter that marked the end of a lesson had quietened off and she'd best get a move on. She didn't fancy finding herself locked into the centre for the night.

Veronica set about putting her shoes and socks on and then shoving her things into her school bag then pushed her way out of the bathroom. Mummy hadn't stayed to watch her lesson this week like she had all the others. All the other mum's apart from Gabe's and hers talked to one another about what they were having for their tea and that sort of thing but Mummy and Gabe's mum stood off to the side from the others as if they thought they were better than everybody else. Mummy never took her eyes off her and she'd seen her lips moving as she counted the steps along with Miss Laverne. Today though, she'd had to take Abigail who'd been sniffling and coughing these last few days, to the doctors. The appointment had clashed with the lesson and Veronica had been told to wait on the steps of the community hall if they weren't back by the time class finished.

The hall had indeed emptied out and Miss Laverne was the only one left. She was packing her music tapes away and looked up on hearing Veronica. A rare smile softened her features which were made sterner by the bold ruby-red she chose to wear on her lips.

'Ah, Veronica, and how are you enjoying the lessons?'

Veronica didn't need to think about her answer. 'I love them, Miss Laverne.'

'And why is that?'

It was a funny thing to ask her and this time she did think for a moment or two trying to find the words to explain how the music and movements made her feel. 'Because, well because I feel as if someone else has taken over my body.'

'You don't like being in your own body?' Miss Laverne had no eyebrows and Veronica stared at the two arched lines that looked as if they'd been drawn on with a brown felt tip pen. This time she pursed her lips and frowned because normally when an adult asked her a question, she would try her very best to give them the answer she thought they were wanting to hear. She instinctively knew this wasn't what Miss Laverne was wanting from her and so she answered truthfully. 'No, I don't. Sometimes when I'm around other people it feels like it isn't even mine and I'm not good at sport and things like the other girls. I suppose I'd be alright if I could make myself enjoy it but I can't see what the point of trying to snatch a ball off someone else or hit a ball with a stick is. I don't suppose I'd be very good at roller skating either but I'd like to try it. When I'm dancing, I know what to do without having to think about it. I feel as if I could do anything. And I forget about this,' she held her arm out and the teacher made a sympathetic murmur at the sight of the openly weepy patch of skin.

She didn't add that it gave her a break from worrying about her mum and dad and their fights which were getting worse. Her mind emptied of everything and the only thing that mattered was the music and movement of her body when she was here.

Miss Laverne looked pleased by what she'd said, although Veronica wasn't sure why. 'There was a light in your eyes when you spoke, Veronica. It's a light that tells me you're a dancer. Dancers feel the music here.' She put her hand to her chest. Her bust under her leotard was tiny, unlike Veronica's mummy's. Hers jiggled and bounced when she walked and Veronica had seen men in cars staring out their window at her in a way she'd didn't like. She didn't think Daddy would like it much either, even though he didn't want to be around Mummy much anymore. She wondered if she'd have bosoms like her mummy's or small mounds like Miss Laverne's when she grew up. Small mounds would be much more comfortable, she decided, and easier. She stopped staring at her teacher's chest as she realised she was asking her a question once more. 'You feel the music in your heart too, I think. Yes?'

Veronica nodded, she wasn't sure if she did or she didn't but she did know dancing made her happy. It was simple. The dance teacher patted her on her shoulder in a gesture of affection that seemed an uncomfortable fit and returned to her task. Veronica hovered, in no rush to leave. Mummy had shown her a book she had at home after her first lesson. Veronica had never seen it before given it was right at the top of the book shelf. Mummy had gotten it down and dusted it off, telling her to be careful with it because it was heavy. She'd also told Abigail she wasn't to touch it. It had made Veronica puff up proudly to be trusted with the book and it had been most satisfying when Abigail began to cry that she wanted to look at the pictures and Mummy had told her to cut it out.

The book was full of colourful, shiny pictures of ballerinas and men with legs that looked like they had ropes under their tights. Veronica had turned the pages slowly, in awe of the dancers' elegance as they were frozen in mid pirouette or as they leaped airborne across the stage. Velvet red drapes adorned the stage, framing the magical beings trapped in the glossy pages. Now it occurred to her that Miss Laverne might have been one of those dancers. Mummy had said she'd been a prima ballerina and there was something about her; it set her apart from other people. It wasn't the fact her hair was fire-engine red either. 'Miss Laverne, did you ever dance on a stage with red velvet curtains?'

She looked taken aback by the question, as though she'd expected Veronica to have gone by now and amusement flickered in her dark eyes. 'I did. I was with the Royal Ballet for many years. Then my mother got sick and my body was tiring of professional dancing even though my spirit wasn't so I came home and decided to teach.'

'Did you dance for Princess Diana?'

'No, but I did dance for the Queen.'

Veronica wondered if she should courtesy or something.

'Do you miss being on stage?'

'Sometimes, yes.' Miss Laverne would not tell this child who was all long gangly, limbs and hopeful bright eyes she missed it with all her being. A child couldn't understand, nor should they, how it felt when part of you died because you could no longer do the very thing that defined you. A recurring injury to her hamstring had culminated in a labral tear in her hip and her time in the spotlight had faded into the wings, to watch while younger dancers took her place. It was akin to being a great beauty and growing old. It was a cruel thing to have a passion and to no longer be able to fulfil it. But, as the saying went, it was better to have loved and lost than never to have loved at all. There was something about this girl, Veronica, that sparked a memory of her younger self. The child was looking at her now, an expectant expression on her pretty features. 'But now I get to pass on all I've learned to my students, and to teach is a wonderful thing.'

Veronica nodded, satisfied by the reply.

'I'll see you on Thursday,' Miss Laverne said by way of dismissal. The girl was stirring emotions in her she'd long since buried when her decision to end her professional career and move into teaching had been exacerbated by her mother's illness.

'Yes, see you on Thursday.' Veronica remembered her manners. 'And thank you, Miss Laverne.' She thudded across the floor, her feet no longer fairy light now she wasn't wearing her magic slippers, and out the doors.

Now

VERONICA AND MARGO sat quietly, both lost in the past. Slowly, Veronica became aware of the sounds around them having changed. There was the clatter of tables being set and the aroma of something hearty that made her think of beef and red wine was growing stronger. Danika caught her eye.

'Is it that time already?' Veronica said to her. 'I'd best be heading off.' She put the costume back in the bag and liked Danika all the more for her not asking as to what the relevance of it was.

'Mum, I've got to go now.' She stood up and kissed her mum on top of her head. 'I love you.'

Margo had begun to cry and Veronica swallowed hard. She hated leaving her when she was upset.

'Come on then, Margo. It's nearly time for your tea. Shall we get you settled at the table? I'll get you a nice glass of juice.' Her voice was cheery and had a reassuring effect. Veronica watched gratefully as her mother put her hand in Danika's with the same trust a child would and allowed her to help her up from the chair. She knew better than to drag out the goodbye even though she was filled with the urge to hug her one last time. As her mum was led toward the dining room, she mouthed a thank you at Danika who'd glanced back at her with a smile to say it would be alright. She blinked back her own threatened tears and the need for fresh air assailed her. Her temples had begun to throb, it was a tension headache, they always came on after these visits. Who'd have thought things would have turned out this way? Who'd have thought her beautiful, opinionated, capable, and at times overbearing mother would slowly begin to wither, a flower slowly dying before her very eyes.

Chapter 12

Isabel

ISABEL PUSHED THE GALLERY door open the following Saturday afternoon having finished a busy morning at The Natural Way. She blew Rhodri, who was chatting to a customer, a kiss before making a beeline for the back stairs. She was starving. The week had flown, she thought, hooking her bag on the back of a dining table chair and hoping there was some of that lovely ham Rhodri had picked up from the butchers earlier in the week left. She'd avoided looking across the road to the post box each morning and afternoon as she went to and from work and a guilty twinge assailed her as she grabbed the loaf from the bread bin. She'd been avoiding Constance too because she knew she'd be in for a talking to over the letter still being in her bag. She couldn't take the next step and just post it and she didn't know why.

She'd retrieved the cheese and, yes, there were two slices of the honey cured ham left, when she heard Rhodri pounding up the stairs. 'Sandwich?' she asked assuming he'd come looking for lunch now the gallery was empty.

'Ah, no thanks.' He crossed the room putting his arms around her and she leaned her head back against his chest. 'Actually, Isabel, I need to talk to you.'

She turned around, his hands settling on her hips. She searched his face for a clue as to what was coming but he was unreadable. He also needed a shave she thought absently.

'I rang Sally.'

'Oh, yes?' She pulled away from him busying herself by slicing a wedge of cheese. She felt bilious, a word her mother always used when nausea hit, and for some reason right at this moment it fitted. The sandwich she'd been looking forward to now held the same appeal of shovelling in handfuls of sawdust and she couldn't meet his eye.

'Yeah. We decided the next step is for me to meet Austin. Isabel, I don't want to waste any more time. So, I'm heading to Manchester.'

'When?'

'Now, if you'll watch the gallery for me until closing.'

'Now?' she repeated, sounding idiotic to her own ears but she was having trouble registering what he was saying. 'But it's after twelve. You won't get there until this evening,' fell out of her mouth. She backed it up with a swift, 'Shut the gallery or ring Nico and see if she can come and help out. I'll come with you.'

Rhodri put his hands on either side of the tops of her arms and she looked up to meet his steady brown-eyed gaze. 'I'd love you to, Isabel, but I need to go on my own. Can you understand?'

No, she bloody well couldn't but this wasn't the time to be argumentative. 'It's very short notice.' She floundered around trying to put the questions she had in order. 'Where will you stay?' *Please, not with her, please, please, please.*

'I've booked a hotel for the night; it's not far from where they live. There's a ferry leaving in forty minutes. I'll throw a change of clothes in a bag and head off. It won't take more than five hours to drive from Portsmouth. I can be there in time for dinner, hit the hay and be up early to spend the day with Austin. I'll drive home tomorrow evening and catch the last ferry back. You won't even know I've gone I'll be back that fast.'

It all sounded perfectly plausible but she knew she'd feel every single minute of his being away. The excitement in his voice at the thought of meeting his son was one she wanted to be part of and the thought of the three of them together, Austin, Sally and Rhodri playing happy families was too much.

He knew her too well. 'Isabel, this isn't about Sally, this is about Austin and what's next. You do know that?'

She swallowed hard not wanting to seem mealy-minded and nodded. 'Of course I do.' She understood the circumstances surrounding bringing a child into the world and who brought that child up weren't always black and white. There were so many shades of grey. This was something she knew thanks to Constance and to her own mum and dad. Sally might have been unhappy with Rhodri, she might have been frightened when she found out she was pregnant, afraid she was going to be stuck in a partnership she no longer wanted to be in. Darian might have provided her a means of escape but she had gone about it all underhandedly and put her own feelings above anyone else's. That made her selfish in Isabel's book. She was the sort of woman who'd have no qualms about trampling over another woman to take back what she wanted and Isabel was frightened.

She nodded. 'I know. Go and pack, you've a ferry to catch.'

Rhodri kissed her, taking it as her having given her blessing and she watched him head for the stairs wishing with all her heart he'd turn around and say he'd changed his mind and wanted her to go with him. He didn't, and when he left ten minutes later she felt very alone.

Chapter 13

Veronica

VERONICA PASSED THE white gauzy gown to her mum who stared at it like a foreign object. Danika had said she'd been a little unsettled today. Nothing to worry about as such, it was just a side to the illness of which there were many. Perhaps hearing her talk might help, she'd added, her smile a mixture of compassion and encouragement.

'This was one of my favourite costumes, Mum,' Veronica said now. It was plain compared to some of the outfits she'd danced in and she'd worn the white tutu with its floaty skirt for a recital when she was around ten. She loved it for the way it had made her feel every inch the princess and she could recall the way the skirt would float around her like a cloud when she pirouetted.

Margo had begun to stroke the fabric and Veronica watched her, wondering what was running through her head as her fingers touched the material she'd laboured over. She opened her mouth and began to carry on with her story, picking up from where she'd left off last week.

1985

THE LIGHT WAS IN BETWEEN afternoon and evening with the sun dipping low and the street outside the community centre a busy stream of smelly cars on a street too narrow for them, full of people on their way home from work. Veronica looked at the blurred faces and supposed they were in a hurry to get home for their tea. She wanted her tea, she was starving and hoped it would be fish fingers and chips because that was her favourite quick dinner. She was always starving when class finished; hopefully Mummy would have thought to pack her a couple of biscuits to chomp during the walk home. There was no sign of her she saw, casting about and spying Gabe sitting on the steps by himself. He was still in his T-shirt and shorts with a jacket thrown on overtop. He'd swapped his dance shoes for trainers.

'Hello,' she said, plonking down next to him whether he wanted her to or not. 'I'm waiting for my mum. She's late.'

'Hello.' His voice was quiet and unlike the boys in her class at school who all tried to talk over the top of one another. 'Me too and my mum's late because she had an appointment at the hairdressers. She's going to an important dinner with my dad tonight and says she has to look her best for it.'

'She's very pretty, your mum. She wears lovely clothes.' A surge of loyalty swelled up. 'So's my mum, pretty I mean.'

Gabe looked unsure of what he was supposed to say and Veronica decided to risk the question that burned every time she saw him, now they were on their own. 'Did your mum make you come to ballet? Because mine did.'

His hair was too long and fell into his eyes as he looked at her quizzically swiping it away with a practised hand. 'No, I wanted to come. I love to dance.' His eyes flashed, daring her to say something.

'Oh!' was all Veronica could come up with.

'The boys at school make fun of me about it.' He kicked at the concrete step upon which a solitary cigarette butt had been left to smoulder down to its tip.

Veronica wondered if Megan's mum had dropped it there. She eyed Gabe. Being on the outside was something she could understand. 'It's only because they don't understand. There's nothing wrong with a boy doing ballet.' And she meant it, she'd gotten used to having him in class.

'Male ballet dancers are athletes as much as those that compete at the Olympic Games but the boys at school say I'm a poof.' He kicked the butt off the step.

'Well, I don't think you're a poof.'

'Thanks.'

'What school do you go to?'

'St Trinian's; it's a boy's school. My dad went there.'

'I go to Abernathy Bridge. Maybe the kids would be nicer if you were at a school for boys *and* girls because the boys leave me alone at school but the girls can be mean. Not in a name calling way but in a not letting you be part of their group way.'

'I don't think my parents would let me.'

They were silent for a moment, both lost in thoughts of how unfair parents could be.

'Do you have any brothers or sisters?' Veronica spoke up first.

'No, it's just me. I'd like a brother.'

'Well, I've got a sister and it's not all it's cracked up to be. I think you're lucky. My sister, Abigail, she gets her own way because she's the baby and she's always following me about at home when I want to be on my own. She takes my things too without asking. She's very annoying.'

Gabe didn't voice that he thought it would be nice to have a shadow around his echoing big house. It wasn't all it was cracked up to be being the sole focus of his parents' attention, either. He felt the weight of their expectations for him keenly, even at eight years old.

'Why didn't you want to come to ballet?' he asked instead.

'I don't know.' Veronica shrugged. 'I suppose I didn't think I'd be any good at it because there's not many things I am good at. I wanted to go to Brownies or maybe learn piano.'

'Why can't you do them as well as ballet?'

'We don't have enough money,' Veronica said bluntly, recalling an argument her parents had had two nights ago which had culminated in her dad slamming the front door and not coming home until she and Abi were in bed. She'd pretended to be asleep when he peeked in on her and when he closed her door, she could still smell beer and something else. Something sweet and cloying. 'My Dad's not working he got made redundant.'

Gabe looked at her, his brown eyes showing surprise. 'My dad's a surgeon and he's hardly ever home. I'm good at rugby but I don't like it much. It doesn't stop Toby Wright and his gang picking on me though.' He turned his brown eyes on her then. 'You're the best in our class, my mum says. She used to dance like Miss Laverne but she stopped when she had me. She says you're a natural.'

'Truly?' Veronica felt warm inside at the thought of the beautiful creature in the Zara-Lee outfits thinking she stood out. What's your surname?'

'Darby-Hazleton.'

'Gosh that's a lot to say.'

Gabe nodded and opened his school bag to produce a lunchbox inside which was a lonely Penguin biscuit. Veronica loved Penguin biscuits and her mouth filled with water as she watched him tear it open.

'Do you want a bite?' He waved the chocolate biscuit in her direction and she took it gratefully trying not to take too big a bite out of it. She handed it back and let the chocolate melt on her tongue.

'Are you glad your mum made you come here now?' Gabe asked flicking his head in the direction of the building behind them before polishing off what was left of the bar.

'Yes. I count down the days between lessons. There's nowhere else I want to be.'

'Me too.'

They smiled at each other and there was a connection in that instant. It was in the unspoken understanding passing between them. Inside the ugly sixties brick building behind them was a reprieve. It came twice a week in the form of Miss Laverne's ballet class and it was a time in which it didn't matter if Veronica's mum and dad fought or if Gabe's dad was never around, because they got to forget and be the people they sensed they were supposed to be. The music spoke to their bodies in a way it didn't to the others and it was wonderful. The stuff of magic. They'd found a kindred spirit in each other.

'Would you like to come to my house one day after class for tea?' Gabe blurted out, hope plastered on his face.

'I'd like that.' She would. Gabe's world would be very different to hers and she'd like to see it for herself. Glancing past him she saw her mum puffing up the street with Princess Abigail reclining in her pushchair. She looked harassed and Veronica didn't hold out much hope of their being biscuits tucked away anywhere on her person. A tooting jolted them both and they looked to the shiny red car that had slid in alongside the kerb. His mum, Mrs Darby-Hazleton, as shiny as her car, was gesturing impatiently at Gabe. He got to his feet, picking up his school bag which he slung over his shoulder. 'I'll see you on Thursday and I'll ask my mum about tea.'

'See you Thursday,' Veronica echoed, watching him skip down the steps and clamber into the passenger seat. She was aware of the concrete, cold beneath the skirt of her uniform which was getting too short for her. She'd asked for a new one but Mum had said she'd let the hem down. He gave her a wave and she waved back watching the sleek red car merge into the traffic. There was a stirring within in her she didn't understand. It would only be as an adult she'd recognise what the feelings bubbling up in her that long-ago afternoon were.

Now

MARGO'S HANDS WERE still on the costume and Veronica patted them. 'You thought they were terribly posh the Darby-Hazleton's but there was always a lot more love and laughter in our home than there was in theirs. I just didn't appreciate it at the time. Shall I get us a cup of tea, Mum? They've put afternoon tea out and I quite fancy one of those buttered muffins?

Margo began to sing *Don't Cry for Me Argentina*.

Chapter 14

Isabel

'ARE YOU BUSY, ISABEL?' Babs Stark asked her daughter.

She wasn't, not really. She was perched on a stool behind the counter of A Leap of Faith. The gallery was quiet apart from a woman browsing through the stack of watercolour prints. Rhodri had been gone a couple of hours and she was still in a mild state of disbelief he wasn't here. 'No.'

'Good, you've time for a quick chat then.'

There was never anything quick about her mother's calls, Isabel thought, staring at the grooves in the varnished driftwood displayed down the far end of the counter.

'We've stopped for a pub lunch in Swindon. We're on our way to your dad's cousin Mick's youngest daughter's wedding in Bristol. It's a bit of a slight you not being invited but there you go. I always said Mick's lot were an ignorant bunch.'

'Mum, you don't need to shout. I can hear you.' Her mother did this whenever she was out and about making a call on her mobile. She couldn't quite grasp its powers of reception. She also did it whenever she spoke to a person who didn't speak English as though shouting would make it easier for them to understand her.

Babs dropped her volume half a notch. 'Anyway, we're not banking on a big spread because Mick's not known for his generous spirit so we thought we'd best fill up beforehand. Do you remember Jez? Big girl with a penchant for jelly babies? You used to drag that smelly blanket around everywhere you went when you were little but with Jez it was jelly babies. Her poor mum had to have a packet to hand at all times or there'd be murder. She'd bite the heads off them first too, says a lot about a person that does. We used to call her Jellybaby Jezzy. I wouldn't dare call her that now. The family she's marrying into are a rough lot, they might take umbrage. She's a year younger than you are too, Isabel, and you know what that means.'

'No, Mum, I don't, but I'm sure you're going to tell me.' Isabel had answered her phone against her better judgment. She knew from experience though, if she didn't pick up, her mother would begin ringing down her list of contacts to check she was alive. She'd start with Rhodri then Delwyn and work her way down to Brenda at the pub. It was easier to talk to her and find out what she wanted. Now, knowing what was coming next, she wished she hadn't.

'It means they'll all be on at me as to when you're getting married.' Her voice took on a sly quality. 'So, what should I tell them?'

Isabel was saved from answering by her mother suddenly shrieking. It was swiftly followed by, 'Isabel! Your dad's only gone and slopped his pint down the front of his trousers. I told him not to have one because he'll be knocking the beers back at the reception and he's had three coffees this morning too. You know what he's like. He'll be weeing every five minutes. He'll probably miss the service because he'll be off for a visit. Oh, I don't believe it, he looks like he's peed himself.'

Isabel heard her father tell her mother to keep her voice down.

Babs Stark was unperturbed. 'They're his good going-out slacks too, the tan chinos. You know the ones. I told him, I did, I said, 'Gary, you can't wear jeans to your cousin's daughter's wedding.''

This time she overheard her father mutter about chinos not being masculine and how Bruce wouldn't be seen dead in them. It made her smile despite herself.

'Tell him to go and waggle himself around under the hand drier in the loos that will sort him out, Mum'

Babs repeated Isabel's advice and she heard her dad muttering but couldn't make out what was being said. She figured her mum must have her hand over the phone.

'What did he say?'

'He said he's not risking burning the crown jewels and I told him it might jolt the old boy back into life.'

'Mum! I don't need to know.'

'You young one's all think you invented sex.'

Isabel tuned her out, waving a goodbye to the woman leaving the shop.

'Isabel, did you hear what I said?'

'Sorry, Mum, I missed that, there's a lot of background noise your end,' she fibbed.

There was a weighty sigh. 'I might as well talk to myself. At least you listen, don't you?'

Prince Charles, the family corgi, woofed by way of reply. They must be in the beer garden, Isabel thought. She should have known he'd be going to the wedding too.

She heard her father say, 'Everybody's bloody well listening.'

'Ooh, lunch is making its way across the garden,' Babs said, adding, 'Say hello to Prince Charles before I go.'

'Do I have to?'

'He'll sulk if you don't.'

She heard panting which signalled her mother had put the phone down by the Corgi's ears.

'Hello, Prince Charles, be a good boy at the wedding.'

There was a yipping reply and the last thing Isabel heard before disconnecting the call was, 'Leave off with the paper towels would you, woman!'

She'd no sooner put her phone down when it pinged to signal the arrival of a photo. It was the sign for the Swindon Arms confirming her parents' current location. A photo of a scampi basket was hot on its heels and, the grand finale, a shadowy, tan, chino blur. Isabel shook her head she would not be texting her mother back for an explanation as to that last picture.

Babs Stark had turned into a menace since upgrading her phone. She'd made do with her slowpoke Vodaphone mini for a long time. Her mantra had been she'd grown up in an era when people talked to one another face to face and the mobile phone should be used for emergencies only. End of. Since the smartphone had arrived on the scene, she'd taken to ringing Isabel for no other reason than because she could. Anywhere, anytime, to tell her anything that popped into her head. She'd also turned into an emoji nightmare. Yesterday, Isabel had received a text informing her she was making steak and kidney pudding for her and Dad's dinner. It had been followed by five cartoon images of a sloth doing everything from hanging off a branch to meditating. She had no idea what that had to do with what her parents were having for dinner and even less idea why she needed to know in the first place.

She'd no doubt get the run-down of Jellybaby Jezzy's wedding later that evening she thought, checking her watch to see there was another hour until she could close the gallery. Not that she knew what she'd do with herself for the rest of the day and evening looming ahead once her time was her own. What she wanted to do was climb into bed and pull the duvet up over her head. She couldn't face showing her face at The Rum Den for a drink on her own and having to fend off questions as to where Rhodri was, which was her only other option, so it looked like she was in for a night of wallowing. The thought of him in Manchester with Sally and Austin stabbed at her once more and she had no idea how she was going to get through the hours until he came home without driving herself mad.

Chapter 15

Veronica

VERONICA LOOKED UP from the order she was in the middle of to see him standing there, Suit-man! This time he was wearing a double-breasted, cobalt suit. His hair was clipped short and an oily stain decorated his tie, the type she knew would be a sod to get out.

'Hi, I was in a couple of weeks ago,' he said as she took stock of how that particular shade of blue made his eyes pop.

'I remember.' She'd not long since sucked a polo mint into oblivion, so coffee breath was not going to be an issue. She smiled to convey that she hoped there wasn't a problem with his purchase.

He'd grinned that grin, the one that made her knees go all trembly, as he gestured toward the MAC stand. 'I gave the young man over there a fright.'

They'd both looked over at Tyrone who'd given them a flutter of his fingers before returning to his inventory of the eyeshadows.

She'd smiled, wishing she could think of a witty comeback but her mind was like a field that had been ploughed, empty.

'This time, I'm looking for a women's fragrance.'

'Oh, right.' Well that was that. She should have known he wouldn't be single even if he did get about with coffee and grease stains on his tie. It was 2020 after all. Women were no longer expected to keep their other halves clothes clean nor had they been for decades. She suspected Jason hadn't been informed of that. He was single once more which meant he was more inclined to turn up unexpectedly on the doorstep wanting to take the boys out for a McDonald's lunch or the like. Only a few weeks back he'd shown up offering Big Mac combos with a shirt draped over his arm along with a pleading look as he asked her to try and get the Marmite stain out of it. Worst of all she'd obliged, pathetically grateful to him for taking his own sons out.

'And I wondered if you could help me choose something? I'm not very good at that sort of thing.'

'Of course.' Veronica mustered a smile as she donned her professional hat and told her roving eye to behave itself. She prided herself on being part of the sisterhood. As such she'd never covet another woman's man and, stepping out from behind the counter, she moved over to the array of colourful bottles and boxes she spent so much time lovingly arranging.

'What's she like? It helps to have an idea of what a woman enjoys doing and her personality,' she explained. 'Because perfume should be an extension of who she is.'

'Oh, um, I don't know her that well.' He shifted awkwardly as if he hadn't thought this through properly and was regretting his off the cuff decision to gift his new lady friend with a French perfume.

'Well, is she outdoorsy, you know into rambling and camping that sort of thing? Or, does she enjoy being dressed up and fine dining?' Hopefully he wouldn't say both and make the choice tricky.

He shrugged looking like a little boy lost. 'What do you like?'

'Me?'

He nodded.

'Oh, er, well I like different fragrances for different moods.' It was true in theory and made her sound rather exotic. Either that or a right moody mare. She could tell by his bewildered expression he didn't get where she was coming from. Men are from Mars and all that. 'What I mean is, if I was going out for dinner, I'd wear this.' She took the classically shaped glass tester bottle of Chloe Love Story off the shelf along with a cardboard strip from the container and, holding it away from herself, sprayed the tip. She let it settle enjoying the neroli, orange blossom and jasmine notes floating on the air. 'This perfume was inspired by Parisian romance and the padlocks on the Pont des Arts bridge.' It was incredibly romantic she'd thought upon listening to the rep get passionate about the company's latest offering a few years ago.

She gave him the card and he inhaled the heady scent looking at her for an answer because it was clear he was uncertain as to what he should say.

'It's quite simple,' Veronica said. 'Do you like it?'

He nodded. 'It's lovely. I think it would suit her and I'd definitely like to take her out for dinner.'

Lucky bloody cow. 'What woman doesn't love Paris?' She got the box down from the shelf and gave it to him so he could check the price. 'This is the eau de parfum which is a concentrated version. It lingers on the skin longer.'

'Paris is one of my favourite cities.' It was said in a manner that told her he was the sort of man who'd take his lady friend on a romantic city break there as well as out for dinner. *Super lucky bloody cow.*

Veronica wasn't normally green eyed but sometimes life could be unfair and resentment toward this unknown woman surged. She'd never got further than a caravan in Cornwall with Jason. She thought about her ex's Ibiza tan and a flare of resentment shot through her.

'Have you been?'

It annoyed her, the assumption that she should be able to flit off to European cities without a care in the world, or perhaps she was being overly sensitive. 'Once, a long time ago now. I suspect I'd see the city differently through adult eyes but I've teenage sons and there's not much time for the likes of Paris these days.' Her voice sounded clipped and defensive.

'I thought you must have visited. It was the way you talked about the perfume, you sounded like you were familiar with the bridge.'

Veronica daydreamed about the sort of man who'd write his and her names with a love heart on a padlock securing it as a declaration of love to overlook the Seine for eternity. Or, at least until the bridge collapsed from the weight of all those locks. She'd seen the photos. Gabe had been that sort of boy. Full of romance and joie de vivre and somewhere on that bridge were his and her names, together forever. Except they hadn't been. 'I visited it, yes, and I enjoy the stories as to how the different fragrances come to fruition.'

A coiffed, silver-blonde woman in pearls materialised at the counter to clear her throat then, drumming talon-like, coral nails on the countertop. Her fingers were a mass of oversized, sparkling rocks.

Veronica excused herself. 'I'll let you have a browse. Feel free to test anything you like the look of. I'll be back in a moment.'

'I've decided. I'll take this one,' he said with the box of Chloe, Love Story she'd recommended in his hand, and then lowering his voice, 'but I think you'd better serve her first or she's likely to break a nail and we don't want that to happen now, do we?'

They shared a complicit smirk and she hurried over to serve the self-important customer who demanded a sample of the latest Chanel fragrance, Chance. Veronica knew her type. She was perfectly capable of locating the tester and spraying her own cardboard stick but she'd rather have Veronica run around after her. She was probably going to stick the strip in her knicker drawer when she got home, she thought, obliging her. All the time she could feel Suit-man's eyes on her as he waited patiently to one side. The uppity woman took the sample from her and unclipped her handbag, dropping it in there barely managing a thank you as she clipped her bag shut once more. Veronica watched her make a beeline for Tyrone with satisfaction. He had a way with the dowager duchess types. He could put them in their place without them ever suspecting a thing.

'Would you like it gift wrapped?' She turned her attention back to Suit-man who'd moved over to the side of the till; he passed her the box.

'Yes, please if you don't mind.'

'Not at all.' She was all fingers and thumbs and wished she could think of some sparkling banter but it was taking all her hand-eye coordination skills to put the Sellotape in place and how she managed to slide the scissor blade up the curling ribbon without slicing her finger was a miracle.

'That looks great, thank you,' he said as she dropped the parcel into a carry bag for him.

'I'm sure she'll be delighted.' Veronica's teeth were gritted as she took the credit card he was proffering to swipe through for him. She wished she could hold onto it long enough to read his name but he'd wonder what she was up to if she were to begin inspecting his Visa. *And besides, Veronica,* she told herself sternly, he was spoken for. He took his receipt and hovered until things began to feel awkward.

'Thanks, then.'

She smiled up at him and was about to ask if there was something else when he turned on the heel of his polished, brown brogue and walked off. A bereft feeling, as though she'd been cheated, somehow settled over her as she watched him weave his way through the store towards the main entrance. She had to smile when he knocked into the table scattering the display of crocodile skin handbags which together could have paid for the deposit of a house. Sandra from handbags was not impressed. Handsome and a natty dresser he might be but he was also a messy eater and a klutz and she liked that. She liked it a lot.

She went back to the order she'd been, unpacking catching a glimpse of herself in the mirror behind the shelving. What had Suit-man seen looking at her? A nondescript middle-aged woman she mouthed at her expression. Definitely not the sort of woman a man would spend his lunch break sourcing the perfect perfume for.

Perhaps she should make a hair appointment, splash out and try a new colour. She'd always loved experimenting with different looks but hadn't done so in a long while. It might perk her up, and her hair in its current au naturel state was a boring brown. Yes, she decided she'd ring that new salon, the one that had opened up where the overpriced shoe shop had been, what was it called? The Theory of Colour, that was it, and book in for one of their late-night appointments.

Yes, she'd gotten to the crux of the problem, she decided. This was why she'd been feeling invisible. She was losing sight of who she was. Veronica the independent woman was being suffocated by being all things to others, daughter, mother, sister, employee and she might as well toss in ex-wife while she was at it. It was time to be proactive.

Chapter 16
Isabel

'I BET YOU THAT'S MUM.' Isabel said out loud to the empty room. She'd been watching at mindless reality show to stop herself thinking about Rhodri. He'd rung an hour ago to say he was having dinner in the hotel restaurant and then was planning on an early night. She'd found the conversation hard and knew she'd been stilted with him but she didn't know what she was supposed to say. He'd sounded weary from the long drive and so she'd told him to enjoy his meal and to call her tomorrow when he got the chance. She fancied she heard relief in his voice at not having to have to try and chat further as he told her he loved her before hanging up.

'Hello, Mum,' she said now, answering the call.

'Hello, we're not long in the door. I've a cup of tea made and I'm kicking my shoes off as we speak. Your father's flopped in front of the tele watching a *Top Gear* special. Ooh, that's better, my feet are killing me from all the dancing we did.'

Isabel pictured her mum doing ankle rotations. She might as well get comfortable too she thought, leaning back into the sofa's overstuffed cushions. 'Was it a nice service?'

'It was. Jez had a lovely, old-fashioned church wedding and she wore white although I'm betting it's the first time Jez and Darren, that's her new husband's name, have seen the inside of God's house in a long while. He had an earring in his chin, Isabel. Why would you want to do that to yourself? Your Aunt Janice said she wouldn't be surprised if he had his you know what pierced too. It's a thing you know, Janice said, although I don't know how she'd know. Anyway, I thought the poor lad had a pimple on his chin but when I put my glasses on I saw it was a silver stud.'

Isabel shook her head trying to keep up. 'What about Jelly Babies? Did Jez carry a packet of those instead of a bouquet?'

'No, she had roses, but there was a miniature packet of Jelly Babies by everybody's place settings at dinner time.'

'And how did the reception go?'

'Well, to be fair, Mick did Jez proud although the portion sizes were on the mean side so I'm glad we'd stopped off for something to eat beforehand. The free bar ran out earlier than your father would have liked too. And I'll have you know, Isabel, by the time the desserts were rolled out I was fed up to the back teeth of being asked if you were going to be next. I didn't know what to say.'

'I'm sure you thought of something.'

'I said I didn't think it'd be long before we were all meeting up in a church again.'

'Mum!'

'What? It's what you'd call clever deflection because your dad's Great Aunt Ada is looking very frail although she's still a bite. Mark my words we'll be gathering again soon enough to see her off. So you see, clever deflection. It'd be nice to know what Rhodri's intentions toward you are though, Isabel.'

'He's not here at the moment, Mum, so I can't ask him. What were the speeches like?' Isabel did some deflecting herself, steering the conversation away from her mother's latest bugbear as to when her daughter would be married.

'They didn't drag on too long which was a blessing. The best man could barely string a sentence together but not because he was drunk. Like I said the free bar ran out early, but because he was a bit of a missing link, to be honest. Oh, and I got stuck next to your dad's Great Uncle Fred at dinner. He's a one alright, his hand kept accidentally slipping to my, knee under the table and I could hear his false teeth clacking all through the meal. It wasn't very nice, Isabel. It nearly put me off my roast beef.'

'Ugh, I can imagine. Did Dad get his, erm, problem sorted.'

'His chinos were dry by the time we arrived and nobody would have noticed the staining if he'd left himself alone. I told him to stop fidgeting about pulling at them all the time or people will think he's got some sort of problem going on down yonder.' She sighed weightily. 'He hasn't been this bad since he had the jock itch. He's not had another bout of that once since he gave up the football. I was right all along. It was the sweaty shorts causing the problem.'

'Good to know.'

'We got to show off our salsa moves on the dance floor too, Isabel. They had a DJ not a band. It went down a treat. We got a big round of applause.' Her mum had finally talked her father into giving up playing football after an ankle injury and talked him into salsa classes by forgoing her week in Benidorm so he could have a Premier League season pass.

'Did you?' Isabel was surprised anything with a Latin American beat had been on the playlist and relieved simultaneously that she wasn't there to witness her parents breaking out their moves to it. 'From memory, Mum, Jez would have struck me more as a heavy metal music fan.' The image of a moody girl, clutching a packet of Jelly Babies, clad in a black AC/DC T-shirt with black jeans and Doc Marten boots sprang to mind. Mind you it had been years since she'd seen her.

'Oh yes, we had the old Acca Dacca and a spot of Motorhead. Your father's not going to be in a good way tomorrow. I think he might have whiplash from the headbanging he did to *Ace of Spades*. Where's Rhodri tonight? A pub quiz down at The Rum Den is it?'

Did she want to have this conversation? Isabel chewed her lip and then decided there was no time like the present because it was seemingly likely Austin was going be a fixture in their lives given things had gone well today.

'Erm, Mum, there's something I should probably tell you.'

'Oh, yes?' Babs sounded wary. 'You're not p—'

'No! Rhodri's in Manchester. He's gone to meet his son for the first time.'

'What? Gary turn that television off. Rhodri has a love child. Isabel, I'm putting you on speaker.'

By the time she'd explained the situation to her parents the clock was inching towards eleven pm and she stifled a yawn.

'And how do you feel about it all, Isabel?'

'Frightened, Mum.'

'Of what?'

'Things are going to change.'

'Yes.' Babs was silent for a moment. 'But you know it doesn't mean they're going to change in a bad way, Isabel. Austin's the one who's going through the most change from what you've told me and he and Rhodri are going to need you to accept him into your life too.'

Sometimes her mum could be a wise woman. 'Yeah, you're right. Thanks, Mum.' Sally didn't feature in the equation and it made her feel better. 'I'm going to head up to bed now.'

'Say night, night to Prince Charles before you go.'

'Put him on.' She stood up, stretching, waiting patiently for the deep breathing. She didn't have to wait long. 'Hello, Prince Charles, did you have a nice time at the wedding. I hope Mum slipped you a few treats.'

He woofed and Babs came back on. 'I almost forgot, what with all your news. He marked his copy book with your dad's side of the family because he decided to do his business outside the front entrance of the venue. Jez nearly stood in it when they came back from having their photographs taken. I only turned my back on him for a few seconds. Honestly, it's the sort of thing you did when you were little, Isabel'

'What, poo in the entrance of wedding reception venues?'

'No, but you went through that phase of taking your nappy off and leaving deposits for Dad to find in the back garden when he went to mow it. Didn't she, Gaz?'

'*Night,* Mum. I love you.' Isabel had heard enough and, ending the call, she waited a second and wasn't disappointed when photos pinged through. She scrolled through thinking Jez would have carried her sparkly white, flouncy dress off better if she didn't have tattoos covering every inch of her bare shoulders. Her betrothed's gold tooth was very distracting in the photographs too. It was the last picture that made her grimace however and she stared at her father, frozen on her screen, hip thrust forward in a dance move that looked more *Saturday Night Fever* than salsa.

She took herself off up the stairs to get ready for bed, the image of her father burnt onto her retinas. Grateful for the distraction her parents had provided.

Chapter 17
Veronica

'THANKS FOR SQUEEZING me in.' Veronica flopped down in the chair, Avery, her designated stylist had ushered her over to. She'd made an appointment at lunchtime. Now she was grateful to take a load off having read somewhere she was a prime candidate for varicose veins thanks to what sometimes felt like a lifetime of standing behind the perfume counter at Blakeley's. It had been a long day which had involved meeting several reps from the different perfume houses and lots of sniffing at fragrance cards. Her day had peaked early with Suit-man's pre-lunch appearance at her counter.

She loved perfume, she adored it in fact, because she believed wholeheartedly in scent having the power to conjure emotion. To change sadness to joy. But some days when she left the department store, she could almost taste sandalwood, rose and musk lodged in the back of her throat ready to taint anything she tried to eat. On days like that, all she wanted was go home to her perfume-free zone where she didn't have to be chatty and friendly with anyone. The boys didn't appreciate chatty and friendly these days, interpreting it as nosy and needy, and as for their particular scent, smelly socks and sweaty armpits hardly counted as perfume.

Avery looked like she'd rather be at home with her tea on her lap watching the tele than about to transform a middle-aged woman. Nevertheless, she mustered a smile as she flapped the cape out around her new client. Veronica had come straight from work, texting the boys to tell them she'd be home later than normal and to sort themselves out something to eat if they didn't want to wait for her. She planned on whipping up a shepherd's pie and if they weren't hungry then she could freeze what was left for another night. Right this minute they were probably microwaving spaghetti noodles.

She caught Avery's quizzical gaze in the reflection of the mirror she was plonked in front of. 'You're booked in for a colour and cut right?'

'Yes, and just a trim off the ends, thanks.'

'Is this natural?' She picked up a clump of mouse brown hair and rubbed it between her fingers. 'It's in good condition.'

'Erm, thanks, and yes I'm au naturel at the moment.' She knew if the boys were listening in they'd be muttering on about her being *cringe*. She could see several silver threads in amongst the brown, and squinting into the mirror, saw they were more like silver ropes. How had she not noticed them? It was pretty amazing the boys had refrained from pointing them out. She knew allowing one's hair to silver naturally was a big trend at the moment but she was away off allowing that to happen and she didn't want to be a mottled mix of grey and brown like a tabby cat either, thank you. She was too young in her opinion to start resembling Scruffy-bum. 'I'd like something different, please, Avery. Something that makes me standout.'

Avery pursed her sticky, glossed lips. Her hair was a white, bleached, chin-length bob and she was obviously a self-tanning devotee because the expanse of skin on display was a tell-tale orange, brown. She had several piercings in her nose which made Veronica clench her bottom cheeks at the thought of having something like that done. Avery was also wearing a black skirt that would ensure she was hard to miss even without the peroxide blonde hair and piercing. It was a skirt her nana would have called a belt and she found herself adding, 'But not in a ridiculous way because I am in my forties.'

Avery gave her a withering look, suggesting this was going to be a tough call. She moved from one cherry red Doc Marten booted foot to the other and appeared to be in pain as she pondered what to do. Veronica was almost ready to apologise for being such a difficult client when she piped up with, 'What about azure?'

Veronica blinked. Azure brought to mind the Greek Islands and swimming in the Med not hair. 'As in blue?'

'Yes, the blue shades are hot right now thanks to Kylie Jenner.'

Veronica was more au fait with Kylie Minogue having spun around to the Australian's hot-pants hit when she and Jason had whiled away Saturday nights clubbing, than Kylie Jenner but she was listening.

'Your eyes are a bluish-green and with your fairish colouring I think you could rock it.'

She could rock blue hair? Avery thought she could rock something. Veronica liked that idea and the younger woman's faith in her. She'd wanted something different so, why not? She decided to throw caution to the wind. 'Go for it, Avery!'

Poor Avery took a step back at the vigour with which Veronica gave her the green light. Even Veronica had to admit it was *cringe*, but she was too excited to be contrite.

The young woman gathered herself and was about to disappear out the back to mix her potion when she paused. 'Do you mind me asking what perfume you're wearing? It's lovely. It makes me think of Starbuck's Vanilla Bean Cream Frappuccino. I lived on them when I went to Orlando last year. They were delish.'

'Oh.' Veronica wasn't sure that was the analogy the nose at the YSL headquarters in Paris would've had in mind but it was an interesting one. 'It's Black Opium by Yves Saint Laurent. I manage the perfume counter at Blakeley's. The fragrance's keywords are floral, energetic, coffee accord and white flowers.' She wasn't sure if she had them in the right order but was certain the company would be proud of her recall, nonetheless. She'd definitely be on their goody bag Christmas list. 'So, I can see where you got the whole frappe connection from.' Avery, she knew from her chats with the rep, was the reinvented fragrance's target market for the perfume. When she'd been her age, she'd splashed Opium everywhere knocking everyone out with her overtly sexual muskiness, convinced it turned her into a goddess especially after a few pints. Jason had asked her to stop dabbing it between her boobs because he didn't need an invitation to visit and it took forever to the get the taste of the stuff off his tongue.

Avery's eyes had already glazed over and she thudded off to the potion room leaving Veronica to relax into the seat.

'Would you like a tea or a coffee? I can make cappuccino.' A young girl with a broom, still in her school uniform, appeared alongside Veronica. She looked eager for an excuse to stop sweeping the hair off the salon floor.

'I'd love a cappuccino. Thank you.' She put the magazine she'd been aimlessly flicking through down and smiled at her.

The teenager puffed up importantly and then she too disappeared behind the dividing wall leaving Veronica alone with her thoughts.

Veronica was about to mull over today's visit to her counter. Relive the moment when she'd turned around to see Suit-man once again but she didn't have time to dwell on their conversation because she was being presented with a cappuccino. Avery picked that moment to reappear with a brush in hand ready to begin the bleaching process.

One and a half hours later, Veronica was angled uncomfortably over the sink while Avery washed the last of the colour out. She was fed up. There were only so many women's magazines to be flicked through and she was more up to date with the seedy goings on of the celebrity world than she'd been in years. She was also fed up with looking at herself in the mirror. She was hungry and her stomach was beginning to make itself heard, loudly. There were one hundred and one other things she could be doing instead of getting a numb bum at the hairdressers. If she'd had an inkling as to what a palaver this new-look business was going to be, she'd have gone for boring old highlights. It was too late now though, she thought, following Avery's direction and sitting up as she towel-dried her hair off.

'It's come up well,' the stylist said, dropping the towel into the sink and inspecting her handiwork. That was something, Veronica thought, following her lead obediently back to her chair in front of the mirror. 'What do you think?' Avery demanded before she even had her bum on the chair.

Veronica sat down and with trepidation met her gaze in the mirror. She blinked rapidly at the initial shock of change and then her mouth twitched with the beginnings of a smile. If she were to see herself as a stranger would, she'd think she looked good. The colour gave her a whimsical look and she liked it. She remembered the long-ago sunshine holiday when her parents had been happy and she and Abi had whiled away their days playing mermaids in the clear blue water. It looks great. Thank you, Avery.'

Avery gave a pleased nod. 'Right then, I'll dry you off and then you can be on your, way.' She picked up a barrel brush and the hairdryer and began to dry her hair with those practiced strokes she knew she'd never be able to emulate at home. By the time she'd finished, Veronica's hair hung in a blue sheet grazing her shoulders. She wanted to swing her head from side to side like the models did on shampoo ads but she'd been here long enough and there'd be time enough for that in the privacy of her own bathroom later.

She gathered her bag up and tried not to show the horror she felt when Avery informed her how much the last three and a half hours had cost her. It was the most money she'd spent on herself in a very long while and guilt stabbed as she remembered the consent form the boys had brought home a few nights ago along with the request for a ridiculous sum so they could go on a science field trip. They needed new summer uniforms too. She'd have to talk to Jason. Her temples began to throb and a rattling anxiety at having to go cap in hand to her ex coursed through her system. She hated asking him for extra money. It made her feel like a failure who couldn't manage her finances. She did her best but it was hard. This one was on her though because nobody had twisted her arm to go and spend a small fortune at the hairdressers. Vanity and a need to be seen were what had motivated her.

Ah well, she'd cross the bridge of field trips and uniforms when she came to it. For now, her immediate concern was what her sons would say to their mother's new do. Would they ban her from the upcoming parent teacher evening? That might not be such a bad thing given how the last one had gone, she thought, digging deep once more in her bag for her keys.

Chapter 18
Isabel

ISABEL STOOD IN THE bathroom and inspected the eczema that had flared up overnight, her arms turned out. It itched and burned and she chewed her bottom lip in an effort to stop scratching at it. Sunday stretched long, especially given the dreary day she'd caught sight of pulling back the bedroom curtains a few moments earlier. She'd try soaking in a bath of colloidal oats and see if that took the irritation down. She was always trying new natural remedies for her eczema because she liked to be able to recommend tried and true treatments to customers. Putting the plug in the tub she turned on the taps and then opened the vanity drawer to retrieve the sachet of oats she'd brought home from The Natural Way. She ripped it open tipping the contents under the running taps.

Rhodri hadn't phoned and while the tub filled she went to retrieve her phone from where she was charging it. There were no new messages and she put it down in disgust. She'd hoped he might ring before he went to Sally's but given it was ten o'clock she didn't think it was likely she'd hear from him now. She pulled the bedding up and fluffed the pillows before shoving the clothes she'd stepped out of last night into the wash basket. The bathroom was steaming up she saw, venturing back in there and turning the taps off. She ran her hand through the water testing the temperature and made her mind up to go and see Constance. She was being silly avoiding her because of the letter. So, with her mind made up she climbed out of her pyjamas and slid into the water, allowing the milky mixture to calm her skin's irritation and wishing it would calm her mind too.

'AND WHY DO YOU HAVE a face on you like the proverbial wet weekend?' Constance asked, looking up from the remains of her lunch to take stock of Isabel who was standing rather bedraggled in front of her.

Isabel had found her in the dining room at her table near the window, not that the view was up to much today. She shrugged off her damp coat and hung it on the back of the chair before sitting down. She could smell roast chicken and was guessing that was what had been on Sea Vista's lunch menu. 'Because it *is* a wet weekend, have you not looked out there,' she gestured to the oppressive sky outside. 'And, Rhodri's gone to Manchester to meet Austin but I didn't come to talk about him. To be honest, Constance, I'm fed up thinking about it. I hardly slept last night playing all the different scenarios out in my mind. I came to talk about your party and to check we've got everything in hand.'

'I see, so that's why you're knickerish and out of sorts.'

'It is.' She forgot she didn't want to talk about him. 'He didn't ring me this morning either. I thought he might have.'

Constance made a noise that sounded like air being let out of a fizzy bottle, before adding, 'Isabel, you should have realised by now men and women are fundamentally different. Men for instance can only focus on one thing at a time. His mind will be on meeting his son. Whereas you, my dear, overthink things.'

'I suppose so.'

'I know so. Here, have my raspberry slice.' She patted her middle before sliding her side plate towards Isabel. 'I've had spotted dick and custard for pudding, I don't need this as well. The coffee will still be hot in the pot, go and help yourself.' She pointed to the tray in the serving hatch near the entrance to the kitchen. Isabel did so, in need of warming up after the brisk walk through the drizzle she'd had to get there.

She smiled at Lesley who helped in the kitchen as she cleared Constance's empty pudding bowl away.

I enjoyed that, Lesley. You can't beat a good old spotted dick.'

'Terrible name for a pudding if you ask me,' Isabel said, placing her cup and saucer down as Lesley moved on to another table.

'Only if you've a mind that dwells in the gutter,' Constance batted back. 'Now then, have you posted your letter?'

Isabel busied herself stirring her coffee.

'Oh, Isabel!' Constance sat forward in her chair, her raised voice causing one or two curious silver heads to turn their way.

Isabel didn't look up from her drink; she was worried she might cry if she did. She was beginning to wish she'd gone with her first instinct upon waking this morning which was to stay in bed until Rhodri got home.

Constance, sensing she was fragile, backstepped, reaching over to rest her warm hand on top of Isabel's. 'It's a big step reaching out to her. I understand, Isabel, I do, but if you don't take that step, how can you ever know what happens next?'

Constance was right, Isabel knew, chomping into the slice and resolving to post the letter, just not today when all this other stuff was going on with Rhodri.

ISABEL LAY ON HER BACK in bed, eyes wide in the dark despite being tired from her restless sleep the night before. She was straining for the sounds that would let her know Rhodri was home and knew she'd only sleep when he was here lying next to her. At last she caught the sound of a door squeaking followed by his familiar tread on the stairs. She rolled to her side and flicked the bedside light on.

'Hi. I thought you'd be asleep.'

'Couldn't, not until you got home.' She studied his face which looked drawn from the driving and no doubt the emotion of meeting his son.

He put his bag down, unzipping it to retrieve his toothbrush. 'Back in a sec.'

She heard him going through the motions in the bathroom.

He was back a minute later and she watched, propped up on her elbow, as he clambered out of his clothes before climbing into bed beside her wearing nothing but his boxer shorts. He rested his head on the pillow. 'God, it's good to stretch out.'

She leaned down and planted a kiss on his lips. 'So, how did it go?'

He smiled. 'He's brilliant, Isabel, you'll love him.'

She could hear the wonder overriding his weariness and wished she'd been there to witness their meeting for herself.

'He was shy at first but as the day wore on he warmed up. I took him to an indoor playground. God, the noise of the place but he had a great time.'

'Did Sally come too?' She hoped her pitch hadn't gone up a notch.

'No, she stayed at home. She thought it would go better if Austin and I had a chance to be on our own together.'

Isabel exhaled, not realising she'd been holding her breath.

'Did you discuss what happens next?'

He closed his eyes and she stared at his lashes fanned out, knowing as soon as she put the light out he'd be out for the count.

'Sally's wanting to book a holiday and for us to have Austin for the week.'

It took all her strength not to let rip with a derisive snort as Rhodri told her Sally needed a break. Again she had to hold back as he added, 'It hasn't been easy for her this last while, parenting on her own.'

She flicked off the light, not trusting herself to speak, and lay next to him stewing, as within minutes his breathing slowed to a steady rhythm. Constance had made mention today that men and women were fundamentally different. She was right. Men could fall asleep no matter what was going on around them. Meanwhile she was destined to hours staring into the dark as she pondered what kind of woman entertains offloading her son on her ex-husband who despite being his father doesn't know him? Not just that either—what kind of woman leaves her son with a stepmum, or whatever she was, she's never met? Isabel knew the answer. The kind of woman who would run off with her husband's best friend and not tell him the truth as to who the father of her child was. She didn't think she'd like Sally very much when they met, as they were bound to do so at some point in the future.

Chapter 19
Veronica

VERONICA WAS RELISHING the second glances she'd been on the receiving end of for the past two days thanks to her new look. She'd grown used to it to insomuch as she no longer wondered who it was staring back at her from the mirror. She wasn't sure the boys had though. Haydn's first words when she arrived home from the salon had been, 'Mum! What the fuck?' Normally the use of such language from her children would have sent her off on a spiel about it being a sign of low intelligence to use bad language instead of finding another appropriate adjective. She had, however, left the house a brunette and come home with mermaid blue hair so she'd decided to let her son's expletive slide—almost. Hunter when he'd mooched down the stairs to see what had his brother dropping the 'f' bomb had shown his superior intelligence by adding, 'Your hair's blue. It looks, *cringe*.'

Her phone began to vibrate and with a glance at the screen, she saw it was Abi wanting to FaceTime her. She could well imagine what she'd have to say about her hair. She debated not answering because she'd only just put her feet up and part two of the ITV drama that had had her checking and re-checking the front and back doors were locked last week, was about to come on. She sighed as the big sister in her reared her head. She put her cup of tea down on the coffee table in front of her, and Scruffy-bum mewled his irritation at being squashed as she bent forward. She supposed she'd better check everything was okay.

'Hi, Abi, how's it going?'

'God, Veronica it's not 1988, you know! What were you thinking?' Her blue eyes bugged as she stared out the phone at her sister.

'I fancied a change. We don't all want to have the same hairstyle we had when Oasis was big you know?'

'What did the boys say?'

'Fuck and you look cringe.'

'I don't blame them.'

'What are you doing with your face?' Veronica stared hard at her sister's screen image. 'Are you trying to frown?'

'I am frowning.'

No, you look like you've got some sort of problem but you're not frowning. Oh my God, Abi! Have you had Botox?'

'No! I look young for my age that's all, everybody says so.' Her voice took on the squeakiness it used to when they were younger and Veronica would ask her whether she'd helped herself to her makeup. Abi would get the same tone she had now and annoyingly swear black and blue she hadn't touched it. This, even though her lips were an unnatural shade of pink and there were streaks of blue eyeshadow smeared across her lids.

'You flipping well have.'

'My life is very different to yours. You wouldn't understand, Ronnie.'

'What, hashtag Botoxlife?'

Abi pulled a face, or tried to. 'There's a lot of pressure on me, as an influencer.'

'A what?' Veronica thought she'd said influenza but that couldn't be right.

Abi sighed as though dealing with an imbecile—it was reminiscent of Haydn and Hunter when she asked them to help her with her phone or the ancient lap- she kept a hit and miss record of their budget on. 'An influencer is someone who has built up a reputation on social media for their knowledge and skills in a particular subject.' She parroted this as though reading the Wikipedia definition.

'And what skills do you share?' From what Veronica had seen of her Instagram posts it involved lots of pouting selfies and not much else.

She did that peculiar thing with her forehead again. 'I promote the various beauty products I use.' She held a hand up to the screen and waggled cappuccino coloured nails, 'See these? They're the result of a manicure I made an online video tutorial for, using the Gelato gel nail kit. I got a year's supply of gel polishes as a thank you. And, you know, people mistake me for Patsy Kensit, back when she was still with Liam,' she hastily added. 'All the time. I owe it to her to keep up standards and then there's Brandon. He's in the music biz and needs someone who looks good in his Insta pictures.' She smoothed her blonde locks with her free hand, tucking them behind her ear as though assuring herself she was photo ready.

An image of her sister's on again off again partner, Brandon, sprang to mind. He might be something cool, or at least that's what she'd thought the twins meant when they'd heard what he did in the music industry. Any man pushing forty who got around in hoodies with chains around his neck and jeans slung so low you could see his underwear brand, Calvin Klein of course, was not to be trusted in her opinion. 'Alright, alright, I get it,' Veronica said, trying not to laugh because she could see Abi had embraced the world of social media as much as any Gen Z'er.

'Aside from having succumbed to the needle what else is up?'

'Don't ask.'

Veronica sighed; it was going to be one of *those* calls. She shouldn't be surprised, nine times out of ten, Abi only rang when there was a drama in her life. 'What's happened?'

'Brandon's being mean. That's what's happened. I might come and stay with you if he doesn't sort his attitude out.'

Unfortunately, it was Brandon's name on the lease of the London Docklands flat he and Abi shared—this of course meant each time they rowed it was Abi who had to pack her bag and load the Range Rover she (1) totally did not need, nobody needed one in London for that matter, and (2) would be paying off from here to eternity, to head out of the city.

'You're not ten, Abi. You can't come running to me every time he annoys you. Work through whatever your issues are. And anyway, what about your job?' Once upon a time before their mother had gotten sick, Abi would've run home to her for some TLC at the first hint of heading into stormy waters. She laid the blame for her tempestuous relationships on having had a father who, firstly, abandoned her and, secondly, died on her when she was small. Okay, yes it didn't do much for one's ability to trust in the opposite sex or feel confident about making long-term commitments, but Abi was no saint. She deserved a title though and Drama Queen fitted nicely. She was, in Veronica's opinion, prone to self-sabotage.

Brandon and Abi had been together two years, having met when she'd temped at the record company he worked at and they'd been apart for at least three months throughout that time due to their volatile disagreements. Abi had flitted around friends and sunned herself in Tenerife for some of that time but one whole nightmare month had been spent on Veronica's couch while her sister waited for Brandon to apologise. She'd parked herself on the sofa, cluttering the small living room with her things as she sulked over something or other, Brandon had done. She'd tried to get poor Haydn to move out of the room he'd shifted his gear into the moment his nana moved into Holly Grange but her eldest twin, who'd waited years to have his own space, quite rightly refused to budge. Thus, this 'I might come and stay' business would be nipped in the bud.

'The job at the ad agency's finished and I'm in between positions.' Abi had never stuck at a job longer than a year, preferring to take long-term temping positions. She enjoyed the freedom it gave her. It was another sign of her inability to commit to things properly so far as her elder sister was concerned. 'And you're not in a position to give out relationship advice, Ronnie. You've no idea what Brandon's like to live with. He's so demanding and,' she lowered her voice, 'I think he might have OCD.'

'No, he doesn't, Abi, you're just messy.' There wasn't much she could say to the other stuff because it was true. She wasn't a shining example of how to maintain a healthy marriage but she did know what it was like to live with Abi and she erred toward Brandon's side, even if he was a prize chump. Besides, demanding? Ha! Pot, kettle, black that was.

Her sister put on her wheedling, whiney voice. 'I want a break from the city anyway Ronnie, the pace of life in London is crazy. I need some me time.'

Play It Again, Sam, Veronica played a mental violin and squishing in with them was hardly going to give her me time.

'And I'd be able to visit Mum while I'm there with you and the boys too. How is she?'

There was a tug at her heart at the mention of their mum. It would do her good to see Abi. Her face always lit up at the sight of her youngest child. 'Honestly?'

Abi nodded.

'She's slipped a bit since you last saw her. She has longer periods where she's locked inside her head but if you visited her more often you'd see that for yourself.'

Abi's voice was small. 'She'll still know me though, won't she?'

'She might not know your name next time she sees you but she'll know you alright.' Maybe it wouldn't be so bad to have Abi here if it meant she went to see Mum, Veronica thought, but Abi was and always had been a demanding presence determined not to be overlooked which might mean she'd get in the way of Veronica's attempts to connect with their mum and put the past to rest. Either way she could hear the underlying distress in her sister's voice and, demanding as she may be, she was also her baby sister. 'She's still Mum, you know, Abi.'

'I want her back the way she was,' Abi sniffed.

'So do I.' They didn't have much in common but they did have a shared childhood and a mutual need for their mum. And this ugly illness was robbing them of her.

'Mum would love to see you. You know that, but try and smooth things over with Brandon first. Listen, I have to go. It's time the boys handed their phones in. House rule.'

The boys and their phones were the bane of her life. It was a constant battle to separate them from the flipping things which were seemingly superglued to their hands. Haydn in particular was a menace and would argue that he should be allowed it in his room at night because all his friends were. He was the only one, according to him, who had any sort of boundaries and as such his, life sucked.

She'd caught him out, one night still fresh in her mind, having been woken in the small hours to sounds no mother should have to hear coming from her son's bedroom. She'd followed the noise tiptoeing into Haydn's room where she'd found him star-fished across the bed. His head was turned to the side and his cheeks were soft with sleep. He looked like a young boy trapped in a young man's body. His phone was on the floor beside the bed glowing brightly and the moans and groans that had woken her were emanating from it. She started as it let out a particularly orgasmic squeal and then bent down to snatch it up. Jason should be dealing with this not her, she thought, stabbing at the phone until the porn channel her son had exhausted himself watching disappeared from the screen. She was still waiting for Jason, who was more tech savvy than her to put some sort of parental lock on them.

'Helicopter parenting in my opinion, Ronnie.' Abbie made a funny expression with her face. 'They've got to learn to take responsibility for themselves.'

'Oh, sod off, Abi, and sort your own life out.' She ended the call watching with satisfaction as her sister's face faded from the screen.

Chapter 20
Isabel

ISABEL'S MOOD WAS BUOYANT as, pleased with the image in the mirror, she decided it was time to make tracks to Sea Vistas. She gathered her things and took the stairs carefully, given the height of her new wedge heels. Hats off to Meghan and Kate, who were both fans of the wedge.

'Well, will I do?' she asked Rhodri, having made it safely to the ground floor. She'd done a sweeping check to make sure the gallery was empty before twirling.

Rhodri, who'd been about to pick up his paint brush, got up and gave her a slow once over, the work in progress of Osborne House, Queen Victoria's holiday home on the easel a colourful backdrop behind him. He gave a low whistle. 'You look gorgeous.'

Isabel preened at the praise, loving the way his Welsh accent made a compliment sound melodious. Now that she could understand him that was! When she'd initially moved in she'd barely understood a word he was saying. He could have been speaking a foreign language but she'd grown used to his lengthened vowels. 'Thank you, kind sir. Now, I'd best get myself off down to Sea Vistas.'

'Not before I get a kiss.' He held out his arms.

'You'll wind up looking like the Joker with my red lippy.'

'Ah, but you complete me.'

She recognised the line from the Dark Knight and pulled a face. 'That's creepy.' Nevertheless, she moved towards him and raised her lips to meet his.

'You smell divine,' Rhodri said when they broke apart. 'I don't recognise it, what is it?'

'I'm amazed you can you still smell it.'

'I can and it's lovely.'

'Shalimar, it's by Guerlain. I called into Boots to pick up the compression stockings Constance needs for the flight and the saleswoman on the perfume counter gave me a squirt.' Isabel had been enamoured with the story the woman had told her as she sprayed it on her wrist telling her not to rub her wrists together or she'd bruise the fragrance. It was created as a tribute to a shah and his wife, whose name meant Jewel of the Palace. They'd had thirteen children and she died having the fourteenth when she was thirty-eight. The devastated shah had the Taj Mahal built in memory of their undying love. The name Shalimar, the sales woman, who was fighting an uphill battle despite the charming story due to Isabel's finances not being flush enough to splurge on French perfume, was chosen because the Shalimar Gardens in Lahore were the shah's late wife's favourite.

She remembered something else she'd been told. 'It earned a bad girls' fragrance reputation because the nineteen twenties flappers adored it when it came out.' She sniffed her wrist and inhaled the warm, spiced perfume now mellow on her skin.

'A bad girl, eh? I like that.' Rhodri grinned and pulled her close once more. She recognised the wolfish look on his face and pushed herself away.

'There'll be none of that, the gallery's still open for another couple of hours for one thing and for another, I can't let Constance down.'

She wiggled her way teasingly across the gallery floor for his benefit, turning as she reached the door to say, 'I'll see you in a couple of hours.' She gave him a Marilyn Monroe styled blown kiss goodbye.

ISABEL TAPPED LIGHTLY on Constance's door.

'Isabel, is that you?' her familiar voice called back.

'It is indeed.' She opened the door and entered the room, putting the bag with the compression stockings for Constance's flight, along with her makeup supplies, down on the bed. She turned to her friend. 'Your hair looks lovely.' She knew she'd had it set in Sea Vistas' salon that morning. The gentle white curls danced around her face becomingly and she preened at the compliment before, in true Constance fashion, getting straight to the point.

'Be sure to post that letter, Isabel. I won't be here to keep tabs on you so I'm telling you now.'

Isabel busied herself retrieving her cosmetic purse. 'How do you know I haven't done so already? I might have sent it this week for all you know.'

'Aha, but I do know because I know you, Isabel. Have you told your parents you're going to contact your birth mother?'

'No, it feels a bit,' she shrugged, 'oh I don't know, faithless, somehow.'

Constance tutted and shook her head. 'You're allowed to have lots of people who love you in your life, Isabel. Nobody has exclusive rights on the emotions.'

'I know. I don't want to hurt them, that's all, well more Mum. It must be strange for her.'

'Yes, it would be but Barbara is your mother, Isabel.'

'Your birth mother wouldn't expect you to replace her. I had to come to terms with knowing Teddy would always think of another woman as his mother. But because he was raised by someone else doesn't mean there isn't a place for me in his life and I'm grateful he wants me in it. It will be the same for you. You'll find where—?'

'Veronica.'

'Veronica fits. It's not a competition as to who you love more. Barbara will know that, even if she's not ready to admit it to herself yet.'

Isabel mulled over what she'd said, knowing it made sense as she announced the light where Constance was sitting was perfect for her to do her makeup. 'That dress is beautiful,' she said, admiring the cerulean blue fabric with its lace overlay which was even lovelier than she'd remembered. The vibrant colour suited Constance's vivacious personality. It had been Isabel who'd pulled it off the rack initially. They'd called into their favourite boutique in the Royal Victoria Arcade where they always did well. Constance trusted young Tara who worked there's judgment and Isabel felt, looking at her now, she'd done her proud. Her eyes were drawn to the seahorse brooch she'd pinned to it as the myriad of Swarovski crystals danced in the sunlight. 'Oh, that brooch is quite something, Constance.' Edward had brought it with him from Hong Kong on his last visit, telling her Olga had helped him pick it out.

'Olga did well.' Constance wasn't sure about her daughter-in-law. This carefully chosen gift was winning her over, though. Olga was Russian and had met her son via the internet a concept Constance struggled with but Edward adored her and Olga seemed to adore him.

'It will be good for you two to get to know one another properly and to spend time with Tatiana.'

'Yes.' Constance nodded, the gleam of excitement in her eyes at the prospect of being with her family not escaping Isabel. She knew she still pinched herself over the fact she wasn't just a mother, she was a grandmother too, now it was time to add mother-in-law to the equation.

Constance remembered herself. 'Your dress is very pretty too, Isabel, it reminds me of—'

'The sea?'

'It does. Look out there today at all the different colours. You're like a mermaid.'

Isabel liked the analogy and she moved over to the window to look farther out to the Solent where she could see shades of denim blending into pools of green. 'It's beautiful.' She could see why Constance was happy to sit here and look out of her window. The view was never the same from one day to the next. It was like peering into one of those children's kaleidoscopes and giving it a twist. She wasn't here to stand about waxing lyrical though.

'Right, well I'll set to work.'

'Isabel, dear, you don't have to make it sound like a Herculean task,' Constance tutted as Isabel retrieved a mascara wand. She did as she was told though and settled herself back into her seat. 'I saw Iris this morning. She said her and Jean are coming this afternoon. Worst luck. She'll moan that there weren't enough sausage rolls or sandwiches or something. She won't be able to help herself. You know what she's like.'

Isabel giggled. Constance was right, Iris's reputation as a world class moaner preceded her. Constance had done a wonderful imitation of her adenoidal voice once as she mimicked her standing up at the monthly resident's meeting to complain that people were taking more than one cake to have with their afternoon tea. It took all sorts.

'Ah, well, you can't very well exclude them.' She held the wand steady. 'Right, now close your eyes slowly.'

'I could,' she murmured mutinously doing as she was told. 'I'm ninety-one, I can do what I like.'

'And you can open them.'

Isabel sifted through the purse finding the lipstick she was after and winding it up was met with a, 'No, not the pink, Isabel, that's too bright.'

Her eyesight was phenomenally sharp for ninety-one, Isabel thought; nothing got past her. She unwound it and popped it back fossicking around for the paler coral tube she knew was in there somewhere. 'What about this?' she asked, locating it and applying a streak of the colour to the back of her hand to show Constance.

'Much better. I'm far too long in the tooth to look like I'm soliciting for business.'

Isabel snorted. 'Don't make me laugh, I need a steady hand.'

'I wasn't trying to be funny.'

'Don't talk either.'

Five minutes later, Isabel stood back to admire her handiwork. 'There,' she said pleased. 'The finishing touches are done. You look stunning if I do say so myself.' She picked up the hand mirror with its mother of pearl inlay and passed it to Constance so she could see her handiwork for herself.

She looked pleased with the end result. 'Thank you,' she said, angling the mirror to a flattering position before passing it back to Isabel.

'We'll give it a few minutes and then we'll head down shall we?' Isabel put it back from where she'd gotten it.

'Walter's calling for me, I hope you don't mind. He wanted to escort me.'

Isabel raised an eyebrow at the mention of Walter. He was such a debonair sort she couldn't help visualise the days of old when guests arriving at parties were formally announced.

'And you can get that look off your face, young lady.'

She grinned. Walter had known Constance from way back when she'd run her herbal shop on the ground floor of Pier View House and he'd run an antique store a few doors down. They'd been competitors rather than friends but that he was smitten with Constance was plain to see. As for Constance she enjoyed the attention and playing hard to get.

'What look?' Isabel feigned innocence.

Constance narrowed her eyes but didn't say anything.

'If Walter's escorting you to the party, I might as well go and make sure everything's in order.'

'Yes, make sure him over there,' Constance pointed to her door and Isabel guessed she was talking about her cantankerous neighbour opposite, Ronald, 'doesn't start helping himself to the club sandwiches.'

'I will do.' Isabel left Constance to wait for Walter, a grin on her face at the thought of gouty, grumpy old Ronald stuffing a sly sarnie down before the festivities began.

Chapter 21
Veronica

VERONICA PUSHED HER front door open and, weighted down by Tesco bags, she kicked it shut with her foot. She thudded up the hallway nearly tripping over Scruffy-bum who howled his greeting. It was the best thing about having a cat, she often thought, there was always someone pleased to see you. This was especially essential when entering into the teenage parenting years.

It was a relief to be home because she'd had a wobble in the supermarket. It hadn't happened for a while but she'd frozen statue-still in the baking goods aisle at the sight of a young woman, her hair falling across her face as she compared two boxes of ready-mix cakes. Veronica could feel the blood surging through her veins like a racing tide and her breath came in short gasps. She wanted to call out and speak to the girl but what would she say? And then she'd put one box back on the shelf and walked away from her with the other in hand. Veronica had watched her go and had only moved on when a woman said excuse me, jolting her back as she reached past her for a bottle of vanilla essence.

She'd finished her shop without incident and the bags she was carting into the kitchen were full of the necessary ingredients to whip up a spag bol, down a glass or two of red while doing so, provide milk for the morning's cereal, bread for the lunches and to whip up a cake to take in for morning tea tomorrow. It was Tyrone's birthday and he loved all things chocolate. She planned on making him her trusty chocolate cake, the go-to 'best ever chocolate cake' recipe was scrawled on a piece of paper having been noted down at a mother's group many moons ago and was tucked between the pages of a recipe book with pages stuck together by her efforts over the years. She still made the cake for the boys each year and the thought of their faces as tots blowing out the candles made her smile.

She dumped the bags on the kitchen floor, retrieving the beef mince before Scruffy-bum had a chance to attack it. He had a food disorder that cat, no matter if he'd stuffed his face a moment earlier, he always had room for more. Mind you, the same could be said of her. 'Did they feed you?' He looked up at her with a baleful expression and the answering mewl would break your heart, she thought, already opening the cupboard to retrieve his biscuits without even glancing at his bowl. No wonder he was getting fat. He got fed on demand.

She added a small scoop to the remnants of his dinner which was evidence Haydn had done as she'd asked and fed him before heading off to footie practice. She held her breath and opened the dishwasher, the sight of it having been emptied had her victory punching the air. The trifecta would be if they'd brought the washing in. Her gaze swung to the kitchen table. Yes! The washing basket was sitting on top of it They'd done their jobs. This didn't happen every day, in fact most days she had to cajole until she wound up shouting but she'd learned to take the small things like today's efforts as big wins. Her mood picked up. They were good boys even if they always left the loo seat up and had difficulty with their aim.

She'd had a sod of a day at work with no bright spots such as a visit from Suit-man. She'd had to content herself with wondering what he'd make of her hair as she nibbled on her sandwich in the staff room at lunchtime. What puzzled her was why it mattered to her especially given his romantic status. Her day had picked up when her phone bleeped a text. It had been a timely distraction from going down that rabbit hole and to her surprise it was from Saskia. She hadn't heard from her friend in ages and, she read with a smile, she wanted to catch up for a coffee. Perhaps there was trouble in paradise, she'd wondered, texting back that sounded great and she was free after work any night except Thursday if she'd rather make it wine. She'd sort something out for the boys; although technically they were old enough to stay home of an evening by themselves she still didn't like the thought of them home alone past nine pm.

Saskia had texted back a minute later suggesting Harry's Wine Bar on the high street and they'd arranged to meet on Friday outside the department store. Gosh it had been forever since she'd ventured anywhere other than straight home on a Friday evening and she'd found herself looking forward to it.

It had almost been enough to make her forget Heidi's snippy comments first thing that morning. It had rankled being called in to her office as if she were a high school student being summoned to the head to explain what she'd been doing behind the bike sheds. 'Is there a problem, Heidi?' she'd asked, having a fairly strong inkling as to what it was. She'd seen the young woman's look of horror as she'd stalked past her counter shortly after Blakeley's had opened its doors for business. There'd been silence for a moment as Heidi finished jotting down whatever it was she was scribbling on that pad of hers. This was a deliberate power play on the younger woman's part, Veronica was sure of it as she stood there having not been asked to take a seat, shifting from the sole of one hush puppy to the other. It was her way of telling her that her time was more important. Her finger had twitched with the urge to tell Heidi exactly what she thought of being kept waiting.

When the line manager had finally deigned to speak, she'd chosen her wording carefully. That was the thing with the younger generation Veronica thought, listening with a frown, they knew exactly how far they could go without getting rapped over the knuckles or slapped with a lawsuit. Heidi had managed to convey, without essentially coming right out and saying so, that blue hair was didn't fit the image of a well-established, department store. She was sure it was discrimination of some sort.

Veronica had chewed her bottom lip, zoning her out as she'd mentally penned a letter of complaint about the line manager overstepping the mark to head office. She'd never do it though, because that would take energy and she didn't have enough in reserve to take on the uppity miss. The patch of eczema in the crook of her arm that refused to go away had begun stinging as she'd waited until she'd been dismissed.

She'd hotfooted it through the department store scratching all the way, feeling curious eyes on her from fellow members of staff but it had been Tyrone she'd sought out. He loved her new look having gushed about it earlier that morning. She also knew he couldn't stand Heidi or Heidi of Green Gables as he called her behind her back. Veronica hadn't the heart to tell him he had his classic children's literature confused. So, she'd leaned against his counter and relayed what had been said. He slapped her hand away from where she was worrying at her eczema and was gratifyingly aghast at the discrimination of it all. Together they'd plotted Heidi's downfall both feeling better by the time customers had appeared to distract them.

It had been when she'd sprayed Marc Jacob's Daisy on the wrist of a harried young mum as her toddler strained at the straps of the pushchair that her mood and hopefully the mum's had lifted. It was the burst of daisy tree petals and sugar musk that did it. She played a game sometimes with her perfumes, trying to guess which would be Bel's signature fragrance. She was old enough to be married or she could be single. She could be gay or bisexual. She could be transgender for all she knew. So, she'd create a made-up personality complete with idiosyncratic traits for her. Today, she'd decided Isabel would be the sort of woman who'd wear Mon Guerlain. The fragrance its designer said was inspired by the notes of a woman, created to reflect the choice, emotions and dreams that embody modern femininity. She liked to think Bel was independent and had the opportunity to make her own choices in life. Choices, with hindsight, she could see had been taken away from her.

The rest of the afternoon had passed with dusting, unpacking an order, serving customers, and engaging in a game of who could pull the silliest face with Tyrone during a quiet patch.

The house was silent apart from Scruffy-bum's purring eating sounds. The boys wouldn't be back for another half an hour or so when their dad dropped them back after practice. She'd have to make sure she had a red wine under her belt before she tackled Jason about the funds for the school trip and new school uniforms. She'd finish unpacking the groceries and pour herself a large one in a minute. A louder than necessary knocking at the door interrupted her train of thought and she hurried down the hallway. There was always a sense of unease when someone banged on the door and the boys weren't home.

She pulled it open and her mouth dropped.

'Abi! What are you doing here?'

'I don't know why you're looking so surprised, I told you I needed a break. I'm a woman on the edge of a nervous breakdown and it's nice to see you too.' Her sister pushed past her dragging a wheeled case behind her. She took a hard right and deposited it in the living room.

She looked like she was about to go clubbing and not at all like a woman who was on the edge of a nervous breakdown, Veronica thought, taking in the apparition that was her sister. Her blonde shoulder-length hair hung like parted silk curtains either side of her pretty face, which was made up with a practiced hand. Veronica smoothed her own hair down which had been buffeted on the walk from car to front door. She definitely needed that wine and she stomped back to the kitchen her sister tip-tapping behind her in her heeled boots.

'You might as well pour us a glass of that each.' Veronica inclined her head to the bottle of red before opening the cupboards under the sink to retrieve the big pot she used for pasta. She set it to boil while Abi doled out two large glasses of the ruby liquid. She handed Veronica hers and sat down at the kitchen table retrieving her phone from the pocket of her clingy silk shirt glancing at it before tossing it down on the table.

'You'd think he'd have called or at least texted when he got home and saw I'd gone.'

'Maybe you should text him and tell him where you are?'

'No, no way. I'm not a pushover. It's up to him to apologise.'

Veronica swigged her drink, mentally willing Brandon to swallow his pride and grovel.

'What are you cooking?'

'Spaghetti Bolognaise.'

'But I'm keto.'

'Abi, I'm not catering for you. Sort yourself out if you don't want what we're having.'

'I'll have sauce no noodles then.'

Veronica lowered her hackles. She could feel Abi's eyes on her hair.

'What did they say about that at work?' Abi picked up her glass and drank deeply. 'Oh, I need this after the day I've had.'

'Snap.' Veronica decided there was no point being grumpy; it would go right over the top of her sister's head anyway so after another sip she told Abi about her visit to the line manager's office while chopping onions and crushing garlic.

'God, she sounds a right mare.'

'She is, but I've wasted enough energy on her today and there's nothing she can do about this.' She pulled at a handful of blue strands.

The front door banged and Veronica winced. The panes would shatter one of these days with the hammering they got.

'Mum, I'm starving,' Haydn announced, thundering up the hall, Hunter hot on his heels demanding to know what was for dinner.

'Hi, Aunty Abi,' both boys said seeing her at the table, no hint of surprise in either of their voices. Nothing fazed them.

'Hello, boys.' Abi's eyes widened as she spied their father bringing up the rear. 'Jason, I haven't seen you in forever. How are you?' Her face lit up with pleasure at the sight of her sister's ex-husband.

Abi was a man's woman and she'd always had a soft spot for Jason, Veronica thought, knowing her sister irrationally blamed her for their break-up. She also knew why his easy-smile and banter went down a treat with Abi. It was because he subconsciously reminded her of their dad just like he had her. 'Boys, go and wash your hands,' she ordered. 'We'll be eating in ten.'

'Hey, Abi, long time no see.' He leaned down and they had a quick hug as he kissed her on the cheek. 'I'm doing good. I'm glad I decided to duck in and say hello. It's good to see you. You're looking great. The lads also said you were channelling Gwen Stefani from the nineties, Ronnie. I had to see it for myself.' He appraised her for a moment as she stirred the tomato sauce, mince, garlic and onions brew. 'I like it. It suits you. You always had a penchant for mad colours.'

Despite herself she was pleased by the compliment.

'That smells *so* good. Bolognaise right? My favourite.'

Veronica raised the spoon to her lips taste testing it as if she'd made it from scratch rather than chucking a jar in. She felt his breath on her neck as he leaned over to inspect what was in the pot. Her ex-husband was the right amount of arrogant to think she'd made it on purpose knowing he'd be dropping their sons' home. He was also not shy in coming forward.

'There's plenty there for one more by the looks of that.'

Veronica would've loved to flick the hot sauce at him.

'You've made a mountain haven't you, Ronnie, and I'm not having the pasta. Keto,' she added for Jason's benefit and this time it was her sister's face she'd like to have flicked sauce at. She'd been put on the spot. Remembering she had to ask Jason to cough up the cash she needed for the boys, she decided it was in her best interest to play the hostess with the mostest.

'Oh, go on then but you can set the table.' She donned her oven gloves and hefted the pot of boiling water over to the sink, tipping the noodles into a colander while he did as he was told. He knew where everything was, automatically popping the plates in the oven she'd preheated on low, knowing how she hated serving a meal on cold plates.

It had taken her all her strength to move past her initial anger at him when he'd left but she had. She was only human though, and while they might be a couple attempting to do a Gwyneth and Chris for the sake of their boys, come Friday night she'd be bleating to Saskia how unsettled and resentful the familiarity with which he moved about her kitchen made her feel. It was at times like this she could almost believe the past four years had never happened. She knew Jason would happily park his shoes back under her bed if she gave him the opportunity. She also knew they'd only stay there for as long as it took for the next woman who need her circuit breaker fiddling with to bat her lashes at him.

Yes, it would be easy to slot back into the way things had been but you couldn't go back and it wouldn't be fair to the boys either. She had his number now. He wasn't a bad man, he was a weak man but at least he'd stuck around for his sons which was more than her father had done.

She dished up and put the plates on the table as Abi chatted animatedly to Jason, informing him her boyfriend was a bastard She shot her a look of a disapproval at her description of Brandon. She didn't like the boys hearing words like that but they were oblivious anyway as they sat down and began shovelling their pasta down like someone was about to snatch their plates away from them.

'Any garlic bread, Mum?' Haydn asked through a mouthful of masticated spaghetti.

She shook her head automatically saying, 'Don't talk with your mouth full.'

'You sounded just like Mum then,' Abi said grinning.

'I wasn't.' Haydn pulled a face before carrying on with his slurping up of the noodles.

An hour later, and with the wine long gone, Jason loaded the last of the dishes into the dishwasher while she wiped the table down. Abi had taken herself off, claiming she was going to set up her bedroom, but the theme tune to *Emmerdale* had just drifted down the hall. The boys had shot upstairs, purporting they had homework and couldn't possibly do it in Aunty Abi's bedroom or in the kitchen with their mum and dad buzzing about. She'd let them go because now he had a full belly, Jason might be more amenable to blowing the cobwebs off that wallet of his.

'Abi doesn't change,' Jason said, grinning lazily. 'Always the first to disappear when anything needs doing.'

'She's never been any different.' Veronica tossed the dish cloth in the sink. It was now or never. 'Jason, the boys need new summer uniforms and money for school trips.'

'Has the maintenance not gone through?'

At that moment she hated him. He knew full well everything was ticking over as it should be but he still had to drop that in. He should also know by now she wouldn't ask unless it was necessary. He must have seen something in her eyes however because he backtracked. 'How much do they need?'

She clenched everything as she told him she reckoned she needed about three hundred pounds.

He gave a low whistle through his bottom teeth and she only untensed when he said, 'I'll put it through to your account tomorrow.'

That was easy, she thought, hanging the oven gloves on the back of the cooker door. She made a note to self to check the brand of bolognaise sauce. It must have been good to have him rolling over like so.

'Thanks.'

He shrugged. 'They're half mine.'

Was this the same man she'd been married to? Whatever had gotten in to him, she'd run with it.

'I suppose I should go.' It was said almost as a question.

Now she could see what had gotten in to him. Well, he could tie a knot in it because that was not on the cards.

'Yes, I've a cake to bake and the boys won't be back down now so unless you want to sit through the soaps with Abi—'

'Uh, no thanks, I'll pass on that.' He held up a hand, disappointment flickering over his handsome features.

You better run up and say goodbye to them. She indicated the rooms overhead, and make sure they're not up to anything they shouldn't be up to.'

'Right-ho.' He hovered for half a second longer than necessary but she'd turned her back in a clear signal and was pulling cocoa and flour from the cupboard. She relaxed as she heard him pad down the hall and take to the stairs. A pang passed through her as she rustled about gathering the ingredients for the chocolate cake. Things might have been so different if Jason had kept it in his pants. She shook the rogue feelings away. She was lonely, that was the problem, and getting under the covers with her ex-husband was not the answer. You couldn't look back.

She was folding the dry ingredients through the wet when she heard him call out from the hall.

'Thanks for dinner, Ronnie.' It was followed by a 'Catch you again, Abi. It was good to see you.' Then the front door banged shut.

Veronica scraped the rich batter into the tin thinking about the boys and the hand life had dealt them with a father who came and went. Then she thought about her and Abi's dad. She liked to think he would have gotten in touch with them both. Once the dust had settled he'd have knocked on their door like Jason did, to take them out for the day. She had to believe he would have because if he hadn't then it would mean she'd never really known him at all.

She scraped the remaining mixture into the tin and then popped the wooden spoon in her mouth. Abi's voice behind her made her jump. She swung round to see her leaning against the door frame, a knowing smirk on her face. 'He still fancies you, Ronnie.'

'Oh, sod off, Abi, that ship has sailed.'

'Has it?'

'Yes, it bloody well has.'

'If you say so, and you've got chocolate on your nose and chin.'

Chapter 22
Isabel

CONSTANCE GLIDED INTO Sea Vistas Oceania lounge as regal as any monarch, on the arm of Walter, whose posture would have done Prince Philip proud. All heads turned and conversation was muted. Isabel watched her friend proudly.

'She's very queenly, isn't she?' Nico murmured, and Isabel nodded her agreement. Rhodri was stood behind her near the bowed food table. Brenda was beside him and had undoubtedly been bending his ear in her strident Cockney tones. Isabel hoped she hadn't been giving him the gory details of her recent bunion surgery, business at the pub was suffering because of Brenda's need to share, or so Tilly said. Brenda and her bunions would be enough to put anyone off the mini quiches being laid down alongside the club sandwiches and sausage rolls right at this moment.

'Shush.' Delwyn tapped Nico on the shoulder. 'Constance is going to speak.'

Constance's gaze swept over her loyal subjects and she cleared her throat. 'Thank you all for coming this afternoon and of course to Isabel for organising this get-together. It's lovely of you to come along to wish myself and Jill well on our travels. So, please eat, drink and be merry!'

'Is Jill the nurse who's travelling with her?' Nico whispered.

'Yes. Edward her son's footing the bill for everything, first class tickets included.' Isabel turned, watching the stampede towards the refreshments which was akin to that of the buffalo running in North America. The residents who'd turned out to say cheerio to Constance fell upon the table, bees to honey. Ronald of the gouty legs was already skulking towards a chair over in the corner of the large lounge room clutching a napkin loaded with sweets and savouries. Gollum with his ring.

'Christ, it's frightening,' Delwyn said watching the gathered crowd. 'You could lose a limb if you tried to get in the middle of that lot.'

Isabel laughed. It was true. She spotted Millicent or Joan Collins as she'd nicknamed the new resident, homing in on Rhodri. Should she rescue him? The poor man had suffered through Brenda and was now about to be hit upon by a glamour puss of great years with a reputation for being a tad too fond of the grape. Her wine glass was indeed nearly empty, she noticed, watching the proceedings with amusement. He was a big boy, she decided, opting to risk the melee for a club sandwich.

By the time she'd managed to snag a ham, egg and tomato she saw Alice, who was the leader of their acapella group, had arrived and was mingling amongst the residents. Daisy, their conductor, was at her side and Isabel waved over before ducking and diving past the tables slowly filling up with residents. 'Hi, Alice, Daisy, thanks so much for coming. Have you had the chance to get something to eat?'

'Not yet, I thought I'd wait until the crowd thinned.' Alice's dark brown eyes twinkled.

'Same here.' Daisy grinned, her cheeks dimpling.

'Probably wise. Is anyone else here yet?' Isabel scanned the room

'No, but they're on their way.' Alice waved her phone. 'I just had a text from Jasmin they're all piling into her people carrier mover as we speak.'

'Great.'

'I'm going to see if there're any scones left.' Isabel went in for seconds. There were three and she snatched one, unsure whether to risk an attempt at the jam and cream, she decided to give it her best shot. She caught Nico lunging for a jam tart and choked back a giggle hearing her tell a woman she was being very rude, pushing so. Unfortunately, her rebuff had fallen on deaf ears because it was Nora and Isabel could see she didn't have her hearing aid in. She slipped away from the table having successfully dolloped both jam and cream on the scone.

'Phew, it's a madhouse,' Rhodri said slipping an arm around her waist. 'Mm, that looks good. I haven't been brave enough to help myself.'

'Oh, go on, you need this more than I do after listening to Brenda and fending off Millicent. Who's she chatting up now?' It must be love she thought parting with her scone.

'Last seen heading for the kitchen so my guess is she'll be batting her lashes at the chef and waving her glass about in search of a refill.' He gave her a cheeky grin before eating half the scone in one bite.

Constance, Isabel could see, was lapping up the attention. For someone who'd made out a party was a fuss about nothing, she was clearly having a lovely time and the sight of her holding court pleased Isabel. She wiped the blob of cream from Rhodri's nose and looked to the entrance as more guests piled in. 'Oh, the rest of the girls are here.' She extricated herself to greet the Angels of Wight who were piling into the lounge.

'Come on, Isabel, we'll get organised.' Alice led her and the rest of their merry band over to where she'd decided the acoustics in the lounge would be the best. They arranged themselves in their practised formation and then Alice clapped her hands and waited a beat before introducing them. It took two attempts but at last she had everyone's attention and, with their eyes on Daisy, the Angels of Wight began to sing *Somewhere Over the Rainbow*.

Their voices soared and harmonised and it wasn't long before two couples took to the floor which brought smiles to the groups' faces. Several more decided to take a turn including Constance and Walter when they moved on to Sam Smith's *How Do You Sleep?* They had their set down pat and they glided smoothly into Adele's *Hello* before finishing on a racier note by erupting into *Bang Bang* by Jessie J, Nicki Minaj and Ariana Grande. The song had been Constance's choice. 'I might be old but I'm not over the hill,' she'd said.

Their voices stilled in good time, Isabel thought, noticing one or two of the residents looking as though they might expire and Alice, on behalf of the Angels of Wight, thanked their audience. There were shouts of 'more', 'more' and Daisy leaned in to confer suggesting Peter, Paul and Mary's *Leaving on a Jet Plane* might be apt given why they'd all gathered. There were nods of assent and so, with a wave of her arms and a dip of her head which sent her hair swinging, the girls launched into it. The song went over well with the crowd with one gent banging his walking stick most enthusiastically. It earned him a tap on the shoulder from Nurse Jill who was worried he might put a hole in the floor.

'Will you stay for some cake?' Isabel asked the Angels as they milled about.

'I can't stop, Mum's got Tessa and she's a teething nightmare at the moment,' Daisy said. 'I'll have to love you and leave you.'

Cheerios were said, with Alice and the rest of the group deciding they'd definitely be staying for cake.

Isabel took a deep breath, her heart beginning to beat faster at the thought of standing up by herself to say a few words. *You're doing it for Constance, Isabel, breathe. You're amongst friends.*

She cleared her throat and her voice when she spoke seemed inordinately loud but then again it needed to be given how many of her audience were hard of hearing.

'Hello, everybody.'

'Hello, Isabel,' came back at her.

'Erm, thank you all for coming to see Constance and Jill off on their trip to Canada and,' she gestured to Alice and the others, 'to my fellow Angels of Wight, thank you for coming and entertaining our wonderful audience. I'm sure you join me in wishing them both a wonderful trip.'

A low murmuring of agreement followed.

'So, I'd invite you to join us in a piece of their delicious Bon Voyage cake.'

Constance cut the first slice of cake which she insisted Isabel have after all her efforts with her party. Jill did the honours, slicing up the rest of the ginormous mud cake and passing it out to the residents.

ISABEL STAYED BACK after the party to help with the clearing up and then ventured upstairs to check on how Constance was getting on with her packing. A suitcase was open on the bed and it was half full. As for Constance she was ensconced in her favourite chair with her sapphire blue, ballet flats discarded on the floor next to where she sat. The butterfly diamantes on the side of each shoe glinted. Isabel had been with her when she'd chosen them and Constance had been like a magpie when she'd spotted those diamante clasps. She'd dozed off but her eyes sprang open as Isabel moved across the room intending to finish off her packing for her. They had a list of what she was taking and it shouldn't be too hard to locate the different items.

'I wasn't asleep if that's what you're thinking. I was resting my eyes.'

'With your mouth open,' Isabel said, smirking. It had been a big afternoon what with the dancing too. 'You're ninety-one, as you're so very fond of saying, Constance, you're allowed to nod off.' She glanced at the list lying beside the case. The sweater and trousers they'd bought for the holiday weren't crossed off yet and she moved to the drawers to locate them. She'd taken Constance shopping a couple of weeks ago to make sure she had everything she needed for her trip and they'd both been particularly pleased with the red wool coat they'd found. It looked stylish on her but would ward off the Canadian chill without being too bulky for travel. The matching red beret would ensure she was toasty.

The coat was hanging in the wardrobe ready for her to wear tomorrow. It was going to be such a long day for her with an early start but then fingers crossed, Isabel thought, locating the trousers and carrying them over to the case, she'd sleep for the best part of the flight. Hopefully the novelty of being on an aeroplane wouldn't keep her awake for long.

Constance waggled her foot in Isabel's direction, 'My ankles are a thing of the past. How're they going to manage sitting in what equates to a tin can in the sky with engines for ten hours?'

Isabel pulled the compression socks she'd brought along with the packet of Epsom salts from the bag she'd carted with her and left in the room earlier. 'You'll be fine. I'm putting these in your carry-on bag now and Jill will slip them on for you before you get on the plane. She'll sort you out with a bowl of cool water and these,' she held up the Epsom salts, 'to soak your feet in when you get to where you're staying.'

Constance's eyes sparked, 'Hark at the apprentice telling the teacher what to do.'

'Sometimes the teacher would do well to practice what she preaches.' Isabel finished off what was left of the packing before insisting on a hug. 'It's going to be strange knowing you're not just down the road.' She'd miss her dear friend while she was away.

Chapter 23

Veronica

'SORRY I'M A FEW MINUTES late. I wanted to get changed,' Veronica said, rushing up to Saskia who was loitering outside Blakely's, as fast as the fitted skirt of the bold floral print dress would let her. It had been an age since she'd worn anything other than jeans or her uniform. The dress felt foreign but it also made her feel feminine and she loved its bright colours, they made her happy. Tyrone had said she looked gorge when she'd emerged from the staff's toilets. She'd chosen to take it he meant gorgeous and not that she looked as though she'd stuffed herself. It was strange too, to have grown half an inch thanks to her heels and she hoped she didn't roll her ankle or anything equally inelegant tottering about town.

She'd washed her hair that morning although she'd had to leave the house with it still damp thanks to Abi. She picked her moments to lock herself in the only bathroom, taking far longer than necessary in there given she had nowhere specific to be. So far as Veronica was aware her plans for the day involved calling in on their mum again and then seeing if she could catch up with some of her old school pals, all of whom were married with children these days and wouldn't give a toss whether she had beachy waves or bed hair or whatever. It was unbelievable how long it took to look as though you'd gone to no effort at all, she'd thought when her sister had finally emerged. The boys had been unimpressed at barely having time to brush their teeth let alone fiddle around with their own hair as was their norm of a morning. Abi had told them she was preparing them for when they had girlfriends.

Thankfully *her* hair hadn't kinked or frizzed and was sitting bouncily around her shoulders and looking at Saskia in her elegant pantsuit she was pleased she'd gone to the effort of getting changed and freshening her makeup. Her friend with her sleek brown bob, impeccable makeup and the fashionable wardrobe her teenage daughter helped her choose, was probably the most glamorous nurse in the NHS. She looked fabulous as always and definitely not heartbroken so that was a good sign. This wasn't going to be a bagging men session then. Unless, she got started on the Jason topic.

The old friends embraced. 'Gosh, it's been ages. Your hair, Ronnie! It looks fantastic. It's so you. Much more like the Ronnie of old.' Saskia held her at arm's-length giving her the once-over. 'It's so good to see you. What is that perfume, it's divine?' She was a million miles an hour.

'It's Envy Me by Gucci.' Veronica beamed. She'd chosen it for its tangy wild fruits and musk scent, sophisticated yet subtle, and she definitely didn't feel like the invisible woman tonight. 'I've missed you and you look amazing too.' The pair linked arms and set off down the high street chattering and giggling like girls on their way home from school as they filled one another in on the latest news. Veronica felt positively carefree with the heady mix of an old friend's company and an evening that was far too glorious to stay in watching television—not that she could get anywhere near hers anyway, not with Abi's stuff spread far and wide throughout the living room. Her sister had redeemed herself post bathroom hold-up having announced she'd treat herself and the boys to a curry from the Indian down the road for dinner which meant for the next couple of hours, she had no responsibilities. She was footloose and fancy free.

The street was teeming with people making their way home, and a sense of anticipation and good humour at the impending weekend and the possibility of more sunshine to come hung in the air. The traffic crawled down the narrow old street of the market town with its Tudor facades in a parade of carbon dioxide fumes and a shout went up followed by a burst of laughter as a group of lads left the White Swan pub further up the street. They were starting early, Veronica thought, wondering if it was a stag do. It was as they approached the crossing she saw him.

Suit-man! He was loping down the street towards them like a man who had somewhere to be. A laptop case hung from his shoulder. His hair looked slightly dishevelled as though he'd had a stressful day and had been running his fingers through it. His suit today was tan and lightweight as befitted the summery day they'd had and she watched like some sort of voyeur as the fabric moved with his body. Her pulse had quickened and there was a jitteriness in her stomach. She wondered if he was a lawyer or perhaps in finance? He must do something along professional lines dressing the way he did.

She willed him to look her way wondering if he'd recognise her out of uniform and with her new hair colour and then berated herself for checking out another woman's man. It was the sort of behaviour that lumped her in with Greta the Gremlin whom Jason had left her for and she was not that sort of a woman. Nope, she was a loyal supporter and champion of her fellow females. Despite this mental warfare she couldn't drag her eyes away from him and she gave a tiny gasp as he faltered mid-stride his eyes widening as he clocked her. He clearly recognised her, she thought, unsure what she should do. Was a wave overstepping the mark?

As it happened, she didn't get a chance to debate her next move further because Saskia swept her out on to the crossing. She glanced back over her shoulder. He was still looking her way and he lifted his hand in acknowledgement. She smiled back stumbling over the kerb.

'Look where you're going, Ronnie, you haven't even had a wine yet.' Saskia giggled, oblivious to the drama that had played out, then in a random change of subject, 'Did you know Botox can be used to treat excessive sweating?'

Veronica barely registered what she was saying. Had he seen her stagger? Her cheeks were hot. She was such a fool. She flapped her hand in front of her face to cool it down trying to focus on what Saskia was saying as she pushed open the heavy glass, doors to Harry's Wine Bar.

'This patient who came in today had the worst case of BO I've ever encountered. It stunk the whole surgery out. Honestly, Ronnie, it was worse than Nigel Price's. Remember him? He sat next to you when we were in Mr Humphrey with the comb-over's home room.' She'd raised her voice above the din of voices.

The words washed over Veronica as she nodded in the appropriate places while they weaved their way up to the bar.

'Jeez, Ronnie, you're too young for the hot flushes, aren't you?' Saskia asked, checking out her friend's red face as she squeezed in alongside a high-top stool on which sat a woman with her back to her. She swiped a drinks menu off the bar top. The hum of patrons crowded around tall tables enjoying a post-work tipple was like the steady drone of bees.

'Far too young,' Ronnie affirmed, not offering up an explanation. Saskia grinned, scanning the menu. Ronnie took in their surrounds. She'd only been here once before and that was for an afterwork drink when Lara, Heidi's predecessor, had put a tab on the bar for her leaving do. She'd liked Lara, she was one of those people who always made you feel she was pleased to see you. Unlike Heidi. A barman was handing change to a dark-haired girl in a short dress who looked like she'd only just become legal. Ronnie watched her sway out the doors to the courtyard and as she pushed it open to join her friends a whiff of cigarette smoke floated inside.

'A New Zealand Sauvignon? Saskia asked, before whispering conspiratorially, 'It's cheaper to buy it by the bottle.'

She could always Uber home and Abi could drop her to work in the morning. 'Lovely.'

'My treat,' Saskia said, ignoring her protestations. She beckoned the barman over and told him what they were after. He leaned over the bar to hear her better and Veronica did a quick appraisal. His hair was groomed back from his face, his beard short and neatly clipped. He had the sort of put-together but not too Metro Man, look she hoped her boys would gravitate towards as they got older. No matter she'd once sported dreadlocks, albeit briefly in her late teens, because double standards were part and parcel of parenting. Neither son would ever know about the tattoo decorating a small corner of her left buttock cheek either. It was of two dainty ballet slippers. She'd been drunk and sad when she'd gotten it. She tried not to dwell on what it would look like when her bum sagged.

Veronica watched as the bartender retrieved a bottle of wine from the refrigerator. Behind him was an expanse of brick wall, running the length of the bar, upon which there were two shelves with an array of red wine bottles lined up on each of them, presumably in some sort of order. Two men who looked to be around her and Saskia's ages wearing shirts and jeans were propping up the bar.

The random thought they looked rather like Laurel and Hardy popped into her head and she wondered if it had been casual Friday at work. The realisation that the portly one of the two was grinning at her gave her a jolt. He raised his glass in her direction and she quickly looked away. She wouldn't even know how to take part in flirty banter with strange men these days. It was hard to believe she'd once strutted about the handful of pubs, and single nightclub on offer in St Rebus with cocky, self-assurance. Now she almost felt like an interloper as if somebody was about to tap her on the shoulder and say, 'What are you doing here? You don't belong.' 'I'll find a table. I think there's one over by the doors to the courtyard,' she said to her friend, reaching past her to take the two glasses on the bar top with her.

She settled herself onto a stool, studiously avoiding glancing over at the bar lest Laurel and his pal over there get any ideas. Instead, she watched as a plate with a mini burger and onion rings made its way out of the swing doors leading to the kitchen and was carried past her twitching nose by a girl in leggings that left nothing to the imagination and a white T-shirt. She didn't have to look to know that Laurel and Hardy would have dislocated their necks as she passed them by. She imagined how she'd feel if that girl were Bel and knew she'd want to punch them in the nose given they were old enough to be her father.

The onion smell made her mouth water. Oh yes, she could definitely see herself snaffling an order of that down later. The food was deposited without ceremony on a table where a couple who should still be in their honeymoon period given their youthful appearances were sitting opposite each other. They barely acknowledged its arrival, too busy scrolling down their phones. Sign of the times that was, Veronica thought, sighing and finding it sad.

'Right then,' Saskia said, putting a bottle of frosty wine down on the table and hopping up on to the seat opposite Veronica. 'What's been happening?'

'You go first. How are things with Dave?'

Saskia's face was like a light bulb switching on at the mention of her new beau's name. 'Good. Amazingly good. Sometimes I have to pinch myself, that kind of good.' She poured them each a generous glass. 'He's great with Florence too. She adores him.' Florence was Saskia's daughter from her relationship with Joe. They'd been together sixteen years before deciding to call it quits. It had come as a bolt from the blue for Ronnie, who'd loved her friend's partner like a brother but given she'd known Saskia forever she knew where her loyalties were going to have to lie. The four of them, she and Jason, Saskia and Joe had had some great times together and Jason had kept in touch with Joe. What had upset her the most when Saskia had given her the breakup news was she'd had no idea her friend had been unhappy in her relationship.

It was strange how you could be the best of friends with someone and not know what was going on in their life behind closed doors. No one was at fault, Saskia had told her, they'd grown apart. It happened. The whole street knew what had gone on with her and Jason by the time she'd finished shouting at him. Her mum had taken the boys to a film and as soon as it was just her and him, she'd let fly. As for Saskia and Joe, there was no messy separation agreement and pending divorce if either of them could be bothered. They'd never married and so he'd moved quietly away to Essex which was close enough for him to take Florence every other weekend but far enough for him to start his life afresh. Sometimes she wished Jason had moved away from St Rebus too. His business was here though so it had never been on the cards. It was selfish to think like that anyway. The boys needed to know he was close by, even if he wasn't always available.

'There's a spark there,' Saskia said, sipping her wine and looking coy. 'Okay, that's an understatement because it's bigger than a spark it's a flipping forest fire.'

'What, is that your way of saying the sex is good? Or do you have arsonist tendencies?'

'We're not sixteen anymore so I'll spare you the details but it's fanfuckingtastic, excuse my language.' Saskia laughed.

Veronica couldn't remember the last time she'd had the sort of intimacy that could be described with the same enthusiasm as Saskia just had. Any sort of intimacy come to that. No wonder she had such an inner glow about her. 'Do you love him?' she blurted out. This mattered to her when it came to sex because after Bel, she'd gone a little mad. She'd bonked her way around town and with the benefit of hindsight now she could see all she'd wanted was someone who'd love her and look after her. Someone who'd stop the freefall she was in and make the pain go away because without the ballet, Gabe and Bel she didn't know who she was anymore. Then Jason had moved into town and the ground had steadied beneath her feet.

'I don't know about love,' Saskia said before grinning wantonly. 'I definitely lust him. Ask me how I feel in a month. We've booked a week all-inclusive in Sardinia for the end of the month and his kids are coming too. Flo hasn't met them yet.'

'A boy and a girl, right? Teenagers.'

'Yup, Toby and Alyssa. Toby's sixteen and Alyssa's a year older than Flo. She's the same age as Haydn and Hunter. The twins might know her, she goes to their school. We're all going out for lunch tomorrow and then to see a film so they're not complete strangers.' For a woman who marched through life full of confidence she looked suddenly vulnerable. 'I've my fingers crossed they get on but who knows with kids.'

'They'll be fine,' Veronica reassured her automatically.

Saskia sipped her drink. 'That's delicious.'

'You picked well.'

'Do you remember when life was simple and men came without baggage?'

'No, mine's always been complicated.'

'That was a sigh from the bottom of those stilettos. I have shoe envy by the way,' Saskia said, gesturing at Veronica's hot pink heels.

Veronica mustered up a smile, her legs were crossed and as she waggled her foot the shoe on top nearly fell off her foot. 'These old things? I've had them forever. But thank you.'

'So, what's up?'

'Jason dropped the boys home the other night after football practice and I think he was trying to sidle his way back in to bed.'

Saskia nearly spat her wine. 'Don't even think about it. You'll have me to answer to if you do.' She patted her mouth with a napkin. 'I like Jason, you know that, but he is not to be trusted. He hurt you once and he'll do it again.'

'I didn't plan on letting him.'

'Good, and while we're on the topic of men there's another reason I wanted to catch up tonight. Dave's got this old uni mate, Luis, he's absolutely perfect for you.'

Veronica held up her hand in a stop signal. 'No, not interested. I've told you that.'

'Hear me out.'

Veronica rolled her eyes and tapped the side of her glass with her nails which were a pretty shade of green in honour of tonight's outing. Abi had painted them for her, choosing the colour from one of the many gel polishes she hadn't been able to leave home without.

'I've only met him once but—'

'Well that fills me with confidence.'

Saskia ignored her and steamrolled ahead. 'He's the same age as Dave, forty-six. He's good-looking and jogs to keep fit.' She grinned adding, 'He has his own teeth and hair and no sign of a beer belly.'

'A definite catch then but your idea of good looking and mine are different. We have very different tastes.' Saskia was all about the brawn; she liked Hugh Jackman when he was all beefed up or Channing Tatum in *Magic Mike* while Veronica was a sensitive, brooding Johnny Depp type of woman, or at a stretch, she'd settle for Brad Pitt and at a pinch the chap who'd played a bodyguard to the PM on a TV drama she'd been glued to recently. Ooh the way he'd said 'yes, ma'am' still gave her goosebumps.

'He's definitely your type. Um, what else? He's divorced with no kids, which believe me has got to be a bonus in the world of middle-aged, second time around dating, and he's an interior architect. Which means, he's creative but no starving artist which isn't so attractive to us middle-aged ladies and by all accounts he earns truckloads of money. Perfect, see?'

'Too perfect, and as such he'll totally be up for taking a woman out who has twin boys fuelled by hormones and testosterone, and an ex-husband also fuelled by hormones and testosterone who shows up as and when he feels like it. Oh, and I nearly forgot, a thirty-seven-year-old sister who thinks she's a rock chick even though her boyfriend isn't in point of fact a muso; he works in the industry granted, but he's no Liam Gallagher, currently living with her.'

'You really are showing your age with the Liam references, and Abi's back? Since when?'

'Since Tuesday night. She says Brandon is being 'mean', she made inverted commas with her fingers, 'her words exactly, and she's not going home until he apologises which so far, he hasn't. She's totally taken over the front room, Saskia. I may go up to London this weekend and drag him down to St Rebus by the ear myself to do some grovelling. Look.' She held out her arm showing the patch of eczema that had flared up since her sister's arrival. 'That's down to her that is.'

Saskia laughed. 'Oh dear, and you know better than to scratch it. Have you got something to put on it?'

'Yes, I've been putting aqueous cream on by the truckload. It's better than it was.'

'I'll have to pop over and say hi to her.'

'You've got a spare room,' Veronica said teasingly.

'No, I haven't. It's an office and I love Abi she's like the baby sister I never had but I couldn't handle her chaos or drama.' She shook her head emphatically to prove her point.

'Neither can I and you wouldn't love her if it had been your stuff she was forever nicking when we were younger. Come to that she's still at it. I found the Coco Mademoiselle shower creme I had in the bathroom cupboard for special occasions in the shower this morning. Half of its gone.'

'Special occasions like a date with Luis? Which is why a distraction in the form of a childless, interior architect who jogs would do you good. Say you'll think about it at least?'

'I'll think about it,' Veronica said, having no intention of doing so. She topped up their glasses. 'Shall we order a snack? I saw a mini-burger and onion rings go by earlier that smelt divine.'

'Yum, go on.' Saskia reached for her purse.

'I'll get these,' Veronica said. She might be finding it hard to make ends meet but she'd still pay her own way, she thought, sliding off the stool. 'Back in a sec.'

She visited the bathroom giving herself the once-over. She still started each time she glimpsed herself. It would take a moment to register who this woman with the blue hair was. She tucked it behind her ears, reapplied her lipstick and did the mandatory skirt tucked in knickers, loo roll attached to heel of shoe checks before exiting to place her food order.

She'd swiped her card and was waiting for the bartender to give her the receipt, aware she was a smidge tipsy as she fought temptation to ask for future reference who his barber was. 'Thank you,' she said, eager to make her getaway before the words popped out of her mouth. She stuffed the receipt in her purse and, picking up the stand with their order number on it, was about to make her way back to Saskia when her gaze strayed down the bar to where Laurel and Hardy were still planted. Laurel's eyes lit up at the sight of her and he mouthed, 'love the hair'. He followed this with a wink and to make sure she got the gist of what he was saying he touched his own thinning top.

Oh, dear God, Veronica thought, too polite not to give him a weak smile before hotfooting it across the crowded floor to her friend.

'If he offers to buy us a drink or asks if we come here often, we are leaving,' Veronica said to Saskia who was snorting into her wine at what had transpired at the bar.

'Oh my God, Ronnie, life's never dull with you around.' Saskia grew serious. 'How's Margo doing? Do you and the boys still go and see her every Thursday?'

Veronica nodded. 'She's as good as can be expected. She's plateaued in the illness so there haven't been any big changes in her behaviour which is good so, we'll coast along with that until the next dip and yeah, we do. We were there yesterday.' Credit where it was due. 'The boys are great with her.' Seeing Haydn and Hunter demonstrate such patience and kindness toward their nana each Thursday reassured her she must be doing something right with them. 'Mum loves them, she always smiles when she sees them.'

Saskia smiled. 'That's gorgeous. They're lovely lads your two. How's Abi handling seeing her?'

'She's been to Holly Grange every day which is something. She doesn't stay long but at least she's going. It's good for her because she needs to accept the situation. She can't change it and neither can I, hard as that is to take on board.' Veronica shrugged. 'I've started to talk to Mum about Gabe when I go on my own of a Saturday. I took in my first ever leotard last week and she held onto that while I chatted.'

Saskia reached across the table and put her hand on top of her friend's. 'Good, I'm glad. It's something you need to do Ronnie.'

Tears prickled and Veronica blinked them back. Saskia was a good friend, the best kind, even though she'd virtually ignored her when she was with Gabe. Between him and ballet practice there'd not been time for anything else. Saskia had been there for her though when she'd needed her. The arrival of their snacks moved them on from the potentially heavy conversation and they both tucked in with relish.

THE BIRDS WERE SETTLING down for the evening lining up along the power lines and having a final natter by the time they left Harry's to await their Uber rides home. They exchanged promises to do it again soon and not to leave it so long next time before Saskia's proclamation, 'It was a brilliant evening.' She planted a wine-breath kiss on her friend's cheek. 'And we got chatted up. We've still got it you know, babe.'

Veronica laughed. Laurel and Hardy had indeed swaggered over. Veronica had an entire onion ring in her gob at the time and had been making mmming noises as to its deliciousness. Saskia had a blob of aioli stuck in the corner of her mouth but they'd been undeterred. Veronica had never been the sort to tell anyone who had the gumption to come up and talk to her to go away or to take the mickey out of them if they were respectful about it. Unlike some of their friends who'd delighted in doing so when they were younger. She thought it was arrogant and to steal her sister's favourite phrase 'mean' behaviour. She'd been unable to stop laughing though at what Saskia piped up with when Laurel had leaned toward her placing a pudgy hand on her thigh to steady himself and through wet lips said, 'I can't stop staring at you. It's the hair, you remind me of someone.'

'Marg Simpson perhaps? Because you've definitely got a look of Homer about you.'

Chapter 24
Isabel

'YOU DID WELL TONIGHT, it was a good send-off,' Rhodri said from where he was sitting on the sofa. His legs were stretched, long and crossed at the ankles, resting on the coffee table in front of him and his hands were clasped on top of his stomach. 'That cake went down well. I don't think I'm going to want much in the way of dinner.'

'Yes, I saw you had a second slice,' Isabel tutted in mock disapproval.

'Too good not to. Soup and toast in half an hour or so?'

'Lovely.' She lay her head on his shoulder feeling fortunate to have a man who was not only eye-wateringly sexy but who happily fulfilled her stomach's needs too. She curled her legs up, snuggling in for the evening. The television flickered in front of them with a sitcom that was making Rhodri laugh. She wasn't watching it though, she was mulling over what Constance had said to her after the party. Her phone began ringing, interrupting their tableau and her thoughts. Heaving a sigh, she got up to retrieve it from her bag which was hanging off the side of the chair where she'd slung it when she got home half an hour earlier.

It was her dad and frowning she padded upstairs to their bedroom so as not to interrupt Rhodri's show. 'Hi, Dad, what's up?'

'I want to talk about the chinos, Isabel.'

'Right?' She hated to think where this was heading and was wondering why he had her on speaker. She flopped down on the bed.

'I keep telling your mum they ride up and they're not comfortable but she won't listen. What I want to know though, Isabel, is this. What did your Rhodri wear to Constance's going away party today?'

'Jeans and a shirt, why?'

'See, Babs, Rhodri wore jeans to the party Isabel went to and that was at that posh retirement village.'

'Yes, but, Dad, it was a party not a wedding and besides when Rhodri wears jeans he manages to look well turned out. You know casual but dressy at the same time.'

Her father snorted. 'I don't know about that, jeans are jeans.'

Isabel was on a roll and she sat up from where she'd lain prone on the bed. 'No, they're not, because you by comparison look like you're about to break into *Born in the USA* whenever you wear your favourite pair, and you weren't, you were born in Southampton,.'

'She's right, a wedding's no place for jeans and there is nothing wrong with your chinos that a dab of stain remover around the crotch won't fix. They fit you like a glove,' Bab's called out her penny's worth.

'A five-year-old's mitten more like,' Gaz muttered.

'Dad, I'm going now, goodbye.'

With a shake of her head she went back downstairs where there wasn't so much as a whiff of soup on the go. She found Rhodri where she'd left him only he had a strange expression on his face and the television was off.

'Everything alright?' she asked, perturbed.

'Sally rang.'

'What did she have to say?' She tried to keep her tone light but her insides twisted like a wet towel being wrung out at his ex's name.

He scratched his head. 'She asked if Austin could come the day after tomorrow for a fortnight.'

She hadn't expected that and blurted, 'What?'

'She's got a last-minute deal to the Greek Islands. A fortnight in Rhodes all-inclusive.'

Bully for her, Isabel thought, managing to swallow the sentiment.

'I've arranged to meet her and Austin in London, she's flying from Heathrow and I'll bring Austin back here to stay with us.'

'But the room's not ready and what will you do about the gallery?' She was bringing up problems that were easily remedied because he'd thrown her and she didn't know what else to say.

'It's not a big deal is it?' Rhodri's expression turned to one of confusion. 'Besides,' he carried on, saving her from having to answer, 'I don't see why we can't check out Oasis over in Brading tomorrow afternoon. They're open until four so that should give us plenty of time after I close the gallery. Nico's often said she's happy to run the place for me if I ever I need a hand. If you speak to Delwyn and explain the situation I'm sure she won't mind you shortening your hours for the time Austin's here so we can juggle one of us always being with him for the fortnight.'

'Yes, of course. You're right it will be fine.' She injected an enthusiasm she didn't feel into her voice. 'And yes, Oasis is a good idea, they have some lovely things.' Her brain was whirring. Sally had kept the truth of Austin's parentage from Rhodri all these years and now at the click of her fingers they were expected to drop everything and come running when she wanted them to. What right did she have to disrupt their lives? Stop it, Isabel, it's not about her it's about a little boy getting to know his father, she told herself, wishing she could shake off her unease where Austin's mother was concerned.

Chapter 25
Veronica

VERONICA HELD HER HAND up to the scanner to let herself into Holly Grange's residents' lounge. She hoped Jason had gone to watch the boys play their respective matches this afternoon as he'd promised. As for Abi, she was in treaty negotiations with Brandon who'd made contact. Veronica had sent up a silent thank you prayer upon hearing this news. He'd texted her last night and Abi had barely looked up from her phone other than to mutter, 'He says he misses me,' when Veronica had gotten in from her evening out with Saskia. The kitchen had smelled like butter chicken and vindaloo and there was no sign of the boys, just evidence in the rice on the floor that they'd definitely eaten. She'd finished what was left of the rich chicken dish eating it straight from the container before rinsing it out. Seeing Abi was still employing her thumbs and wearing that peculiar trying to frown expression, she'd left her to it, going upstairs to check on her sons. Their grunts assured her all was well in the world and so she'd gone to bed.

It had been hard work getting Abi up in the morning and she'd made her a coffee, wafting it back and forth under her nose until she'd finally managed to rouse her. She'd driven her in her pyjamas to Blakeley's, muttering all the way about it being an ungodly time of the morning on a Saturday and how she'd have bags under her eyes all day which was catastrophic given Brandon was coming to see her. 'Put haemorrhoid ointment under your eyes, that will sort your bags out,' Veronica had said, getting out the car. It was a tip Tyrone swore by, not that she'd ever been game to try it out for herself.

She heard the door click and pushed it open wondering if Abi had taken her advice. The thought of her sister, who liked to think she oozed cool, standing in Boots asking for pile cream made her grin. She wouldn't be waving that about on her Instagram feed!

'You're looking very cheery,' Helen said, smiling up at her. She had a large piece of jigsaw puzzle in her hand. 'And I love the hair. It's great.'

'Thanks, Helen.' Veronica's hand automatically fluffed at it.

'Has Margo seen it?'

Veronica nodded, 'Yes. I called on Thursday.' She'd gotten more of a reaction from Danika, who'd fussed over her, eager to see Margo's reaction when she saw her daughter's new look. 'What do you think of Mum's hair then, boys?' she'd asked the twins. Haydn had mumbled something about it being alright and Hunter in his usual fashion had grunted. Danika had smiled. 'You can always count on your kids for a compliment.'

'Tell me about it,' Veronica had replied as the caregiver took her aside to tell her how Margo's week had gone. It was her usual practice to do so and she'd said how lovely it had been for her to have her other daughter calling in every day. 'Your sister was telling me she's on a break from her boyfriend which is why she's down from London. You're nothing at all alike, are you? She's a very pretty girl.' Veronica must have looked startled because Danika's hand had flown to her mouth as she realised how that had sounded. She'd stumbled over her words apologising but Veronica had seen the funny side, and laughing told her not to worry about it. 'There's five years between us,' she'd informed her, not adding that most of the time if felt more like twenty-five years.

Mollified, Danika had said, 'She reminds me of someone, and it's bugging me because it won't come as to who it is.'

'Patsy Kensit,' Veronica stated as Haydn and Hunter searched out their nana.

'Yes! That's who. Thank you. It's been driving me round the twist.'

Margo hadn't so much as blinked when Veronica sat down opposite her, the boys already having pulled up chairs either side. It had made her sad insomuch as the mum she'd known not all that long ago would have had plenty to say on the subject of her daughter's hair once upon a time. She'd always liked it when she wore it up but Veronica suspected that was only because it reminded her of her dancing years, lashings of hairspray, bun nets and bobby pins.

'She took it in her stride, Helen. I don't think she registered it to be honest.'

Helen smiled, 'Well, it looks great.' Next to her, a woman Veronica knew to be called Fran was staring intently at the half-completed image on the table in front of her. Sunlight streamed in through the doors which were open to let in the fresh summery breeze. A family were out in the garden clustered around an elderly gent and two youngsters were playing a game of tag. Residents were dotted about the place, some pushing their walkers as they went on a fruitless search for something or someone, others dozed in chairs or were seated alongside friends or family.

Veronica could smell coffee. She wouldn't mind a cup, she thought. She could do with a jolt of caffeine; wine and butter chicken had proven not to be a good mix at three in the morning when she'd woken up boiling hot, her poor liver working overtime. Her counter had been busy today too, and her feet ached. First things first, she'd find her mum. She spotted her sitting at one of the tables in the dining area. Adesh, a carer who had the gentlest of smiles, was keeping an eye on her and the two other residents also at the table all engrossed in the colouring in they were doing. 'She's doing a good job,' Helen said, following her gaze.

'Thanks, Helen, it's such a gorgeous day, I'll go and say hello and see if she wants to sit outside.'

'It is.' She went back to the puzzle then and Veronica made her way over to her mum, the bag with the tutu inside it rubbing against her leg. She observed her for a moment, her head dipped, silver hair needing a trim falling forward about her face. The pale lemon blouse suited her and she was wearing white, three-quarter-length pants, as befitted the weather. She had a red crayon gripped in her hand and was shading in a butterfly's wings with grim determination. It was a shame to interrupt her when she was settled at a task.

'Look who's come to see you, Margo,' Adesh said, reaching over to touch Margo's hand. Her mother looked at Adesh. 'Veronica's here, your daughter.' She turned her head dreamily to Veronica as she pulled away from her colouring in, trying to process what was happening.

'Hi, Mum, you're looking lovely in lemon,' she said brightly. 'That's a pretty picture.'

Margo smiled and began to get out of her seat. 'What a silly colour your hair is. Are we going out? I like to watch the, the...' she frowned.

'The planes, Mum.' Once a week on a Wednesday morning, a mini-van took those residents who were well enough for an outing on a drive. Sometimes they went to watch the small planes take off and land by the roadside of the private airfield, at other times to admire the ever changing countryside. This week, they'd gone and had ice cream at a local farm shop.

'Yes.' She nodded, pleased the mystery was solved.

'We could go and sit outside in the garden if you like, Mum. It's a glorious day.' Veronica took her hand. 'Would you like that?'

'I don't mind.'

Veronica smiled at Adesh before steering her mother over to the doors and into the garden beyond. The grass was spring grass, soft beneath her feet and she'd have loved to have kicked her shoes off and run across it like the young girl visiting with her family was. A cartwheel might be beyond her these days, but then again you never knew. She'd read somewhere that your muscles retain memory of what you'd done in your youth.

There was a bench seat near the white lilies but not so close she'd start sneezing as she was prone to doing and they made towards that. 'Aren't the flowers pretty?' Veronica said, indicating the elegant blooms. It was hard to believe something so simple and beautiful could be toxic, the yellow stamen shrouded by those soft petals was—to cats at any rate. Her mother nodded and Veronica smiled. Margo had always had an appreciation for beauty. Their back garden had been full of colourful cottagey blooms, at odds with the austereness of the council house they'd eventually moved into AD. To her mind the time when her father was in her life was BD and then, when'd he gone, life had become AD. Margo had looked after Veronica's garden for her too, never failing to deadhead and trim back the blooms in a back garden that otherwise would have been left to its own devices.

A sudden shout of laughter made her startle and Veronica soothed her, 'It's alright, Mum, it's just some children playing.' She sat her down and once she was comfortable said, 'I've brought something to show you.'

'For me?'

'Yes.' She opened the bag and pulled out the tutu, the pale, pink tulle scratchy to the touch. Shaking it out, she held it up for her mum to see. The sequins Margo had hand sewn onto the leotard sparkled and danced. Oh, how she'd loved the way they'd glittered under the stage lights. 'You made this for me, Mum, when I danced *The Nutcracker*. I was the Sugar Plum Fairy and Gabe danced the role of my Cavalier.' Veronica closed her eyes against the bright sunlight momentarily. She'd been fourteen and something had changed in her relationship with Gabe as they rehearsed their performance day after day. His hands spanning her waist felt different and she'd feel the imprint of each of his fingers encircling her, wanting them to linger there forever. She'd become aware of his presence in a way she hadn't understood before.

She'd started with pain in her ribs not long after the *Nutcracker* performance and had been X-rayed and diagnosed as having a stress fracture. It wasn't uncommon for girls of her age who danced apparently, but that hadn't done much to console her. She'd not been able to practise for over six weeks and it had left her feeling at odds with herself, ballet had become her world and Gabe an extension of herself.

There was so much more to this costume than an awakening though, Veronica thought, as Margo reached out and rubbed the tulle between her fingers. She hadn't appreciated her mother's efforts back then to the degree she should have. Teenagers were a selfish lot. This was due to the wires in their brains not being connected properly or something like that. She'd learned this at a talk on parenting these mystical creatures at the boys' school. Her two were no different. It was only when you were an adult, a parent yourself, you understood and fully treasured the sacrifices that had been made on your behalf.

'My daughter danced,' Margo said, as Veronica began to talk.

Chapter 26
Isabel

IT WAS A WILD AND WINDY Tuesday afternoon and Isabel was unpacking an order of Bach Flower Essences wondering how Rhodri was getting on. Her phone was in the pocket of her jeans and she pulled it out to check for any messages. There was nothing other than a series of Pocket Fox emojis and a short video clip of the kitchen back home in Maybush showing a puddle on the floor—she assumed it was courtesy of Prince Charles. The corgi was no longer just needy, it seemed he had selective incontinence. A short text blaming the telling off Jez's mother Pauline had given him after the poo outside the wedding reception entrance followed. It had made him nervy, Babs said.

Gawd, her mum was in fine form today, she thought, scrolling down to the final picture. It was of her in her Asda uniform and the look of surprise that she'd managed to take her first selfie made Isabel laugh. She quickly sobered though. She'd thought Rhodri might've updated her when he'd collected Austin but nada.

The idea of him meeting up with the woman he'd once been engaged to at the London hotel where she and Austin had stayed last night stirred a gamut of emotions. The way she'd treated Rhodri was appalling, the way she appeared to be using him for her convenience now was, to Isabel's mind, appalling but the fact she'd once come close to marrying the man she loved and was the mother of that man's child terrified her. What if he decided it would be in Austin's best interests for them to give things another go? She stomped on the thought before it could grow legs. She knew it was irrational and Rhodri would be appalled to know she'd ever think such a thing.

She hadn't heard from Constance either. She was under strict instructions to telephone once she'd arrived safe and sound in Vancouver and by Isabel's calculations, she should be there any time now.

The door to The Natural Way jingled, startling Isabel and, looking up from her task she saw, as if she'd conjured him by the power of thought, Rhodri. Her heart leapt at the sight of him. His hair was windblown, his cheeks reddened by the sea breeze, and the look on his face was one of pride. Isabel's gaze travelled down to the little boy who was clutching his hand. She didn't mean to stare but knew she was because he looked exactly like the photographs she'd seen of Rhodri as a small child. How must Rhodri have felt seeing Austin for the first time? Glimpsing his younger self in the little boy's features? There was something so trusting about the way Austin was holding his hand too. It was as if he knew instinctively that this man would look after him now he'd been given the chance.

Rhodri's other hand was wrapped around the handle of a wheelie-case upon which a car seat was precariously balanced. He had a small backpack slung over his shoulder. His grin was wide, and his eyes were shining. 'Austin, this is Isabel. Isabel, Austin.'

Isabel put the box she had hold of down on the ground and then plastering her cheeriest smile in place she said, 'Hello, Austin, I've been so excited to meet you. It's lovely you've come to stay with us.' She reminded herself of a children's show entertainer, all faux jolliness and bonhomie.

'Hullo,' Austin said in a small voice, turning his body toward Rhodri as he looked up at her from under a fringe that was a tad too long. He tugged on his father's hand and looked up at him. Rhodri leaned down to catch what he was saying. Whatever it was it made him smile and he said, 'Yes, she does. I think it's pretty.'

Austin looked at her again and Isabel, having twigged he'd said something along the lines of 'she's got pink hair' could see the uncertainty in his eyes. She reminded herself what a big thing it was for him to travel to stay with his dad who he barely knew and his dad's girlfriend whom he was meeting for the first time. He was only four and he'd been left with veritable strangers.

'We came straight from the ferry,' Rhodri explained. 'It's been a big day so I think we'll head home now but we wanted to come here and say hi first, didn't we, pal?'

Austin looked doubtful as to this having been the case.

'Well, I hope you like your room, Austin.' Isabel knew Rhodri was eager to show Austin their efforts and it did look lovely. They'd picked out a very cute duvet set called Apple Tree Farm. She'd fallen in love with the prancing horses decorating it and Rhodri had said all kids wanted to have a ride on a tractor. She couldn't recall it being on her wish list when she was a child but she hadn't said anything. They'd also bought him a rather plush teddy bear with a tartan hat and scarf; he was perched on the bed waiting to be given a name and cuddled. They'd picked up a nightlight in case he was frightened of the dark and then Isabel had panicked that they had no toys. They'd raced over to Newport and Rhodri's wallet was considerably lighter when they left the toyshop there carting a whizz bang, Paw Patrol something or other, a Magformers car thingamajig, and a Cheeky Monkey board game. They all came highly recommended for four year olds, the woman behind the counter assured them.

As for food and the like, another cause of sudden panic on Isabel's part—what did four year olds eat?—Rhodri had thought it best to take Austin with them to the supermarket so they could pick up things he was used to. In the meantime, they'd made sure to have spaghetti hoops, alphabet shaped pasta and a box of Shreddies cereal in. It would be Rhodri who'd be doing the cooking anyway, Isabel had told herself, so she didn't need to worry. They'd none of them starve.

'Okay, I'll see you both in an hour or so.' She attempted another winning smile in Austin's direction but he was studying his shoes.

'I thought I heard your voice. Hi, Rhodri.' Delwyn appeared from where she'd been tidying the back store room. 'And who've we got here then?' She knew exactly who they had there because Isabel had been prattling on about Austin coming to stay for the best part of the morning.

'Hi, Delwyn, this is my son, Austin. Austin, this is Delwyn.' The poor kid was looking overwhelmed Isabel thought, as Delwyn went up and crouched down to shake his hand. 'Hi there, Austin, it's nice to meet you.'

He shook her hand back and gave her a shy smile. Isabel wished she'd thought to do that.

'Did you enjoy the ferry ride? I hope it wasn't too choppy with that wind.'

He nodded and lisped, 'Yes, we sat at the top of the boat and it was very bumpy but it was fun.'

No wonder they looked like they'd braved a gale, Isabel thought.

'And, Daddy bought me a cake and we got to meet the captain.'

Isabel stared. He was quite the chatterbox when he got started. It sounded so strange to hear this young boy referring to Rhodri as Daddy, and the look on Rhodri's face made her want to cry. He was entranced by Austin and it was lovely to see.

'We did a bridge visit,' Rhodri explained.

'Wowzers, you're a lucky boy,' Delwyn said, straightening up. She was clearly at ease with children and knew how to talk to them. Isabel felt an uncharacteristic stab of envy. 'Isabel, why don't you head off with these guys, it's been quiet this afternoon. I can manage.'

But I'm not sure I can, Isabel thought. 'Are you sure?'

'Positive, go.'

'That'd be brilliant, thanks, Delwyn.' She put the last of the bottles of essences on the shelf and picking the box up carried it out the back to where her bag was. She tossed the holdall over her shoulder, hearing Delwyn ask if Austin went to nursery school. 'I'll see you tomorrow, then,' she said reappearing in time to see Austin nodding his head and making a note to self to ask him what he liked doing best at nursery school. Perhaps he enjoyed painting, it was in his blood after all. She could pick him up some children's paints if he did. That would win her brownie points.

'Enjoy yourselves.' Delwyn grinned, watching the trio as they headed out the door.

Isabel was unsure what to do as they exited the shop onto the street. Should she offer to take Austin's other hand or would that be too much too soon? She couldn't bear the thought of him shaking her off so she took the car seat from Rhodri and walked alongside him. They strolled down the street at a pace suitable for pint-sized legs with the wheelie-case rolling along obediently behind them, all the while being buffeted by the breeze. People smiled at you more when you had a child with you, Isabel noticed, her mouth beginning to ache with reciprocating. Rhodri was in his element as he chatted on about the things they'd do while Austin was staying with them.

'Here we are then, this is us.' They came to a halt outside the gallery entrance and Rhodri pushed the door open. Austin followed behind him, his eyes wide at the new surroundings, Isabel saw, closing the door behind them.

Nico was eagerly waiting to be introduced to Austin and she too, seemed equally comfortable as she chatted to him about the ferry and then showed him his dad's paintings. 'He's very clever. Do you like painting?'

Austin nodded.

'Well then, I happen to have some paints I bought for my niece when she came to stay. They'll be all dried up by the time she comes back for another holiday. Would you like me to bring them with me tomorrow?'

'Yes, please.'

'You and your daddy could do a spot of painting outside, take a picnic somewhere. The weather's supposed to be lovely.'

Isabel was crestfallen, that had been her idea. Her way of winning over this boy who was now looking adoringly at Nico. Even Rhodri was joining in. 'What a good idea. We could take a picnic down to Appley Folly and set you up with my easel. You could swim too if it's warm enough. Would you like that?

Austin was nodding enthusiastically. Isabel wanted to tell them both he was four years old, he didn't need to be set up with an easel. Finger painting would suffice, but she didn't say anything, she just stood on the periphery surplus to requirements while they all stood about looking pleased with themselves.

'I'll pop the kettle on,' she said, taking to the back stairs. Nobody replied.

Austin and Rhodri appeared a few minutes later. "I've poured you a glass of milk, Austin, and there's some crackers and cheese there if you'd like it.' She pointed to the dining table proud of the healthy afternoon tea she'd whipped up.

'I'm not hungry,' Austin said.

Isabel wasn't sure if she was imagining the belligerent tone or not.

'He did have a big piece of cake on the ferry,' Rhodri explained, and Isabel nodded. 'But I don't mind if I do.' He helped himself.

'It's fine. You'll need to make room for your tea won't you, Austin. Shall we take your case to your room?' Again she was like the chirpy children's presenter. She was liable to burst into the opening songs for *Postman Pat* or

Bob the Builder if she wasn't careful. She took his case by the handle deciding to be assertive as she trundled it behind her in the direction of the stairs. She carried it up, pausing to look back to see if he was following her.

Rhodri let go of Austin's hand. 'Off you go. There's someone on your bed who's been waiting for you to arrive.'

Austin hung back, clearly wanting his daddy to be the one to show him where he'd be sleeping.

Rhodri flashed Isabel a smile. 'We'll all go, shall we?' He headed to the stairs, Austin shadowing him. Isabel carried on to the landing of the top floor where the bedrooms and bathroom were. She pointed out the bathroom once the other two had joined her. *He would be toilet-trained, wouldn't he? Most four year olds were, weren't they? Who'd do his nightly bath or did he have showers?* She told herself to calm down and then pointed out her and Rhodri's room. 'We're right next door to you if you need us,' she added brightly before opening the door to where he was going to be sleeping. 'Here we are, Austin, this is your room.' She flattened herself against the door to let him and Rhodri pass. The toys they'd purchased were in a basket in the corner and Austin hovered, torn between checking them out and picking up the teddy who was sitting on the bed.

He chose the teddy and bounced up and down on the bed in a way that would have had Babs Stark telling Isabel she'd break the thing if she wasn't careful when she was small. He held the teddy tightly in his arms.

'Shall we give him a name do you think?' Rhodri asked.

'Benny.'

'Benny the Bear,' Isabel chirped. 'Perfect.'

'No, just Benny. Benny's my friend at nursery.' Nursery sounded like nurswee and Austin was looking at her like she knew absolutely nothing about his life. Which of course she didn't.

'Benny it is.' Rhodri rubbed his hands together.

She wasn't doing well, Isabel thought glumly, but she was nothing if not a trier. 'How about I unpack your case?'

Austin stopped bouncing and shook his head. 'I can do it.'

'Here we are, pal,' Rhodri unzipped it. 'Why don't we do it together.'

Once again Isabel found herself standing on the outside looking in.

Chapter 27
Veronica
1992

GABE WAS SPRAWLED ACROSS his bed, lying on his stomach with his feet hanging over the edge of the navy covers as he scanned the back of the Nirvana CD cover, *Come as You Are*.

He looked up at Veronica who was sitting on the chair by the window, her legs pulled up in front of her as she blew cigarette smoke out the window. She wasn't listening. A study of moodiness, clad in black, frustrated by not being able to practise because of her stupid fracture and sick to death of soaking in baths full of the Epsom Salts her mum swore by. Her body was brimming with twitchy energy which had no outlet. It was like an itch she couldn't scratch and she knew all about scratching itches, she lifted one leg out straight and rubbed at the patch behind her knee.

'You'll make it worse, Ronnie.'

She poked her tongue out at him but, knowing he was right, she folded her leg back up and watched the bluish, grey smoke twirl out the window. She didn't even like cigarettes but it made her feel like a normal teenager doing normal out of bounds things. A bit like playing Nirvana way too loud. Besides, ballet dancers were supposed to smoke, everybody knew that. It kept them thin and helped with the stress of always having to perform to the peak of their abilities, or so Megan said. She was a know-it-all, Megan, and where once Veronica had admired her and been desperate for her acceptance and friendship, she now found her grating.

For her part, Megan was not interested in playing second fiddle to her and Gabe. Veronica knew she had a crush on Gabe who was oblivious to her and she also knew it annoyed Megan no end because she was used to being noticed. Nor had she been gracious at being relegated to mechanical doll dance moves in the *Nutcracker* by Miss Laverne while Veronica was transformed into a fairy.

Hayley, thank God, had long since given up on ballet and was more inclined to hang around the precinct shops after school with a group of girls who didn't have much going on in the way of aspirations. They were all about the boys and would pose with a bored air, their orange legs on display thanks to the waistbands of their uniforms being rolled up so their skirts sat mid-way up their thighs. Mum would tut that they'd all be pushing prams before they were twenty when she saw them.

This was incredibly hypocritical of Margo but Veronica knew that to mention this would earn her a slap across the legs. Her mother seemed to have forgotten she'd found herself in the family way with Veronica and had married her father before she was twenty. Had she been like Hayley and the others with her skirt worn too short, hanging about waiting for trouble? Veronica wondered. She also wondered if her mother blamed her for the way her life had turned out. She'd never know because it wasn't the sort of thing you could come right out and ask, mostly because if she were honest with herself, she was frightened the answer would be yes.

She did know Margo had left the umbrella of the Catholic church she'd attended with her parents and siblings her whole life, resentful at being pushed into marrying a man who wasn't ready to be married. Something Dad had gone on to demonstrate by leaving them, only by then of course, she had two children not just one. Veronica didn't like to dwell on these thoughts too long because they'd inevitably lead her to ponder an alternative reality where their dad hadn't left and was still alive. She turned her mind deliberately back to Hayley.

Just as she and a handful of the other girls who'd been enrolled in those first classes seven years ago had gone, so too were the days of lessons being held at the community hall twice a week. Miss Laverne had her own studio now having leased a warehouse space on the edge of town. She'd converted its interior into an expanse of polished dance floor with changing rooms off to the side. Another woman, with a barky voice and what Veronica's mum deemed risqué moves given the age group she was teaching, ran jazz ballet classes there too. The demand for dance tuition in St Rebus and its surrounds had grown rapidly. It seemed there were a lot of young girls with dreams of being Nina, Pretty Ballerina like the old ABBA song but other than a boy who thudded about like an elephant, Gabe was the only male enrolled.

The dance school was a home away from home for both her and Gabe, because these days it seemed they spent more time there practising than they did anywhere else. It was why times like this spent doing not much of anything other than hanging out, were precious.

It wasn't just the premises that had changed, the mood in their lessons had too because the girls who'd once giggled in the changing room of the community centre were now whispering behind their hands. A competitive edge as to where they wanted to take their passion had begun kicking in as the classes began to sort out those who had the passion and raw talent to be professional from those who'd never be offered the lead roles. The mums watching from the sidelines were just as bad, her own included. Gabe's mum, Mrs Darby-Hazleton came now and again to watch. A glamour puss who always held herself slightly aloof from the other parents who, knowing her background as a professional dancer managed to behave in a ridiculous star-struck manner. Even Miss Laverne was solicitous toward her. Her mum wasn't. Apart from a curt hello, she ignored her and Veronica fancied she was envious of Mrs Darby-Hazleton and the fact her daughter spent what sparse free time she had at the woman's house.

There was none of that bitchy rivalry with Saskia, her friend from school, but this was probably because she had no interest in ballet. It was nice to have someone to talk with about other things, like boys and clothes at lunchtime. There was no antagonism between her and Gabe either. They'd never have to worry about being pitted against one another in a recital. Sometimes, she was convinced he was the only person in the whole universe who understood her. He got her in a way nobody else did because music and dance consumed him the same way it did her.

This last year their pointe work had begun and they practised fifteen hours a week. Miss Laverne was hard on them, exacting in what she tried to push them to do, but they knew why. She'd made no secret of the opportunities that would open up for them if they gave it everything they had. Her mum reckoned they were like a young Fonteyne and Nureyev and Gabe's mother who didn't hand out compliments readily had been impressed with their performance's in the *Nutcracker*. She'd danced the Sugar Plum

Fairy pas de deux once upon a time too. Gabe had been happy she was there. It was the one thing she showed interest in when it came to what was going on in his life, he reckoned. As for Miss Laverne, she'd never heap such lavish praise on them. She was a believer in keeping their feet firmly on the ground, so to speak. And right now, much to Veronica's absolute frustration, that's exactly what she was doing and it was making her crazy.

From her window seat she could see the fat green leaves of the oaks that lined the street Gabe lived on. Expensive neighbourhoods were always full of trees, she mused, and the foliage she was looking at now was so dense she could almost believe she could walk across them like one of those treetop forest walks. Or, even better dance over them. She half shut her eyes picturing herself performing the split leap ciseaux over the top of the trees. It would be like flying.

'Ronnie?' Gabe tossed a sock at her.

She swivelled to face him. 'Oi, I hope that was clean!'

'*Come As You Are*.' He waved the CD cover.

'Yeah, great.'

Gabe's bedroom walls were an interesting mix of ballet and Nirvana, Soundgarden and The Red Hot Chilli Peppers. She watched as he rolled over and pulled himself up to a sitting position, aiming the remote at his CD player. The rack went through the shuffling motion before the song began to blare and he lay back down, this time on his back with his eyes closed. He fancied himself a kind of Kurt Cobain anti-hero. Gabe's eyes were brown but he had the singer's blond good looks and he'd been growing his hair so it hung in his eyes. School, he'd told her, was on his case to get it cut. It could do with a wash, she thought, knowing he'd have liked to have stubble decorating his chin and upper lip but all he could produce was a shadow moustache. She'd thought quietly he might be cultivating his grunge look to hide behind because the boys at his school were liable to understand that image more than the dancer side of him.

As for her, she was no Courtney Love but she had been going heavy on the eyeliner and the attitude much to her mother's annoyance. She'd taken to leaving the makeup off until she got farther up the road and putting it on at the bus stop. It was a good job Abi was still at primary school because she'd have been the first to tattle tale on her.

'Do you want the rest of this?' she asked above the pounding beat, holding the smouldering fag out. He stretched his arm back over his head taking the cigarette from her, dragging deeply before exhaling a lazy plume towards the ceiling, uncaring as to what his parents would say. They were never home anyway, their lives very much their own, and by the time they got back from whatever function they were at he'd have aired the room out and given it a liberal spray of Brut deodorant.

Veronica thought he was lucky. His house was her sanctuary. It was a bolthole where she could breathe and had room to think. She liked the way the place smelled too. Her house smelled of frying and cats. His smelt elegant. She'd never known this was something you could detect in a scent but you could. It was in the fresh flower fragrance from the bouquet on the occasional table in the hallway. A fresh arrangement was delivered to the door each Monday. It was also in the rich subtle odour of leather and furniture polish and the faint whiff of wine and whisky left over from the drinks Gabe's parents enjoyed as a precursor to dinner.

How amazing it would be to have a woman who came and cleaned your house from top to bottom every Thursday. A woman who didn't hold up your bed's valance to peer at what was housed on the floor beneath it and bellow at you to get up the stairs and sort it out before you brought the mice in. There was so such much space in Gabe's home, you weren't forever tripping over things or living on top of one another like at her house. His parents were always off out somewhere black tie and when they were home, they left him to his own devices. His basic needs were taken care of in the form of meals and if he needed to go somewhere his mum or dad would usually drop him off in one of their big shiny cars but for the best part he was left alone.

There was none of this knocking on the door to see if they wanted a drink or something to eat like her mum did. Veronica knew it was a thinly veiled excuse to see what she and Gabe were up to, not concern as to whether they were fed and watered. Her mum had a thing about boys in bedrooms but when she broached this Veronica had said, 'But he's not a boy, he's Gabe, Mum.' There was a difference, because he was her best friend. In the end her mum had let it go because there was nowhere else, they could go. Nine times out of ten Abi would be lying on the floor of the living room, her sock-clad feet kicking at the air, hands cupped with her chin resting in them watching the television. The kitchen was Margo's domain and so, the only place where they could chat in peace was her room. Yes, she much preferred it when they went to Gabe's.

She also thought it would be wonderful to be the only child. Gabe tried to tell her it wasn't but she found it hard to believe. What bliss not to have to hide the things you didn't want a nosy younger sister finding. Gabe came and went as he pleased and the only time his parents stepped in was when he wasn't performing as he should be. He reckoned he was a box to be ticked on their life achievement list, have child, tick, ensure child succeeds, tick, but, that was as far as their interest in him went. She thought it would be great to have parents who let you live your own life instead of smothering you with their hopes and dreams. I mean, his mum had been a professional dancer but she wasn't constantly on Gabe's back like hers was. The problem, Veronica had concluded, was her mum had no life of her own. AD, they'd had to move to a smaller house and her mum's world seemed to have shrunk along with their living circumstances. She was bitter and full of regrets. The woman you did not want to strike on the check out when you came to pay for your weekly shop.

Veronica had long since revolved to get out from under her mother's roof as soon as she could. She had plans. She and Gabe had talked about it with Miss Laverne and if they worked hard enough and if this dumb fracture would heal, they could make it happen. Their dream to dance at the Opera National de Paris could become a reality. Élisabeth Platel had danced there. The French prima ballerina was one of her idols. Miss Laverne had said she had friends in the company who would keep her up to date with openings in the Corps de Ballet.

Firstly though, she'd lectured they must continue to work hard and take every opportunity that came their way including attending the Royal Ballet School's intensive summer training. For two weeks they'd be taught a curriculum of ballet, variations, pas de deux, Royal Ballet repertoire and stage craft by former Royal Ballet artistes. She'd be living her dream of dancing full time. How her mum would afford to send her though she didn't know.

She was lost in the music and her musings when Gabe got up, and moved towards where she was sitting by the window. Even when he was simply walking there was a sleekness about him. He leaned past her and Veronica caught the tangy aroma mingled with pine cones of the deodorant he used. She felt a stirring of something unfamiliar in the pit of her stomach at his proximity.

'Come on, dance with me.' He took her hand and dragged her up as the song finished and *Smells like Teen Spirit* began to play.

To hell with her stupid injury, she thought, as he put his arms around her and she locked hers around his waist. Her head came up to his shoulder; he'd gotten tall these last couple of months and she leaned her head against his chest feeling him breathing. They moved slowly almost out of tune and as the music reached its mad crescendo, Gabe pushed her away gently and with a laugh began po-going madly about his bedroom. Veronica cracked up at the sheer madness of him. He didn't care, carrying on letting loose and it was infectious because she began jumping around in a manner that would have had Miss Laverne and her mother screeching at her to sit down and be careful of her injury. She tossed her head about, her hair flying and when the song came to an end, she fell backwards onto his bed a breathless, giggling wild thing.

She bounced up as Gabe flung himself down next to her. 'That was brilliant.' He grinned, his hand patting about until it found hers. They lay like that hand in hand getting their breath back and then Gabe released his grip, rolling onto his side and propping himself up on his elbow. He looked down at Veronica and there was a light in his velvety eyes she'd never seen before. Time slowed as he reached out and with his index finger traced a line from her forehead down her nose, over her lips and chin until it came to a stop at the hollow in the base of her neck. 'I love you, Ronnie,' he said, his voice gruff. 'We're soulmates you and me.'

So, simple so natural, so perfect. 'I love you too.'

'I've got something I want to give you.' He scrambled off the bed and went to his leather jacket hanging on the back of his door. He pulled a box from the pocket and clambered back alongside her. His eyes shining as he handed it to her.

She studied the small lilac box for a moment, her stomach fluttering with unfamiliar, exciting new feelings. 'What is it?'

'Open it and see.'

She did and her eyes widened at the silver band with a pearl, set like a daisy nestling amongst the silver looped leaves. Pearl was her birthstone, he knew that. 'Gabe, it's beautiful.'

'You're beautiful. You're everything to me, Ronnie. Promise me you'll always wear it and we'll be together forever.'

'I will and I promise.'

'Together forever?'

'Together forever.'

He took the dainty ring from the box. 'Give me your hand.'

She held out her left hand and he slid it on her ring finger, raising her hand to his mouth and brushing his lips against her skin. She remembered, fleetingly, that pearl was also for tears but brushed it aside. All the stuff that had happened, her dad leaving and then dying. It didn't matter because she had Gabe now and a promise that they'd be together forever.

She knew what was going to happen next and she closed her eyes in expectation of their first kiss. She was aware of the maleness of him. The scent of sweat mingling with the cigarette they'd shared. His lips settled on hers, tentative and searching at first and as she responded he grew bolder. Veronica pulled him down closer to her wanting something more, knowing he did too. The rumbling of the garage door opening broke the trance and they sat up. She almost felt drugged as she pulled herself into the here and now, tugging her top down and smoothing her hair. She looked at Gabe uncertainly because they'd crossed a line and things could never go back to the way they were. He reached over and tucked her hair behind her ear and from the look on his face she knew whatever happened next it would be okay.

Now

A SCREAM WENT UP AND Margo flinched. Loud, sudden noises frightened her these days and Veronica searched for the source. She saw the young girl who'd been frolicking about the garden earlier clutching her foot, her concerned mum bending down to look. 'I think the poor thing got a bee sting, that's all, Mum.' She rubbed her arm to reassure her. She was still holding the tutu on her lap. The sun had moved across the sky and the seat was beginning to feel hard beneath her Veronica realised, shifting to try and get comfortable. She shivered at the breeze that had dropped from summery to spring cool and glanced at her watch. She'd been here over an hour. It would be time to go soon and catch up with all the things needing doing at home.

'Mum, I wanted to tell you I'm sorry.' She took Margo's hand in hers.

'It's very pretty,' Margo said, her eyes on the tutu.

'Yes, you made it. Weren't you clever?'

'I made this?'

'Yes, and I never thanked you properly. You did so much for me and I never told you how much I appreciated you. I was angry for a long time over dad leaving us and then, well, then he died and you wouldn't talk about it. I had all these feelings churning inside me and nowhere to put them so I took them out on you. It wasn't fair and it was wrong of me. Mum, I'm so, so sorry.' Veronica squeezed her hand gently. She hadn't understood it at the time, the sacrifices Margo had made for her. Not just the long hours at the sewing machine or taking the extra shifts at Tesco's to pay for her lessons. The sacrifices had started when she was still in the womb and she'd gotten married.

Margo and Phil had done the right thing after the pressure had been heaped upon them by their families when they broke the news Margo was pregnant. They hadn't been together long and they were young but they had their big day, a white pretence, and gave it their best shot until there was nothing left to aim for anymore and Phil moved to greener pastures. It wasn't how Veronica had seen it at the time though. Back then she'd seen her mother be short and snippy with her father. He could do no wrong in her eyes and she'd held on to the belief that if Margo had been kinder, spoken to him more softly, he would have stayed and if he'd stayed, he wouldn't have died.

She hadn't understood how things had been for a long time, mostly because she hadn't wanted to acknowledge the reality of the situation. Their dad had left not just his wife, but his children too, not once trying to contact them and that had hurt far too much to accept. It had been easier to blame her mother.

'My daughter was a dancer.' Margo stared straight ahead, her expression blank.

'Yes, she was.'

'She was very good, you know.'

Her mum had always been her biggest champion. As a parent you pushed and encouraged because you saw the potential others might miss. Veronica knew this now. Her eyes burned and her throat tightened until it hurt to hold back the tears. She wouldn't cry though, not in front of her mum it would only upset her and she swallowed hard trying to rid herself of the lump lodged. 'Was she?'

'Yes. I have two daughters.'

'You do, Mum, yes. Abi and Veronica.'

'Abi, I haven't seen her in a long while.'

'She came to see you yesterday.'

'Did she? I don't remember.'

'She did. She's been to see you every day this week.'

'Has she?' Margo shook her head. 'I don't remember things. This,' she tapped the side of her head. 'It doesn't work like it used to.'

Veronica sensed her agitation. 'I love you, Mum. Shall we go and see what's for afternoon tea today?'

'I don't mind.'

Veronica stood up, rolling her shoulders forwards and backwards to loosen the knot that had formed, she must have been hunching while she was sitting there talking. Then she helped Margo up and led her towards the open doors.

'I can hear music,' Margo exclaimed, her face suddenly alight.

Someone was playing the piano, Veronica realised. An entertainer of some description came most Saturday afternoons. This was much better than the trio caterwauling Peter Paul and Mary's hits last week. It was Tchaikovsky she realised, recognising the tune as the waltz from *Sleeping Beauty*. She'd once danced to it and closing her eyes she remembered how it had felt.

1994

VERONICA AND GABE PEERED around the velvety drapes on the stage of the St Trinian's School theatre where they were waiting for their musical cue. Gabe's mother had managed to secure the use of the theatre at the public school he attended for a nominal fee. Out there in the audience, the parents were all sitting forwards in their seats enjoying the spectacle of their offspring on stage while siblings sulkily slouched in theirs, forced to come and watch with the promise of a bag of sweets to keep them quiet. Abi, she knew, would have a packet of her favourite lolly mix. You could hear the rustle of wrappers in between acts. Whoever was employed to clean the auditorium afterwards was in for a good time, Veronica had thought.

This was the pay-off for all the mothers who had, in the weeks leading up to this end of year, Christmas *Sleeping Beauty* performance, been busy sewing the various costumes prancing about on the stage. Veronica smiled, seeing the dodgy looking six-year-old Puss in Boots milling about under the lights alongside the lilac fairy, Megan, and a disgruntled Goldilocks, Hayley. Everybody, no matter their age or ability would have a moment to shine, Miss Laverne had assured her students and their parents alike. It was unspoken but it was known the real stars of the show were Veronica and Gabe in their roles of the Princess Aurora and Prince Désiré.

Veronica, with her tiara and white tutu, shone and she knew it; so too did Gabe who was resplendent in his brocade embellished white jacket, dance belt and tights. This wedding pas de deux, the grand pas de deux was their moment to show everyone what they had, what they'd been working so hard towards. The music tempo changed and Gabe held her hand lightly in his as they moved gracefully across the stage to take their place in the centre of the milling fairy-tale wedding party.

Veronica stepped into her complicated entrée adagio and arced long into port de bras back before the turn where, for the briefest second, Gabe had no contact with her body and there was always the possibility of falling. She had to put her faith in him and he'd never failed when they'd practiced over and over until she'd perfected the steps. She was unaware of the audience or her fellow dancers. There was only her and Gabe as she performed the delicate motions of her opening sequence with a regal grace. The steps grew increasingly technical and daring, building in crescendo until it was Gabe's turn to seemingly effortlessly leap, jump and turn before coming back to her. The dance grew bolder, grander, the pirouettes perfectly executed and the fish dive garnering an audible gasp from the audience. Their steps perfectly mirrored one another's as they performed them in the threes of the classical ballet.

The music calmed and Veronica was Aurora, not just a princess but a girl getting married and she allowed the romance to shine through with her fluttering but precise movements. They presented the flashy, technically difficult steps, all the while building into their finishing and daring climax with her in Gabe's arms.

The applause was deafening and as it thundered about them Veronica was conscious of her heart beating next to Gabe's in sync as if they were one.

Chapter 28
Isabel

THE FIRST WEEK WITH Austin staying was a disaster from Isabel's perspective whereas Rhodri, who in his own new-father bubble, thought everything was going marvellously. He'd been having a wonderful time taking Austin out each morning and the weather had played ball. They'd swum and made sandcastles, and yes, painted before picnicking. Austin's artwork a bright daubing of yellow sun and blue sea with white specks for sails on it was now stuck to the fridge. They'd settled into a routine for him quickly of seven o'clock bedtime, six am rise and shine, some morning television—he was partial to the shopping channel, which had caused her and Rhodri to raise their eyebrows—but Rhodri decided not to rock the boat. So, while Austin sat glued to the screen as everything from homeware to kitchen and DIY was given the hard sell, Rhodri sorted out quick oats and toast soldiers. Isabel had offered to do this but Rhodri was enjoying the novelty of fussing over Austin in a normal morning routine.

She'd sat down next to the small boy and done her best to make conversation each morning as she sipped her wake-up brew. This morning she'd asked him whether he had a NutriBullet at home and if it was as good as they were making out on the tele. He'd just stuck his thumb in his mouth though and continued to stare at the screen. She'd given up, and chomping on a piece of toast headed upstairs to go and get herself ready for work.

She'd have left for the day by the time Nico arrived each morning to open the gallery and then the hours until Isabel got home were Rhodri and Austin's to do as they pleased. Delwyn had been very understanding about her need to finish in time to be back at Pier View House for two o'clock so Nico could go home and work in her studio while Rhodri took over in the gallery. In some respects, she wished she hadn't been, and she disliked herself for feeling like that. The shop had been busy today and she'd felt terrible leaving Delwyn in the lurch but she'd waved her away saying she'd managed before Isabel had come to work at The Natural Way, she'd manage on her own for a couple of hours.

She would've loved to have talked the situation over with Constance when she'd telephoned sounding a box of birds from Vancouver. It wasn't the right time though. She was on the trip of a lifetime and didn't need to be weighed down with Isabel's problems. So she hadn't said a word, just listened and made the right noises as Constance told her all about the meal and service they'd had in first class on the plane. She'd moved on to how the apartment was lovely with lots of room for them all and who'd have thought people lived like that all the time, up high in the sky like so. She was in her element and the knowledge that this was the case lifted Isabel's spirits. True to her word, Constance had demanded to know whether she'd posted the letter.

The hesitation in her voice told Constance all she needed to know but before she could lecture her, Isabel had deftly moved the conversation onto finding out what plans the family had for the week. They would be walking in Edward's father Henry's footsteps revisiting his childhood haunts. All the places Henry had told the young Constance about and the excitement in her voice as she relayed this was palpable. They'd said their goodbyes with Constance promising to send a postcard or two while they were away and a stern reminder for her to send the letter.

Isabel pulled her phone out of her pocket and glanced at the time. She'd nearly run from The Natural Way only slowing as she neared the Esplanade. She couldn't leave mid-sale and so she was running a few minutes late. Today would be different she resolved, puffing as she turned the corner. Today Austin wouldn't sit with his knees pulled up leaning against the arm of their sofa the iPad nestling against his thighs as he watched the flickering screen for the entire afternoon.

The world had changed so rapidly. It hadn't been that long since she was a child and at twenty-seven, she shouldn't be saying, 'Back in my day it was DVDs,' but she found herself thinking it. She'd tried, she had. She'd suggested they go for an ice cream and walk along the pier, but he'd said his mummy didn't like him eating ice cream. A jaunt on the bus to see the rest of the island had been next on her list and seeing that didn't rev his engine she'd taken things up a notch by saying they could head to Newport and visit Tapnell Farm Park. There'd been desperation in her voice as she asked him if he'd like to feed the wallabies. He hadn't batted an eye as he said he didn't like farms because they were smelly.

Rhodri waved her concerns away, saying Austin was worn out from his busy mornings that was all, and if he was content to just sit back and watch a movie so be it. Isabel should be grateful she didn't need to entertain him was his unspoken message. In their own ways they were both tiptoeing around him, Isabel had realised. Neither of them wanted to upset him because both were scared he'd refuse to come back. It was just they had different reasons for feeling like that.

Today though she wasn't going to ask him if he'd like to do something, she was going to tell him what they *were* doing. That was where she was going wrong, she'd decided as she tossed and turned last night. Rhodri had laid his arm across her, a dead weight, and asked her what the matter was. 'You're not normally such a fidget,' he'd murmured sleepily. She'd snuggled closer pressing her back against him. 'Sorry, can't sleep.' He'd kissed her on the back of her head and been snoring a minute later while she pondered how she could get Austin to engage with her because if he refused to spend time with her, other than time spent on his iPad, while she milled around wondering what to do with herself, how were they ever going to get to know one another?

She'd even rung her mother for advice and her wise words had been, 'Buy him a chocolate bar, Isabel. It worked a treat with you every time. A Galaxy bar and you were anybody's.' It was advice she didn't plan on taking on board and she wasn't that much of a pushover, was she? Then again, she did love a Galaxy bar. It was the creaminess that got her.

Today, she resolved, opening the door to the gallery and seeing Austin sitting behind the counter while his daddy chatted to a customer, she was pulling out all the stops because today she was taking him to Blackgang Chine, the island's theme park. How could he not love her after that?

Chapter 29
Veronica

'HELLO, MUM, HOW'RE you today? It's not very nice out there is it?' Veronica put the carrier bag down and leaned in to kiss Margo on the top of her head. She didn't look up as she sat with her hands clasped, seemingly engrossed in the striped pattern of her skirt. She'd spotted her mother on the end of a row of chairs set up in a semi-circle around a woman with a guitar who was strumming her way through John Denver's *Country Roads*. Veronica glanced around, seeing some of the residents were clapping along enthusiastically to the old favourite while others dozed and some, like her mother was currently doing, were studying their laps. She crouched down alongside her and took her hand in hers joining in on the final chorus. She surprised herself by knowing it word for word. Her mum, however, clearly wasn't in the mood for singing.

When the song had finished, she said, 'Mum shall we go and find somewhere quieter to sit. I've brought something in with me I'd like to show you.'

'Are we going out? Will we see...'

The frustration as she tried to find the name she wanted was evident as she pulled at the fabric of her skirt and Veronica took a guess, not wanting her to get aggravated. 'Abi?'

Margo nodded. 'Yes, her. This doesn't work like it used to you know.' She tapped the side of her head.

'She might come later, Mum.' Veronica had high hopes of Abi heading back to London with Brandon but his recent visit hadn't yielded a reconciliation. Abi was playing hardball. 'Saturday afternoon's our time.' She felt a light touch on her shoulder and looked up to see Danika. She was holding the hand of a woman who was clasping the baby doll she knew

172

did the rounds of the residents, tightly to her chest with her free hand. 'Hi, miserable day out there.' She smiled up at the caregiver.

'It is. I'm glad we had entertainment organised. You're in time for afternoon tea too, it will be served in fifteen minutes or so.'

'Great. A cup of tea's always welcome. She's very good.' Veronica gestured to the guitarist who was now strumming *Hey Jude* by The Beatles. She had a lovely voice.

'Mm, better than the chap with his portable electric organ we had the other week. He murdered the Beach Boys.'

Veronica laughed. 'How's Mum been?' She'd seen her on Thursday with the boys and she'd been quiet, Veronica had thought.

'She's been fine, happy listening to her music, you know Margo. You love your music, don't you?'

Margo gave a vague smile and Danika patted her on the arm leaving them to it.

Veronica helped her mum up and picking up the bag once more, she held her hand and led her over to the far end of the lounge where there was a vacant two-seater sofa which would do them nicely. 'Here we are, Mum, we can hear ourselves think now.' She settled her on the seat and then sat down next to her.

'Is she coming today?'

'Abi might come later or she'll call in tomorrow.'

Margo seemed to accept that and Veronica retrieved what it was she wanted to show her. A plain black tunic with no skirt which she gave her mother to hold.

'I wore that to a very important audition.'

Margo turned the costume over in her hands and Veronica pulled out the second item she'd brought with her. It was a photo album and she opened the cheap flower-patterned, hardback cover.

'That's my ticket to London, Mum,' she said, pointing to the stub sellotaped on the inside of the cover. 'I went with Gabe.'

'Gabe was a dancer.'

'Yes, he was, Mum.'

'My daughter danced.'

'I did, yes. You've got my leotard there in your hands and this, here, is the ticket that took me to London with Gabe. We went to the Royal Ballet School's two-week course over the summer. It was held in Covent Garden and we boarded in the school's hostel, Jesbson House.' This time she showed her mum the photographs on the first page. They were pasted down by the plastic film covering them. 'Here.' A matte photo of her roommate, Jessica, who was lying on her stomach with her legs kicking the air, her face cupped in her hands just as Abi always had done when she was watching TV, as she grinned for the camera. They'd thought they were so sophisticated, sharing a sly cigarette down the alleyway after lessons. It made her laugh thinking about it now. There was nothing sophisticated about it at all they'd been positively furtive, terrified of getting caught by one of the hostel's pastoral staff.

She'd looked Jessica up on Facebook a while back, feeling creepy stalkerish but curiosity as to where she was now and what she was doing had overcome her guilt. Jessica worked as an accountant and had two girls a year or two younger than the twins who, judging by the photos on the feed, were keen dancers already. An accountant was as far removed from a career in ballet as you could get, Veronica had thought, staring at her laptop screen. Then again working behind a perfume counter hadn't been what she'd had planned that long-ago summer either.

They'd gotten on well her and Jessica, laughed lots during that fortnight and vowed to keep in touch when they went home. Jessica was from Leeds and they'd written to each other once. Hashing over the fortnight's events on quickly scrawled letters, posted off before they got sidetracked by life. It required an effort to keep in touch back then, in the days when you had to pick up a phone or write a letter to maintain long distance friendships though, and Veronica, once home from London had barely enough time to eat and sleep between school and practising. Oh, and Gabe of course. She'd had time for Gabe.

How grown up she'd felt that sixteenth summer, boarding the train for London with her case. Just her and Gabe. She'd have been terrified if she'd been travelling on her own but with him by her side nothing scared her not even the thought of fourteen days of the most intense dance training of her life. It had been a foregone conclusion that Gabe would go, but money had been an issue for Veronica.

'You took an extra job at the supermarket, stacking the shelves of an evening when I was home to look after Abi for eight months, Mum, so I could go on that course. You worked so hard for me and Abi but especially me.'

'Did I?'

'Yes. Thank you for doing that.'

She leaned over and kissed Margo on the cheek. 'I love you.'

Margo smiled.

'Miss Laverne, she was our teacher in St Rebus.' Veronica stopped herself from saying, remember? It was better to simply tell the story. 'She was our main champion, mine and Gabe's. We were so lucky to have her. She passed away a few years ago.' It had hurt Veronica's heart when she'd read in the local paper's obituaries she'd died after a good battle had been fought. She'd let her down, just the same as she had her mum, and had kept her distance from her former teacher, ashamed of the secret she nursed. She hadn't wanted to see the disappointment etched on her face the way it was her mother's.

'I remember what she said to Gabe and me before we went to London.' If she closed her eyes, she could still see the lithe, ageless form of Miss Laverne, her ruby-red lips pursed as she watched their faces wanting to be sure they'd understood what she'd said. 'She told us to give our all in the technique class, establish rapport with our teachers and to get on with our classmates. We did too.'

Their days had begun with a class at nine thirty and she'd spent her breaks with Gabe and Jessica and Gabe's roommate Dorian. Veronica felt as though she was a caterpillar emerging from its chrysalis to unfurl its wings during that time. With all the heated emotion of a teenager on the cusp of a bright future, she'd known she was discovering her true self. The young woman she was destined to be. She was born to dance. Gabe confided he felt the same way and they'd smiled at one another, hands held tight as they immersed themselves in a world outsiders couldn't relate to. It was theirs and that of the tight circle at the ballet's summer school.

All four of them had spent their one and only free day, a Sunday, exploring London. Having a ball riding the tube to different destinations as they'd laughed in the carefree way only the young can when life is theirs for the taking. She hadn't appreciated that brief time with the fullness it deserved before responsibility and duty began to creep in.

Miss Laverne, through her contacts, heard of an audition when they'd completed their London training. It was for the Opera de Paris for male and female positions in the Paris Corps de Ballet and unbeknown to them she'd sent in their résumés along with the requested photographs. She waited until the positive response with an audition date for the first round arrived to tell them of the opportunity.

Veronica and Gabe had lain side by side, hand in hand on his bed, the sheet covering their naked bodies. A kiss had turned to something more as they whispered, even though no one was about in that big echoing home of his, about what it would be like to dance with the Parisian Ballet. They spoke about things others would have no understanding of because ballet had its own language.

How would it feel to be a quadrille, the beginning level in the Corps de Ballet? To have the opportunity to audition for the concours in order to advance up the rank to the position of coryphées and eventually sujets. They were foreign words but it was a language they yearned to be part of and to embrace. There was the chance too, if they proved themselves worthy of these promotions, and if an opening came up, of auditioning for the coveted post of premier dancer. They'd live together in Paris, realise their dreams and that rarest of rare things in the world of dance, job security.

If they'd been honest with one another, the electricity that sparked between them when they danced hadn't flickered and ignited as they'd fumbled their way through losing their virginity. It was probably the only time since they'd known each other they hadn't been truthful about what they'd done. They didn't know it then but it wouldn't happen again.

'We had the opportunity after we came home from London to go to Paris and audition, Mum, for the Corps de Ballet.' Veronica looked at her mother and rested her hand on her arm. 'You worked so hard again putting in all those extra hours at the supermarket. It was a job you hated but you said it was worth every second of gritting your teeth and smiling as you plucked things off the conveyer because Gabe and I made it through the first round.'

Margo was silent, listening to Veronica as she held the tunic in her hands, her eyes fixed on it as though she'd discovered the eighth natural wonder. Veronica closed her eyes briefly, recalling the long-ago class held by one of the French ballet school's teachers in the Palais Garnier's training studios.

It had been a modern facility with timber panelling along the walls and yet more light, square panels of wood chequering the illuminated ceiling. There'd been no hint of the blood, sweat and tears, no doubt spilled on the polished floors over the years. They were split into male and female groups, given numbers to wear and the voices chattering excitedly around them had accents from as far and as wide as Canada, America, Australia and New Zealand.

The auditions took place at different times and it had helped her to know Gabe was outside the studio willing her on as the pianist, her back ramrod straight as she sat at the sleek, black piano in the corner of the studio began to play. They'd been led through bar and middle floor exercises in front of a jury to whom they were all just numbers in black tunics and flesh coloured tights. How austere the group of people seated alongside the wall with the porthole windows had seemed. She remembered the puddles of light from those windows reflected on the floor with its high gloss sheen. It had been like looking into a pool of water at a reflection. That these overseers were qualified to pass judgment, there was no doubt. They were comprised of the elite. The general director of the ballet school, the dance artistic director, ballet masters, two guests, other artistic personalities, administrative staff and management whose names meant nothing to either her or, she found out later, Gabe. There'd been five dancers representing the ballet too, and it had been them Veronica had kept in her head throughout the arduous routines because, they'd been where she was. They knew how much she wanted this.

'I remember Miss Laverne nodding when mine and Gabe's numbers were called out at the end of the day when the ballet managers announced the numbers selected for the second round,. There was no jumping for joy at all our hard work having paid off. She was cool as a cucumber, and said she'd expected no less. It was such a dream come true, Mum, to be invited to take part in the next stage, but you were so worried as to how we'd afford it and at the same time you were determined I'd go. Miss Laverne offered to help but she couldn't afford to subsidise my whole trip. We even talked about fundraising but then Gabe stepped in and told his parents he wouldn't go if I didn't go with him.'

She knew it wasn't the first time he'd refused to do something because of her. His mother had wanted him to attend the Royal Ballet School on a permanent basis; he was good enough but then so was she, it was just their circumstances were so very different. Mrs Darby-Hazleton had wanted to enrol him when he was fourteen, arguing this was how it had to be if he wanted to progress into a full-time ballet career. He'd seen it as her and his father's way of further fobbing him off. He'd refused to leave behind the one person who was always there for him—Veronica. Besides, he'd argued his case, Miss Laverne was one of the best teachers in the country and she was tutoring them on an individual basis these days. You couldn't get better than the one on one classes they attended.

Veronica hadn't thought how it must have been for her mother to accept charity from the Darby-Hazleton's who'd been equally determined that this time their son would not miss his chance because of Veronica.

She'd had no choice but to do so, Miss Laverne had been looking at Margo, desperate for her to accept their generous offer. Mrs Darby-Hazleton, so aloof in her clouds of perfume and designer pantsuit. The money was no skin off her nose but it must have cost Margo deeply. Perhaps if she hadn't agreed things might have been different and Veronica wouldn't have felt beholden to her when it mattered most.

She recalled how she and Gabe had carried on with their theme, swept up as they'd been in the idea of their grand Romeo and Juliette affair that if one of them wasn't offered a position with the Parisian company, the other wouldn't accept.

Veronica turned the pages of the album on her lap and pointed at the photo of her and Gabe. Miss Laverne who'd travelled to Paris with them as their chaperone for a second time had taken it. They were outside the Palace of Versailles. Her hair had whipped across her cheek but you could still see how wide her smile was. Gabe had his arm draped over her shoulder and he was gazing at her, also grinning. Everything had changed not long after that picture was taken.

It was a photo that made her feel sad, knowing what came next, and she turned the page pointing to the image of the Palais Garnier. It was the opera house where she'd imagined she'd dance, where Gabe had danced many times over the ensuing years. 'This is the Palais Garnier, Mum. Isn't it beautiful? And look this is the Opéra Bastille, such a contrast with its modern design but an incredible facility. And this here is the Opera Garnier where we auditioned that second time. Shall I tell you about that?'

Her mother held the leotard to her cheek, her head tilted slightly as she listened to Veronica tell her a story she'd never heard before.

Chapter 30
Isabel

ISABEL AND AUSTIN TRAVERSED the middle of the island by hopping on the bus from Ryde and jumping off at Newport where they could get their connection. She bought him a packet of crisps which he ate with his legs swinging back and forth under the bench seat while they waited for the bus to take them to Chale. She'd spent the time checking through the rucksack she'd thrown all sorts in before heading off. For once she felt prepared as she located the water bottle, sunscreen and packet of Jacob's Mini Cheddars along with two shiny, red apples to nibble on if they got peckish, although Rhodri said Austin had eaten a big lunch. She'd even packed her swimsuit and Austin's trunks in case he wanted to go on the water slide. She'd had a moment's panic but then felt the towels down the bottom of the pack. Yes, she thought, zipping the bag back up she'd done well. Normally she flew out the door barely remembering her bag let alone to pack it. She glanced down the road but there was no sign of the bus as yet. It should be here any minute though if it was running to its timetable.

Rhodri had looked pleased when she'd told him of her plans. She hadn't missed Austin's baleful expression as he fixed his eyes on his dad, looking like he was hoping for a reprieve. If Rhodri had been the one to announce they were going to an adventure park, Isabel had no doubt he'd have been beside himself with excitement but because it was her, the wicked girlfriend he might as well have been told he was off to the doctors for a jab. She'd not given him time to dwell on it, taking him firmly by the hand and trotting him out the door before he could protest. They would have fun, she'd decided, even if it bloody well killed her.

'Here comes a bus,' Austin said. It was the first sentence he'd uttered since leaving Pier View House and Isabel wondered if winning him over was as simple as a bag of crisps.

She looked to where the bus was chugging towards them and seeing the number said, 'Yes, that's us, Austin.' She opened the front pocket of the rucksack and retrieved her purse counting out some coins as it pulled in alongside the kerb.

The journey didn't take long with Isabel telling Austin to ring the bell as she spied the giant pirate with a rum barrel on his shoulder that signalled the entrance to the theme park. It was the oldest amusement park in the United Kingdom, not that she thought that piece of trivia would be of much interest to Austin. 'Wait until the bus comes to a complete stop before getting up,' she said as it began to slow. He did as he was told, waiting until she stood up and called out a thank you to the driver before hopping off. They made their way to the entrance building to pay the admission.

The park had only been open a few weeks after closing for the winter season. It would be busy but not crazily so, she hoped, and the afternoon was mild which was better than stinking hot. She'd timed their visit well and her mood was exuberant as she handed over her card to be swiped. The excited squeals of children rang out as they ventured forth and she felt a frisson of excitement herself. You couldn't help but feel happy somewhere like this, she thought, seeing hyped small faces racing about the grounds. She risked a glance at Austin, pleased to see he was looking animatedly around him. A girl of eight or so walked past them her face all screwed up and a frozen slush drink in her hand. Brain freeze no doubt, Isabel thought.

'Should we walk around first and see what you'd like to go on, Austin?' As soon as she'd said it she chastised herself for giving him a choice again. She quickly opened the map and glanced over it. 'Let me see, hmm, the Lands of Imagination sound like fun. Let's check out Nursery Land.' She looked up to see a small child with a Mr Whippy almost as big as he was, white creamy ice cream dripping down the side of the cone. Inspired she added, 'And then we could get an ice cream cone.' Like she'd told herself earlier, she was pulling out all the stops and who needed cheddars and apples when there was ice cream? He'd already had crisps, she might as well go the full hog.

'Nursery Land's for babies,' he lisped, looking at where she was pointing on the colour layout and I don't like ice cweam.'

That, Isabel knew to be a fib, she'd seen him slurping on a chocolate cone his daddy had bought him just the other day. She took a deep breath. 'Fair enough, you're a big boy after all. Hmm, do you think we should be brave and visit,' she lowered her voice intending to sound dramatic but coming across like the creepy voiceover for movie trailers, 'Restricted Area 5, where the dinosaurs live?' Ah ha, that got him, she thought, seeing the flare of interest in his brown eyes. 'Come on then,' she held out her hand and he looked at it for a moment before taking hold of it and letting her lead the way.

They entered through the gates of the mystery enclosure and moved stealthily through the wooded area waiting for something to jump out at them. It was Austin who spotted the family of dinosaurs up ahead. He began to jiggle with excitement. 'They're triceratops!'

'Wow, do you know about dinosaurs then, Austin?' Isabel asked, following behind. She was sensing genuine wonder in his voice at what he was seeing as they drew nearer.

'I do, I collect them.'

It was like all the bells and whistles going off on a gaming machine, Jackpot! She, Isabel Stark, had discovered Austin's passion. She felt a stab of regret at having chosen the farm duvet instead of the dinosaur one. It would be too late to take it back now but they could certainly go back to the toy shop while he was here and see what miniature offerings of the Jurassic kind they had. She watched delightedly as he carried on exploring, exclaiming as to who was who in the dinosaur world as other creatures reared out at them through the foliage.

'Look over there!' Isabel got into the swing of things pointing to an enormously fierce T-Rex with gnashing teeth whose head was peeking out between he trees. 'Do you think we should run for it before he gobbles us up for dinner? She expected Austin to laugh but he didn't, he looked terrified at the sight of the fearsome model and he turned and ran off back from where they'd come.

'Austin. It's alright it's not real,' she called after him but it was too late. She watched with her hand to her mouth as his foot caught on a tree root. Things seemed to move in slow motion as he went flying through the air, landing with an almighty thump on the hard ground.

Isabel ran down the path, worried by the lack of noise coming from him but as she pounded up to him, he began to howl. It was louder than Prince Charles when he thought he was being ignored and she didn't know whether to be relieved by the sound or worried in case he'd injured himself badly. She crouched down alongside him as he rolled over and sat up clutching his knee to his chest. It physically hurt her to see him sobbing so. He'd torn his trousers and she could see a nasty graze on his right knee that blood was beginning to ooze out of.

Okay, Isabel, she told herself, there's no point overreacting you'll only upset him further. You need to be calm and not make it into a big deal. 'Come on now, Austin, you'll be right as rain with a spot of antiseptic cream and a plaster.' Where she would get a Band-Aid from she didn't know. They'd no doubt have a box in the main entrance but she had to get him back there first. She could carry him, she supposed, if he'd let her.

Austin stared at her through watery eyes and she tried to give him a cuddle but he pulled away, stuttering as he stared down at his knee, 'There's bl-blood.' They both watched the bright red globule pool and then trickle down his leg.

A woman with an entourage of three youngsters broke the trance calling out, 'Are you two okay?'

'He fell over and his knee's bleeding, you wouldn't happen to have a plaster on you?'

'I do as it happens.' She wandered over, leaving her three frolicking about and knelt down on the other side of Austin. 'Let's have a look at the war wound then. Oh, you poor fellow. That's a nasty cut. It must hurt.'

He nodded and then looked at Isabel with an accusatory stare. She'd come prepared, Isabel thought, watching as she whipped out a travel-sized first aid kit and set about cleaning his knee with an antiseptic wipe before putting a large Elastoplast on it. 'There you go, Mummy,' she said to Isabel. 'Good as new, almost. I can't help you with the trousers, I'm afraid.' She smiled.

'She's not my mummy.' Austin hiccupped.

Isabel wanted to cry herself but she blinked forcibly and seeing the woman was looking at her, gabbled, 'He's my partner's son this is the first time he's stayed with us. Things were going well until he fell over.'

She'd said too much and the woman gave her a cautious but sympathetic smile before getting to her feet. She brushed the dirt from her pants before looking around to rally up her own troops. 'Well that should see him right now.'

Isabel remembered her manners. 'Thank you so much for your help.'

'No problem. Bye.'

She disappeared up ahead and Isabel held out her hand. Austin took it and she pulled him up with an 'Upsy-daisy.'

His face screwed up with pain. 'I want to go home.'

'Are you sure, Austin, because we haven't seen much of the park? There's some super cool rides to go on and there's the Underwater Kingdom.' She didn't fancy her chances of getting him to carry on but she had to try. It wasn't about the forty pounds she'd paid to get them in either it was about finishing their day on a happier note. Although, forty quid, was forty quid.

'I want to go home.' His face set in a stubborn expression she was coming to know well but this time his bottom lip was quivering.

'Righty-ho, then we'd best head out to the bus stop.' She tried to take his hand to walk toward the entrance of the Restricted Area but he brushed it away, standing his ground.

'Not that home, my home. I want my mummy.' He began to cry again, great big heaving sobs and Isabel didn't know what to do. She went with instinct and crouching down put her arms around him feeling his slight body cardboard stiff against her. 'I don't blame you, Austin. You must miss your mum and I can understand how strange it must be coming to stay here with me and your dad. We're very happy you came though and your mum will be back from her holiday soon. Shall we count how many sleeps?'

She thought, but wasn't sure, she'd felt his body relax ever so slightly against her but she definitely heard him mumble, 'Alright,' against her chest.

'Right, well, there's tonight, that's one sleep, tomorrow, two sleeps and then the day after that, three sleeps, the day after that, four sleeps and the day after that, five sleeps and when you wake up Daddy's going to take you back to London to meet her off the plane. She'll be so excited to see you.'

There was a loud sniff followed by, 'I can go to the airport?'

'Yes, of course you can.'

Isabel knew she wasn't imagining it as his body relaxed in her arms. It dawned on her then he'd been worried his mum wouldn't come back for him. The father he'd known had gone away and now he had a new daddy. Perhaps he'd thought the same thing would happen with his mummy and he'd be told Isabel was his new mother. Maybe that was why he'd been set against her. Kids heard and saw things differently to adults. Their thought processes were different. She remembered how when she'd stayed away from home for the first time, she'd had nightmares that she'd be taken away in the night by a nameless, faceless woman, knowing she'd never see her parents again. Children didn't always understand what was going on, especially when they'd had as much change as this lad had. She felt a surge of love for him and pulled him tight and he let her but only for a moment. When he pulled away, he said, 'I think I'd like to go to the underwater place. I like fish. Sometimes I go to the pet shop and watch all the colourful ones.'

Isabel stood up and warmth flooded her as his hand slotted into hers.

'Would you like your own fish?'

Austin fixed her with those brown eyes of his and she saw the tears on his cheeks had dried to streaks. She wished she had a tissue on her so he could blow his nose.

'Yes, but Mummy says not at the moment because we might move to a new house.'

Another change for him, Isabel thought as her mouth opened and the words. 'Tomorrow's Saturday, Austin. When Daddy closes the gallery in the afternoon, we could all go to the pet shop in Newport and see about getting you some fish. When you go home to Mummy's we'll look after them for you until you come to stay with us next time. What do you think?'

'Can they live in my room?'

'Yes.'

'And you'd look after them when I go home but they're still my fish?' he clarified.

'That's right.'

He smiled broadly. 'Yes, please.'

He limped toward the gates holding her hand all the way.

'Isabel?'

'Yes, Austin?'

'Do you think I could have an ice cweam after all. It might help my knee feel better.'

She smiled. 'I think that's a great idea. Ice cream is the best medicine.'

LATER THAT EVENING when seven o'clock rolled around and Rhodri had finished reading the Dr Seuss book, sourced on a visit to the library, Austin asked if Isabel would tuck him in. Rhodri gave her a grin and mouthed, 'You're in.' She smiled back. It had been a brilliant afternoon. Austin had forgotten about his sore knee as they explored the Underwater Kingdom where nothing frightening suddenly appeared. To her relief he'd been too short for the Cliffhanger rollercoaster; those adrenalin inducing rides made her feel sick, and he had gotten over his disappointment thanks to their robust game of Snakes and Ladders where they'd had to spin a wheel to find out if they had to slide down a slide or climb a ladder. By the time they'd arrived home to Pier View House they were worn out and Austin's T-shirt had ice cream stains all down the front of it. With his plastered knee and ripped trousers, he looked like a right ragamuffin and Rhodri's face had been a picture when he saw him.

Isabel felt privileged as she followed Austin up the stairs to his room. She snuggled Benny in next to him and tucked the sheets in for him, under strict instructions to pull them tight. She stroked his cheek and then asked what had been puzzling her since they left the Restricted Area. 'Austin, why were you afraid of the T-Rex but not the other dinosaurs?'

He blinked and pursed his lips. 'Because T-Rex eats meat which means people. Triceratops and the others only eat plants.'

'Of course,' Isabel slapped her forehead. 'Aren't I silly forgetting something like that?'

He nodded his agreement which made her smile and with a kiss on the forehead she said night-night.

Chapter 31
Veronica
1994

IT WAS A GREY DAY IN Paris and Veronica was feeling queasy. She put it down to the flaky croissant she'd had for breakfast. It was rich and buttery and wasn't sitting well with the coffee, which was served stronger than she was used to. She'd felt exactly the same yesterday morning too. Her fingers were crossed inside the pocket of the sixties style houndstooth wool coat she'd bought from a local thrift store before the trip. It was her Paris coat and it made her feel hip and edgy. She'd hung it out to air for a day or two but the faint traces of musty flowers from its previous owner still clung to it. She didn't mind though. Her hair was scraped back in a bun and she'd left her trademark black eyeliner off today. She felt exposed without it.

The pavement they were walking along toward the Palais Garnier was crowded with angular, sophisticated Parisians, all in a hurry to get to wherever they were going. The wide street rumbled with motorbikes weaving in and out of cars that, to the uninitiated, appeared to follow no road rules other than go. For all the chaos though, it seemed to work. Cigarette smoke mingled with exhaust fumes and the smell of fresh bread as people strode past eating baguettes for breakfast from brown paper bags.

Up ahead the palais bustled with comings and goings. The hopes and dreams inside the building were palpable and would be more so this time around, now they were within reach. Veronica looked at the golden statuettes either side of the building's crowning, green dome—all of which was supported by the grand Grecian-style columns. There were sixteen columns. She'd counted them last time as they'd walked across the pedestrian crossing toward the palais to compete in the eliminatory round. It had taken her mind off her nerves. Underneath these columns, she could see the archways, and the orange glow of light beckoning them was welcome on this dull morning.

Gabe was quiet as they approached the building. Veronica knew him well enough to know this meant he was nervous. 'You don't need to worry, Gabe. Your Grand Pas Classique is going to be magnifique!'

He smiled at her faux French accent, both his hands thrust into the pockets of his green Army Surplus parker as he strode along. His hair was flopping in his eyes and Veronica saw a passing young woman take a second look. Miss Laverne, who'd dressed in a belted, red dress coat which made her waist look miniscule but also made her look like a spy or stripper depending on what sort of mind you had, hadn't stopped talking from the moment they'd sat down in the hostel kitchen for breakfast. 'Did you wear your flip-flops in the shower?' she'd fired at Veronica as she'd sipped her too-hot coffee. 'Yes.' It had been drummed into her to do so because a ballet dancer could not risk a fungal infection from the less than sanitary showers the hostel they were booked in to offered. She'd yawned, her sleep had been broken due to the comings and goings of their fellow guests.

She was grateful she and Miss Laverne were sharing a room and not in the dormitory as they'd been on their prior audition visit. Gabe had his own room this time around too. There'd be no chance of any illicit liaisons under Miss Laverne's watchful eye though. Veronica had found it a shock the first morning she'd awoken to see her dance teacher without her lipstick on, that first trip. She looked pale and uninteresting without her signature ruby-red lips.

Miss Laverne was still shooting instructions at them as they walked over the pedestrian crossing once more. 'Be confident and show your passion for the dance, don't deviate from your routine or decide to be clever. Remember to use manners at all times. Most of all,' she said, as they entered the hallowed building, 'perform as though your life depends on it.'

Veronica had had a month to rehearse the company's chosen solo dance and she performed the Soirs de Fête from *Coppélia* with every fibre of her being.

Now

'GABE AND I WERE BOTH accepted into the company, Mum, and you were so excited and proud. All those extra hours you'd done, all that scrimping and going without, all of it had been about this. Veronica stared unseeingly at the photo album, she'd turned the page to the last picture taken of her and Gabe. They were at Heathrow about to embark on their new life in Paris, she was leaning her head on his shoulder and they both were doing peace signs. She remembered, despite the smile, she'd been feeling sick. It was more than nervous anticipation of a new adult life away from home for the first time but she'd swallowed it down as she'd been doing for the previous three months.

I never told you what happened in Paris, Mum. I never explained why I stopped dancing and came home and, believe me, I'm so sorry for keeping it all from you. I've wished I'd come to you and told you everything so many times because it all could have worked out so very differently if I had. We can't go back though, Mum, can we? We can only try and make peace moving forward and that's what I'm trying to do now.

Chapter 32
Isabel

ISABEL'S SATURDAY MORNING at The Natural Way flew by in a flurry of natural remedies for everything from head lice to rosacea. She was eager to get back to Pier View House though, as Austin had talked of nothing but the fish he was going to choose from the moment he'd opened his eyes. He'd also informed her that yes, his mummy did have a NutriBullet but he didn't like the smoothies she made in it because they were always green.

She'd promised him she'd be home after work as quick as she could and Rhodri planned on distracting him with a long walk along the beach to see how many periwinkles they could find. Austin had screwed up his nose when Rhodri explained how you boiled them in seawater and then hooked the mollusc out with a pin to eat it. They'd have fun foraging for them at any rate, she'd thought, giving Rhodri a kiss goodbye and planting one on top of Austin's head. She'd had a definite skip in her step as she'd made her way up Union Street.

She avoided looking across the street at the letter box because there was no time for flagellating herself about sending her letter to Veronica today. Dodging her way through the shoppers, she hared off down Union Street noticing the cluster of white down by the shoreline. The noise of squawking seagulls grew louder the closer she got. She wondered if that meant they were due for some bad weather. She was sure she'd read somewhere that when a large flock appeared like that so close to land it meant a storm was on its way. They'd had a good run and it couldn't last forever, she supposed. At least it wouldn't affect their afternoon if it packed up. She reached A Leap of Faith and burst through the doors.

She waved at Nico who was chatting with a young man about a soft, dreamlike watercolour on display, although Isabel thought it more likely he was interested in Nico and not the watercolour.

'I'm home,' she called, racing up the stairs.

Rhodri greeted her with a smile from where he was standing at the stove by a pot of bubbling water. Austin was standing on one of the dining table chairs observing what was going on from a safe distance.

'Winkles,' he said. 'I've talked this young man into trying one and I plan on having mine on a piece of brown bread and butter. Can I tempt you?'

'No thanks, I'll stick with a ham sandwich.' She wrinkled her nose at the fishy smell.

'When we've had the winkle can we go and get the fish, please?'

'Yes, that's the plan,' Isabel said, as excited as he was to get to the pet store.

IT TURNED OUT AUSTIN had exotic tastes when it came to fish and despite her and Rhodri's best efforts to steer him toward the guppies and goldfish he went straight to the tropical fish tank. Isabel elbowed Rhodri and they both smiled indulgently, seeing him staring through eyes round in amazement at the colourful fish. They all watched the vibrant oranges, reds and blues swirling lazily about in their watery home.

'I like that one there, Daddy, Isabel.'

'Austin, don't touch the tank,' Rhodri said, leaning in for a closer look. 'The one with the purple in its fins?'

'Yes, I'm going to call him Nemo.'

'Definitely looks like a Nemo to me,' Isabel said, squinting at the prices tacked onto the side of the tank. Her eyes began to water. Who knew tropical fish were so expensive? She doubted Rhodri would be exclaiming quite so gleefully over Bubbles, Fin and Fish Finger having also been picked out had he seen it. No wonder Sally had held off. They hadn't even checked out a tank and all the other paraphernalia that would go with it.

Ten minutes later, Rhodri muttered, 'This was your big idea,' to Isabel as he dusted off his wallet while his son yabbered on about how tropical fish had to have warm water. His smile softened his words.

Austin's hand searched out Isabel and at that moment she wouldn't have minded if Rhodri sold all their worldly possessions and bought the entire pet shop because the feel of his plump warm hand in hers melted her heart.

Chapter 33
Veronica
1994

VERONICA SAT CROSS legged opposite Gabe on his bed in the apartment his parents shelled out the monthly rent for. It was a modern and functional one bedder and so much bigger than the garret space she shared with Delia, despite theirs having two bedrooms. Her fellow Brit roommate had been with the corps a year and Isabel had answered the advert she'd pinned to the company's noticeboard, desperate to move out of the noisy, dirty hostel where she'd been paying far too much for the privilege of somewhere to sleep.

Gabe had wanted her to stay with him but she'd known her mum would go berserk if she got wind of that and then there was his mum. Mrs Darby-Hazleton was prone to impromptu visits. Gabe being here gave her the excuse she needed to visit her favourite city whenever the fancy took her and Veronica, having visualised the look on her face were she to be busted camped out at her son's pad, the one she and his father were springing for, had opted for the hostel. They'd both be eighteen in a few months; they could pool their meagre incomes and do what they liked then, get a place together off their own backs but for now it was best not to rock the boat.

Veronica had changed from her leotard and tights into her jeans and a black tee after today's rehearsals. The session she'd come from had been particularly gruelling and her body ached. Where she'd been Miss Laverne's protégé along with Gabe, here she would have to prove herself because all the other dancers in the corps wanted the same opportunities she did. There was no easy route. No shortcut and it was all so much harder than she'd expected. She'd been feeling bone-tired most days which she put down in part to the strain between her and Gabe. It wasn't anything tangible just a subtle shifting of the dynamics between them. She'd thought about refusing his offer to go back to his apartment to grab a Chinese and drink cheap red wine. It would have been nice to beat Delia home and grab the first shower while the water was hot then curl up on the lumpy sofa that had come with their apartment to sleep while the television flickered. She'd seen something in his face that had told her she should go back with him. They needed to address the uneasiness that had been settling between them since they'd arrived in Paris.

She twisted her daisy ring, willing him to meet her gaze but he was staring at the rumpled bed covers. He'd ordered the food in his halting French and would go down to collect it from the takeaway in ten minutes, picking up the plonk from the small supermarché on the corner while he was out. For now though the Crash Test Dummies song *Mmm Mmm Mmm Mmm* was playing softly and she could smell stale cigarette smoke. She could picture him these last few evenings sitting at the window with the sounds of the busy Parisian street below wafting up as he anxiously puffed trying to formulate the things he needed to say to himself. Things that needed to be said out loud.

'What is it, Gabe?' She reached forward and touched his knee. He too had slipped into sweat pants and a T-shirt. Come on, it's me, we tell each other everything, remember?' She was frightened of what was coming but instinct told her she already knew what he was finding so hard to say. She'd sensed the cooling between them, she'd seen the sidelong looks of longing at other dancers and had known he didn't understand it himself.

He didn't speak for a moment and when he did his voice was quiet and she strained to hear his words.

'I love you, Veronica. You're everything to me but I don't think I love you the way I should.' He looked at her from under his too-long hair with pleading eyes. 'I don't want what I've got to say to change things between us but I don't want to lie to you either.'

Her breath snagged. *This was it; the truth she'd known.*

'I think I like men.'

The air was sucked from the room. It was out and it could never be taken back. He looked up then and reached out to her. Veronica wouldn't let him touch her; instead she wrenched the ring from her finger and thrust it out to him, her hand trembling.

'I can't wear this anymore.' She watched the tear dislodge itself from his eye and trace a line down his face.

'*Please*, Ronnie, I love you. I don't want this to change things between us. We're soulmates.'

'No! No, we're not. You can't love me the way I need, not properly. I've seen you looking at the male dancers, Gabe. You don't look at me like that. You never have. Take it. I can't wear a lie.'

'No. That's why I told you because I don't want there to be lies between us. I'm not lying when I say I love you.' He shook his head and she was struck by how beautiful he was. The muscled contours of his athlete's body were bathed in the dying rays of the sun which was illuminating his bedroom in a golden glow. An Adonis but not her Adonis.

She tossed the ring down on the bed and got up. She needed to put space between them and she walked out of the apartment without looking back.

Now

'I THINK GABE AND I would have found a way through it all if I hadn't found out I was pregnant, Mum. We were soulmates him and I, just as he always said. Love isn't always black and white and we were friends before we were anything else.' Veronica twisted her daisy ring on her finger just as she had that long-ago night. She could still remember the cold terror she'd felt a few days after Gabe had admitted his attraction to men to her. She was sitting on the toilet with the peeling lino under her feet, the stick in her hand showing two distinct pink lines. They hadn't spoken since she'd walked out, managing to avoid any contact with each other during rehearsals. She was hurting and she knew he was too, and as the reality of all those missed clues over the last five months, the nausea and the missed periods she'd put down to the intensity of her dance schedule and that all-encompassing tiredness sank in, she'd had to go and see him.

1994

'RONNIE! SHIT, WHAT it is it? What's happened?' Gabe flung the door open staring at her with an expression of relief that she was there and concern as to why she'd come.

Veronica collapsed into him feeling his strong arms encircle her and she began to sob, great big heaving sobs. He stroked her back and led her over to the table pulling out a chair. 'Here, sit down, I'll fetch you a drink.'

She shook her head trying to get a hold of herself. You weren't supposed to drink when you were pregnant, or smoke. He lit up a cigarette and pushed up the sash window to blow the smoke out of it not taking his eyes off her.

'What's going on?'

Veronica looked at him through aching, puffy eyes. 'I'm pregnant.'

He looked at her in disbelief, his spare hand raking through is hair. 'Jesus. Are you sure?'

She nodded.

'But we only—'

'It only takes one time, Gabe.'

'That means you must be what? Nearly five months along.'

She nodded, beginning to cry again because there was no way out of this.

He tossed the cigarette out the window and moved lithely across the room. He picked something up from the sideboard that had come as part of the apartment's furnishings. 'Put this back on, Ronnie. You told me you'd never take it off.'

She shook her head, tendrils of hair escaping the bun she wore her hair in most days. 'No, you gave me that before; it doesn't mean the same thing anymore.'

'I still love you, Ronnie. That hasn't changed. I meant what I said, we are soulmates. Please. Put it on.'

She let him slide it back on her finger.

'We'll get through this together. Alright? You're not alone. I'll ring Mum, she'll help us work this out.'

'What can she do, Gabe?' She knew she couldn't face telling her own mother, not yet at least.

'I don't know. She'll help us out with some money I guess.' It was the need to do something that saw him phone his mother as she lay on the sofa with a blanket he'd pulled from his bed draped over her. She lay there, listening to Gabe tell her their predicament, feeling as though it was someone else he was talking about.

VERONICA HAD ONLY GONE back to her lodgings to get a change of clothing and had been relieved to read in the note Delia had left her that she was out for the night. She didn't want to see her roommate. She didn't want to see or talk to anyone other than Gabe and she couldn't bear to be away from him right now either because she only stopped being frightened when she was with him. She'd spent the last three nights at his place. When she was in his arms with her head burrowed in his chest she believed it would work out okay. She didn't know how but she was clinging to the hope it could, because what mattered when you got to the heart of a family was love, and they had plenty of that.

The knock on the door startled her and zipping up her holdall, she went to answer it.

'Mrs Darby-Hazleton.' She was taken aback at the sight of the glossy woman, who with her blonde hair, impeccable makeup and cashmere, camel coloured coat oozed sophistication standing in the doorway. Her nostrils flared as they were assailed by her distinctive perfume and she took a step back slightly, awed and unsure of herself as she always was in her presence.

'Veronica, I've just come from Gabriel's. We've talked about your, er, well, your situation again.' She glanced to her right as next-door's door banged shut. 'We need to have a conversation you and I and I don't want to do it out here. May I come in?'

She remembered her manners. 'Yes, of course, sorry. You'll have to excuse the mess.' She opened the door wider and the older woman swept past her.

Veronica looked about the poky living room with no hint of the romance of the city outside and silently cursed Delia for leaving her dirty dishes on the table and not having put away her laundry basket full of clothes. What would Gabe's mother think?

Her gaze was desultory as she swept the small living area before gesturing to the sagging piece of furniture serving as their sofa. 'May I?'

'Please.'

She perched on the edge of the seat as though frightened she might catch fleas and Veronica was unsure where to place herself in the room. She didn't want to sit next to her; it seemed wrong, an invasion of space. She'd pull up a chair from their table she decided, but first she'd best offer her refreshments. 'Would you like a tea or a coffee?'

'No, thank you, Veronica. Look there's no point in pussyfooting around. Sit down.' She patted the cushion next to her but Veronica couldn't bring herself to do so. Instead she retrieved the spindly dining chair and, dragging it over, sat down. She kept her hands clasped tightly in her lap unsure what to do with them, wishing she could smoke. She wasn't sure what she was expecting from Mrs Darby-Hazleton's visit but she was disappointed Gabe wasn't with her. There was strength in numbers especially where his aloof and intimidating mother was concerned.

'You'll have the baby of course. There's no question.'

Veronica's hands settled protectively around her middle now as if Mrs Darby-Hazleton bringing up her pregnancy had given her permission to acknowledge it. Her belly showed only the gentlest of swelling but she'd become aware of a sensation, akin to what she'd imagine butterfly wings beating might feel like, deep inside her these last few days. She nodded.

The older woman's lipsticked mouth pursed and in that moment, looking at her hard face, Veronica had wondered how she'd ever thought her pretty. 'Now listen to me carefully, Veronica, because your whole future rests on the decision you're going to have to make. As I see it, there's really only one way forward and that's for the baby to be put up for adoption. There're plenty of couples in a far better position than you and Gabe desperate to have a child to love.'

Veronica blinked. Adoption? She hadn't even considered that. She'd seen her and Gabe somehow muddling along, finding their way through it all, perhaps with a little help on the money front from his parents. Her mother would be shocked when she heard the news initially but she'd come around and be delighted at the prospect of a grandchild. She'd continue to dance and somehow it would work. They'd make it work. But adoption? No. It wasn't an option. She shook her head slowly to convey this.

'Veronica. Obviously I can't make you give the baby up but what sort of a life can you offer a child at this point in time? Look around you. You can barely support yourself.' She flung her arm around the room demonstratively.

'But Gabe would—'

'Gabriel's homosexual, Veronica. Oh, don't look surprised. You must know.' The exasperation in her voice was evident.

'Did he tell you?' Veronica's voice was small she could feel the walls closing in on her as her options closed like a vice.

'No, there's been no impassioned coming out on his behalf but he's my son, I've always known. He's being ridiculous talking marriage and suchlike.' She made an unattractive snorting sound, 'He wants to do the right thing by you. As if getting married would be the right thing to do. A farce is what it would be because he could never be a husband in the proper sense of the word to you.' She didn't wait for a response. 'He's far too young to be a father, Veronica, as you are a mother. Surely you can see that?' She flicked an imagined piece of lint from her coat.

'But Gabriel is sensitive enough and stupid enough to toss his future aside to look after you and the baby if that's what you ask him to do. I've no doubt he'd do his best to try and raise a child your both ill-equipped to care for but he'd have his hand out doing so. He's notions of being noble but there's no nobility in being poor, Veronica. You'd know about that and is that how you want to raise your child?' Her eyes narrowed with the implied threat that she and her husband would not support them in any way as she pinned Veronica in a steely stare. 'Because I won't have it. Do you understand?' She drummed her deep red nails on the sofa arm. It was the act of a woman used to getting her own way.

Veronica sat trancelike as her words continued to shoot forth like well-aimed darts. 'This isn't just about you, understand that, Veronica. Gabriel has a successful career ahead of him doing what he loves—what he was born to do, and so do you. Don't throw that away. Believe me, in life

Page 200

you can't have your cake and eat it too. Choices, difficult choices have to be made and if you don't make the right one now I can tell you your chance to fly will be gone in the blink of an eye. There'll be someone else only too grateful to take your place. Surely you can see that this,' she flung her hand in the direction of Veronica's stomach, 'is a blip on your chosen paths? It can be overcome, sorted out, and then you can go back to what you're destined to do. I'll take care of everything. It's the best possible decision for everyone.'

She'd left after that and the only clue to her having been there at all was in her perfume hanging in the stagnant air. Veronica had unpacked her bag, thrown her pyjamas on and crawled under her bed covers pulling them up over her head. She'd ignored the ringing telephone, knowing it was Gabe, unable to talk to him while his mother's visit was still raw. She'd cried herself to sleep because she knew Mrs Darby-Hazleton was right. Her father had asked her mother to marry him out of duty and pressure from both sets of parents because she was pregnant with her and look how that had turned out. They'd wound up hating one another and her mother had struggled along trying to make ends meet ever since. She didn't want that to happen to her and Gabe, not ever, and she didn't want her life to become a mirror image of her mother's.

Now

'I DANCED UP UNTIL I was thirty-six weeks. Can you believe that, Mum? I was tiny with Isabel though, not like the great big hippo I turned into with the boys. It helped get me through knowing what was coming. Things weren't the same with me and Gabe once I'd made the decision to have the baby adopted. We tiptoed around one another, not sure of what to say or how to be. He was angry at me because he had no say in any of it and I never breathed a word of what his mother said to me when she came calling. I should have told him because then we could have told Mrs Darby-Hazleton, with that carrot stuck up her backside, that we'd manage on our own. Could have, should have. I've been over it in my head so many times, Mum. She took care of everything as she said she would. It was like being on one of those travelators at the airport; things were in motion and heading in one direction. I couldn't get off.

I had the baby privately and I only got to hold her for a few minutes.' Veronica's vision swam and blurred. 'Mum, she was the most beautiful thing I'd ever seen.' She conjured up the warmth of the bundle she'd held briefly in her arms. 'I tried to stamp every bit of her into my memory, her scent, her tiny fingers and toes, and I called her Isabel. The only thing I asked was for her adoptive parents to keep the name I'd chosen for her because it fitted her perfectly, and then, just like that she was gone.' Veronica held the tears at bay. She'd gotten this far, she'd reach the end of her story. She ploughed on with determination.

'I thought everything would go back to how it had been. That I'd resume dancing, Gabe and I would find a way to put Isabel behind us and make a way forward as friends but it changed everything. I didn't want to be in Paris anymore. It was tainted and everywhere I turned there was the memory of her. Of Isabel. I wanted to be home with you and Abi and I didn't care if I never danced again. I'd no idea when I agreed to Isabel being adopted how she would leave a hole inside me that nothing could fill. So, I came home and

201

I ignored Gabe's attempts to keep in touch and tried to carry on with life the best I could. I'm so sorry, Mum. I know you never understood why I stopped dancing and I always felt I'd let you down in doing so but I couldn't bring myself to tell you what happened.'

Veronica inhaled her L'Air du Temps as her mother began kneading the tunic as if it were dough. Fragrance was so evocative she thought, resisting the urge to scratch the patch of skin that had been plaguing her of late. 'It was Joy, Mrs Darby-Hazleton wore, by Jean Patou. I can't stand it even now,' she said, half to her mum and half to herself.

'There was a baby?' Margo said.

'Yes, Mum, there was and she was beautiful. Her name's Isabel and she's not a baby any more she'll be a grown-up woman now of twenty-seven.'

Margo let go of the tunic and it puddled into her lap. 'I don't live with my daughter anymore.'

'No, Mum, you live here. You're well looked after here.'

'There's some very strange people here.'

Veronica looked to where a woman was pushing a walker. It had a stack of books she liked to sit and look at in the basket. A reader in another life who still found comfort in having books close by. She'd seen the woman sitting in the sunshine with a book open as she worked her way through the pages in a lifelong habit. 'Come on, we're all different, Mum. If we weren't the world would be a very grey place to live.'

'Where's the baby?' Margo looked about then, a frightened expression on her bare face. It was hard to recall the mother who'd always refused to leave the house without her lipstick and mascara firmly in place.

'I don't know, Mum. I don't know where she is.' Veronica closed her eyes against the prickling of tears and this time she couldn't hold them back.

Chapter 34
Isabel

'MUM, DAD, THIS IS AUSTIN,' Isabel said. The little boy had tight hold of her and Rhodri's hands as they stood at the door of her pebbledash family home. Cars whizzed by behind them, which still managed to surprise Isabel. It had been much quieter when she was growing up here but a roundabout at the top of the road had gone in, making it a thoroughfare a few years ago, much to the residents' dismay. Her dad's lament for the best part of a year had been you couldn't stop progress.

The Starks had been delighted when Isabel asked if they could stay the night before travelling up to Heathrow the following morning to meet Sally off the plane, and Babs was all smiles as she ushered them in.

'Gary, get out of the way.' She elbowed her husband aside. 'Hello, Austin, it's lovely to meet you. Watch you don't trip over Prince Charles he has a habit of lying exactly where you want to walk.'

Austin held back, tugging on Isabel's arm. She looked down and he whispered shyly, 'What shall I call them?'

'What would you like to call them?'

'Are they my nana and grandad?'

Isabel shot a 'help' glance at Rhodri who shrugged.

Babs having overheard the exchange told Gaz to put the kettle on and to fetch Austin a glass of lemonade then she crouched down in front of him so she was eye to eye. 'Would you like us to be your honorary grandparents.'

Austin gave a small nod even though he didn't know what honorary meant.

'Well we'd be honoured to be, Austin, and I'd be delighted if you were to call me Grammy Babs and —'

'I'm Grampy Gazzer.' Gaz was still loitering in the hall.

Isabel choked back a laugh and saw Rhodri doing the same. *Grammy Babs, Grampy Gazzer?*

Austin looked very pleased with their titles and he let go of their hands to follow Grammy Babs into the living room. 'My mum doesn't let me have lemonade.'

'Well, Grammy Babs does. Grandparents have special powers of dispensation you see, Austin. We're not supposed to make sensible choices. We're here for the fun stuff. So, go on Grampy Gazzer and get Austin his drink.'

Isabel hoped Sally wouldn't think they were overstepping the mark with the titles but as for the lemonade, well she could hardly lay down the law on that, not when she'd spent a fortnight relaxing in the sun.

ISABEL AND RHODRI FOUND themselves surplus to requirements as Babs and Gaz fussed over Austin spoiling him with an array of sugary treats. It was a tonic for Austin who'd been sad to say goodbye to his fish. He'd shown Isabel how much to feed them three times that morning before trooping downstairs to the gallery to fetch Nico. He'd given her the same rundown while Rhodri manned the floor. Goodness help them if anything happened to the fishy foursome between now and his next visit. They'd go broke replacing them for one thing.

Babs whispered to Isabel how it was wonderful being made instant grandparents as Gaz gave Austin a horseback ride on his back. Unsurprisingly, Prince Charles was sulking over all the fuss usually reserved for his corgi highness going elsewhere. He was flopped on his mat with his head on his paws and Isabel felt sorry for him. 'Nobody's giving you any attention are they? Austin, hop off Grampy Gazzer's back and fetch his ball, it's over there in his basket, see if you can cheer him up.'

The corgi's sulk was banished as Austin rolled the ball along the floor to him. He proved there was life in the old dog yet as he came as close to scampering as a geriatric corgi could to retrieve it.

Isabel leaned over and asked Rhodri on the quiet when he'd take Austin to meet his parents because she was sure the, lovely, gentle Welsh couple she'd met a handful of times now would be equally besotted. 'When things are firmed up as to the visitation arrangements,' he'd said.

'Well now, I suppose I should be getting dinner ready. I hope you like pizza, Austin.' Babs said, heaving herself off the sofa and picking up a couple of the empty glasses.

'It's my favourite, Grammy Babs.' He dimpled, loving all the attention and treat foods he was getting.

'I'll give you a hand, Mum.' Isabel got up and stacked the rest of the now empty dishes on the coffee table.

'Its only pizza, Isabel, I can manage.'

'That as may be, Mum, but I'll be well and truly outnumbered if I stay in here.'

'Fair enough. Come on then, kitchen party it is.'

Isabel followed her mum through to the familiar kitchen and loaded the dishwasher while her Mum pulled two pizzas from the freezer. 'You're very good with him,' Isabel said, closing the door.

'He's a treasure, Isabel.'

'Yes, he is.' She bit her bottom lip. It was now or never. 'Mum,' she blurted, 'I want to write to Veronica and ask her if she'd like to meet me.' She didn't want to say she'd already done so. It was better to test the waters and see what her mum had to say on the subject.

Babs froze at the worktop and then she began ripping open the pizza box in a frenzy of activity.

Isabel put her hand on her mum's to still hers. 'Please don't ever think I'm looking to replace you. I have a mum, you, and I love you and Dad with all my heart, you know that. It's something I have to do, though. Can you understand?'

Babs lips puckered and then flattened. 'I worry about you being hurt, Isabel, that's all.'

'I won't be.' It wasn't true. Isabel knew if her letter was met with rejection, or worse silence she'd find it hard to accept. 'And if I am you'll be there for me, won't you?'

'Isabel your dad and I, we'll always be there for you. It's called being parents.'

'It'll be fine, Mum.'

'It's just that you've always been such a sensitive soul and I don't know what you're expecting to get from meeting her.'

'An extended family,' Isabel said simply. 'Look at Austin. You said yourself, he's a treasure. Family doesn't always have to fit neatly in a one-size fits all box, Mum.'

Babs nodded slowly. 'That's true. You're our world though, Isabel, don't forget that.'

'As if I would. I love you, Mum.'

'I love you too, sweetheart and I hope you'll find what you're looking for.'

'Can I have a cuddle?'

'Come here, you.'

Isabel sank into her squishy, booby cuddle, breathing in that mumsy smell that always made her feel better.

An especially loud, 'Yee-ha,' went up from the living room. They were obviously back at the horsey ride game. Babs rolled her eyes. 'I wish he'd put that much energy into our salsa classes.'

'I thought Dad had a bad back?'

'He does and he won't be able to move tomorrow if he continues carrying on like John Wayne or Clint flipping Eastwood.'

Isabel giggled as her mum went back to sorting the pizza. 'Why, howdy partner,' she said doffing her pretend hat. 'I'm a chino trouser wearing cowboy.'

Babs looked at her and her mouth twitched and then she too was giggling. The natural order of things had been restored. It was Babs and Isabel against Gazzer and just like that everything was fine.

Chapter 35
Veronica

'HI,' ABI SAID, PUTTING the tin she'd had in her hand down and waving her fork toward the bowl on the kitchen worktop when Veronica appeared in the kitchen that Saturday afternoon. 'Keto,' she explained.

Scruffy-bum was mewling in Veronica's arms.

'Salmon, spinach, hardboiled egg, pan-fried haloumi and black olive salad with keto friendly mayonnaise dressing. It's a late lunch.' She glanced at the wall clock. 'Actually, it's an early dinner and don't ask if I've called Brandon because I haven't. I'm making him sweat.'

Salmon? No wonder Scruffy-bum was dislocating his neck to see what was on the bench, Veronica thought, putting him down. Normally, she'd have flipped off a smart remark of some sort about her sister's diet but none was forthcoming. Abi too, had expected some such comeback and she stared at Veronica with that funny trying to frown expression. 'Has something happened?'

'Yes.'

'Is it Mum?' Abi put down the fork she'd been flaking the tinned salmon into her bowl with. Her blue eyes were wide and Veronica saw the flash of fear in them.

'No. There's something I need to tell you though.'

Abi relaxed and then her face did that funny trying to frown thing once more. 'You're not sick are you?'

'No, nothing like that.'

Abi finished tipping her salmon into the bowl and cursed as she narrowly missed tripping over Scruffy-bum carrying her salad over to the table.

Veronica picked him up once more and opening the back door told him to go and sniff the air. Abi watched her from under thick lashes.

'Sit down, Ronnie, and get whatever it is off your chest.' She forked up a mouthful of her salad and Veronica sat down. At times like this she wished she could smoke a cigarette more for want of something to do with her hands than a need for nicotine. Perhaps she should take up knitting? she thought idly as she moved the tablemat around.

'I was pregnant before I left for Paris with Gabe. Obviously I hadn't a clue. Anyway, by the time I realised, I was over five months. I had a baby girl called Isabel and she was adopted by a British family. That's all I know.' It came out in a whoosh and Abi would've looked startled had she been able to. Her fork froze mid-way to her mouth.

'Say that again.'

'I got pregnant—'

'I heard you the first time.' The fork clattered down in the bowl. 'Geez, Ronnie, did Mum know?'

'No, I told her today. I needed to tell her why I stopped dancing.'

Abi shook her head uncomprehendingly. 'How could you keep that to yourself all these years?'

'I don't know, Abs. Looking back now I don't know why I went along with everything. I just did.'

'What do you mean?'

Veronica relayed the story she'd told her mother, the whole shebang.

'What a total bitch-faced cow,' Abi said of Mrs Darby-Hazleton when Veronica finished, her salad forgotten.

'Yes, she was. You know, Abi, I've had plenty of time to think about it and Gabe's mother didn't do what was right for me or him. She did what was best for her.'

Abi massaged her temples and Veronica watched her lime nails in fascination. 'How did Mum take it?'

Veronica shrugged. 'As you'd expect. She was confused. I don't normally go on a Sunday but I'll call in tomorrow and see how she is.'

'I want to come with you.'

Veronica nodded.

'I'm sorry you had to go through that, Ronnie. I'm not surprised Gabe's gay but I always wondered, you know what happened in Paris. You were different when you came home. Me and Mum knew you'd broken up with

Gabe, obviously we didn't know why, and we knew how much he'd meant to you but we couldn't understand how you could work so hard for something, the way you had for your dance career and then throw it all away.'

'Well, now you know. I should've told you a long time ago.'

'Yeah, you should have. Do you know anything about her, my niece? Was it an open adoption?'

'No. Nothing. Her records are sealed. It has to be her who contacts me.'

'Do the boys know? Did Jason know?'

She shook her head again, not wanting Abi to feel she was the last to find out about Isabel.

'You told Jason didn't you? I can tell by your face and I bet you told that friend of yours, Saskia.'

She had. They were the only two people aside from Gabe and his mother who knew about Isabel.

Veronica's phone rang, a timely distraction from whatever Abi was working herself up to say, and she picked it up. 'It's Holly Grange,' she said, instantly on alert. Abi too sat forward in her seat.

'THANKS FOR COMING IN, Veronica, Abi. She's not normally so hard to settle but she was agitated after you left today, Veronica.'

Abi shot Veronica a look.

'It's the first time she's been aggressive.'

'What did she do?' Abi asked.

'She tried to bite me.'

Veronica was horrified at the thought of her mum trying to hurt someone who was only doing their best to care for her. Her hand went to her mouth. 'Oh God, I'm sorry, Danika. It's not Mum. You know she's not normally like that. If you'd known her before...' her voice trailed off as the caregiver put into words what Veronica had told herself time and time again.

'It's not your mum, Veronica. It's the disease. It happens.'

Veronica managed to rustle up a grateful smile. 'We should come and see her.'

'Yes, I'm sure you both coming in will calm her. She's in the television alcove. We put the André Rieu video she likes on.'

'Thanks, Danika.' Abi echoed the sentiment and they walked over to where the carer had directed to find their mother sitting hunched over in her chair picking at something only she could see on her skirt. On the table beside her was an untouched chocolate drink. She was oblivious to the Austrian conductor and all the swirling glorious colours on the big screen overhead, the music not managing to capture and hold her the way it usually did. 'Hello, Mum. Have you not been feeling too good?'

There was no response, so Veronica sat down next to her and stroked her arm. Her mum paused in her fussing of the fabric of her skirt.

'Mum it's me, Ronnie. It's alright. I'm here now.'

'I'm here too, Mum.' Abi crouched in front of her.

Margo still didn't look up but she clutched hold of Veronica's hand and held it tightly. 'It was the right thing to do.'

'Of course it was, Mum.' Veronica went along with her, a kernel of hope she was telling her she'd done the right thing having Isabel adopted. Abi shook her head in a what's she talking about? gesture.

'I had to tell them that. What else was I supposed to say?' Margo looked up then and turned her head toward her eldest daughter. Her eyes were cloudy and Veronica knew it wasn't her she was seeing.

'You had to, yes, Mum.'

'I did, yes.' Margo nodded emphatically. 'He left me for another woman you know.'

Ah, God, she was talking about Daddy. 'I know.' She exchanged a glance with Abi.

'It wasn't my fault.'

Veronica had long since resolved those childhood feelings of anger towards her mother where her father was concerned. From her own experience with Jason she knew nobody knew what went on in someone else's marriage. She'd hardly been able to keep up with what was going on in her own, for goodness sake. Her parents were the victims of circumstance and the casualties of doing what others expected of them. Just as she'd been with Isabel.

'No, Mum, it wasn't your fault.' Margo's shoulders seemed to sag but Veronica wasn't sure whether she'd imagined it or not.

'He shouldn't have married her.'

Now she was lost and Abi too was bewildered. What was she talking about? She probed. 'Who did he marry?'

'*Her.* He married her when he was still married to me. He shouldn't have done that.'

Veronica tried to process what her mother was saying. Her father married the woman he'd left Margo for? That couldn't be. It didn't make any sense. Margo was confused and the past was playing tricks on her, that was all.

'It was illegal.' She knotted and unknotted her fingers. 'What he did was wrong. I couldn't have my girls finding out so, I did what I had to do.'

'And what did you have to do?' Veronica was suddenly chilled despite the temperate air which always erred towards being set too warm in the residents' lounge.

'Yes, Mum, what did you do?' Abi asked.

Margo's expression cleared and Veronica had the eerie sensation of talking to her mother as she'd been thirty years earlier. It was as if a curtain in time had been pulled back. 'I lied. I told them both their father was dead.'

Chapter 36
Isabel

THE DAY AUSTIN'S MOTHER flew back from the Greek islands, the weather was blustery with a definite nip in the air and by the time they were circling the short-term parking the rain had turned from a light spit to a steady drizzle. Isabel, her nose pressed to the window scanning the rows of parked cars for a vacant slot was glad it wasn't her arriving home from all that whitewashed, sun-drenched Mediterranean scenery to this gloom. *How depressing.*

She'd been quiet on the journey up to Heathrow from her parents', content to mull things over as she sucked on a continual supply of toffees which were making her teeth feel furry. So too had Rhodri and, glancing over her shoulder, she saw the reason why. Austin. He was still asleep having nodded off by the time they drove through Winchester. His head, with its shock of dark tousled hair, longer in just two weeks than it had been when he'd arrived, had lolled to the side and his cheeks were pink and soft with sleep. Her heart tugged. She'd miss him. It had been a privilege getting to know him and gaining his trust. It had filled her with awe each time he'd slotted his small hand trustingly into hers and she hoped it wouldn't be long before he came to stay with them again.

She wasn't sure how Rhodri and Sally would work things out but Rhodri was determined now Austin was in their lives, he'd stay there. He'd asked her how she felt about him staying with them regularly and it had been a no-brainer, she'd love it. Austin was a part of Rhodri therefore she loved him.

His son would have his father in his life, he'd told Isabel quietly but with a grittiness she hadn't heard in his voice before.

She was in a strange mood, she thought, wiping away the patch on the window that had fogged up with her breath as Rhodri began another circuit. The mixed emotions were sadness at saying goodbye to Austin and the twitchy knowledge that with opening up to her mum yesterday she'd run out of excuses for not sending her letter.

The windshield wipers swished hypnotically and Isabel spied the reversing lights on a blue hatchback, 'They're pulling out, over there.' She pointed and Rhodri drove closer, flicking on his indicator to wait.

'I'd like to come in with you both if that's okay? I think Sally should meet me.'

Rhodri nodded. 'You should.' He pulled into the parking space and turned the lights and windscreen wipers off before stilling the engine. His eyes flicked up into the rear-view mirror. 'He's still sound asleep.'

'Dad and Prince Charles wore him out.'

'Gary was great with him.'

'Grandpa Gazzer, and yeah he was.' Isabel grinned and Rhodri returned it. They hatched a plan as to how to get the slumbering child in the back inside the airport. Rhodri, it was agreed, would carry Austin in to the Arrivals Hall and she'd bring his case and car seat.

THE HALL WAS TEEMING and the scent of wet wool mingled with coffee as people went about their business. Isabel raised a hand to her hair hoping it hadn't frizzed in the rain. She didn't know why it mattered that she be presentable but it did. She had an image of Sally as one of those women who always made other women feel inferior. Like they'd somehow gotten it wrong with their hair and makeup or choice of outfit. She was nervous at the prospect of meeting her. What would Sally, the successful lawyer make of her.

Austin had woken up now and insisted on being put down on the basis of his being a big boy and he stood leaning against his father's legs. There was a flurry of activity as the doors opened and a slow but steady stream of suntanned people in clothes more suited to the beach than the damp London day awaiting them trickled forth.

She'd only seen a handful of photographs of Sally. She had long blonde hair like a golden sheet and was beautiful, but they'd been taken over five years ago now and she wasn't sure she'd recognise her. Austin was standing to attention, all traces of sleepiness gone as he eagerly scanned the faces appearing one after the other. Isabel stood back as he broke away from Rhodri and ran to a woman who abandoned her trolley to crouch down with her arms outstretched. Her smile was white and bright against the flush of her smooth, honey skin. She wore her hair short these days and reminded Isabel of the woman who was in the *House of Cards* series. She'd also had the common sense to put a cardigan over her white tank top.

Rhodri waved and, giving her son a kiss, she stood back up and taking him by the hand steered the trolley one-handed over to where they were standing.

'Good holiday?' Rhodri asked, kissing her awkwardly on the cheek. It was a gesture that made Isabel feel odd.

'Brilliant, thanks.' Her blue eyes travelled past Rhodri to Isabel. Sizing her up in one sweep before lingering a split-second longer on her hair, she took a step closer.

Isabel caught a whiff of sunscreen and a light fresh smell that reminded her of the sea. Sally held her hand out. 'Hello, I'm Sally. You must be Isabel. Love the hair by the way.'

Isabel was pleased her voice came out sounding normal as she replied. 'Yes, thanks. It's nice to meet you.'

The two women circled each other mentally as they shook hands, sizing one another up, all the while smiling. Rhodri, Isabel knew would be oblivious to this undercurrent because it was a primal woman thing.

Austin tugged at his mum's capris managing to get chocolate on the white pants but she didn't seem bothered as she listened to him gushing, 'Isabel took me to a park with dinosaurs and we got fish. Daddy and I painted and swam lots and I ate a winkle. It was yucky.' His excitement at having his mum home was hyping him up. It was nothing whatsoever to do with the chocolate bar, Grammy Babs had slipped him for the journey.

'Well, you sound like you've had a wonderful time.' She ruffled his hair. 'I missed you.'

He grinned up at her.

'He's missed you too,' Isabel said, careful not to sound accusatory.

'Thank you for having Austin.' Sally said to both of them.

'We had a great time,' Rhodri replied, his hands thrust in the pocket of his jeans.

THE DANCER

215

'We did,' Isabel reiterated.

It wasn't the time for deep discussions about visits and the like and they were only allowed to park where they were for fifteen minutes, so Rhodri hefted the wheelie case on top of Sally's bags before taking the car seat from Isabel and doing the same. He gave his son a hug. 'I'll see you again soon.'

Austin clung to him.

'Can I have one too?' Isabel moved in to join them.

'The train's leaving in a few minutes. Sorry to rush you,' Sally said, and they broke apart. 'I'll call you in the next day or so,' she said to Rhodri. 'Austin, what do you say?'

'Thank you for having me.'

'He doesn't have to thank us, I'm his father,' Rhodri said quietly and there was a moment's awkward silence until Sally said, 'Right, well we must make tracks.'

Isabel and Rhodri waved goodbye, Austin's voice asking his mum if he could have lasagne for tea because his daddy made lasagne and he liked it slowly fading away.

Isabel rubbed Rhodri's arm. 'You okay?'

'Yeah.' His face looked drawn and she wanted to make him feel better but knew there was nothing she could say or do.

'Come on. I don't want a parking ticket.'

She slid her hand into his as they headed back to the car.

Chapter 37
Veronica

VERONICA NEARLY RAN a red light as she drove home on automatic pilot from Holly Grange. She slammed her foot on the brake to come squealing to a stop in the nick of time.

'For God's sake, Ronnie, pay attention and get us home in one piece,' Abi said, lurching back in her seat.

'I can't get it out of my head.' Her mind replayed the words her mother had said. *'I lied. I told them their father was dead.'*

'Me neither.'

It had taken every ounce of Veronica's being to stay seated there in that cosy nook next to their mother after she'd offloaded the news her father wasn't dead, or at least that he hadn't died when Margo said he had. Nothing they thought they knew was true. Her own revelation had paled into insignificance as her mother worried over the lie she'd told. Abi had gone white beneath her tan makeup and told Veronica if she didn't get outside into the cool evening air, she was going to be sick. Veronica had waved her away biting her lip as she choked back the questions vying for attention knowing it was futile to ask them because she could see the window to the past had closed once more. The conversation she'd just had with her daughters was lost to Margo. Instead, Veronica had been the dutiful daughter whispering soothing platitudes as she stroked her mother's arm until, gradually, she'd settled, becoming engrossed in the waltz music on the big screen in front of her.

She'd gotten up and left then, avoiding Danika's questioning gaze as she walked swiftly through the lounge to the exit, desperate to escape the walls of Holly Grange and the horrible thing she'd learned inside them. She'd found Abi leaning against her car, arms folded across her chest.

'Do you think it's true, what she said in there?' she'd demanded as soon as she saw Veronica.

Veronica aimed her keys at the car. 'Yes, I do.' There'd been a rawness on her mother's face, a peeled back honesty when she'd said what she'd said.

She'd not been sure she should drive straight away as she felt punch drunk and so she'd slunk low in her seat, Abi clambering in next to her as they silently mulled over what to do about what about what they'd learned. Their father was a bigamist—what could you do with that? The boys would be at football practice and Jason had been talking about taking them to Nando's for dinner. There was no way she could pretend everything was normal and she couldn't very well tell them what her mother had just revealed. They'd have to stay the night at their dad's, she decided, and retrieving her phone she texted Jason. The message something urgent had come up with her mother, telling him not to worry she was okay but asking if he could have the boys to stay over tonight pinged off. His reply had bounced through a few minutes later.

'Can do – you ok?'

How tempting it was to type 'no'—to go to her ex-husband, lay her head on his shoulder and feel the arms that had once held her wrapped tight around her once more as she poured out what she'd just learned. She couldn't give in to the temptation though. So, she sent a quick response saying she was fine and just had to sort something out for her mum. Nothing came back so she assumed, he was satisfied with her reply. She'd turned the key in the ignition then and begun the journey home aware of Abi sitting statue still next to her.

'WHAT ARE YOU DOING?' Abi stood in the hallway knocking back a glass of wine she'd helped herself to the moment they'd gotten in the door. She watched as Veronica unhooked the latch and pulled the ladder down from the loft.

'I want to get up in the attic and I need you to stand at the bottom here so I can pass some boxes down to you so when you've finished that,' she pointed to the wine, 'put your glass back in the kitchen and help me. I'm going to see if I can find any clues as to where Dad is now in Mum's old stuff.'

Abi's eyes narrowed. 'Mum always said he went to Devon but then who knows if that's true. Who knows if any of what she said tonight is true and anyway, what are you going to do if you find something?'

A thought occurred to Veronica as she tested the ladder. 'You saw her face, Abi, it's true. He might have tried to contact us and she never told us. Have you thought of that?' Her stomach contracted at the thought. Would she have wanted to hear from him? The answer was yes, because then she'd know it wasn't her and Abi he'd left, that he'd loved them after all. It mattered to her to know that. 'I want to see him with my own two eyes.' She hadn't thought this through, not at all, and it was pure adrenalin she was running on but she also knew without a shadow of a doubt it was what she wanted to do. Needed to do.

'He might be dead you know, Ronnie. What then?'

'At least we'll know for sure.'

'And what if he's alive and well, happily living his double life with another family he wanted more than he wanted us? How do we deal with that and do you upend their lives too? He could go to prison you know.'

'I know and I don't know. Stop talking, drink your wine, and help me.' Veronica clambered gingerly up the rungs and poking her head into the darkened space, she felt like one of those meercats stretching her neck long and gazing about.

'Watch out for the rats,' Abi called.

'Shut up,' Veronica hissed back, retrieving the torch she'd shoved in the pocket of her work trousers. She shone it about half expecting to spy small shapes scurrying into the shadows but there was nothing to see, only the boxes she'd shoved up here, out of sight out of mind. She pulled the rest of her body up and crawled the short distance to where the boxes she'd sealed with masking tape, and had the foresight to label clearly with permanent marker, were. She'd learned the hard way if she were to try and straighten up she'd smack her head on the rafters.

For a moment she toyed with the idea of pulling the boys' two boxes of pre-school memorabilia down. She felt a tug of longing for those precious years. It had been a time of certainty when she'd understood exactly who she needed to be because the boys had made it clear to her. A mother. They were growing up too fast, she thought, recalling Haydn's flaming face when his voice had cracked alarmingly as he answered Sophie's question about a band they were both into while they waited for her to finish work on Thursday afternoon. She'd felt for him. It was such an awkward age and once they were through this boy-man phase she suspected it wouldn't be long before girls started making an appearance on the doorstep.

How tempting it would be to sit on the floor of the living room, if she could find space amongst Abi's crap, and rifle through their old paintings, to smile at a favourite toy like an old friend. She could pretend the bombshell her mother had dropped was a bad dream. She'd like nothing better than to marvel over how small her boys' shoes had been or the size of a teeny-tiny hand-knitted jumper she'd once pulled over their heads and gently pushed their pudgy arms through the sleeves of. The evening would disappear if she went down that rabbit hole and the time to do this was now while the boys were away for the night. 'Stick to the task at hand, Veronica,' she told herself.

'Did you say something?'

'No.'

She shone the torch, scanning the handwritten labels until she located what she was looking for and, pushing the first of the three boxes along in front of her, she crawled back to where the light was shining up through the trapdoor.

'Abi, I'll pass it down to you.'

There was no answer.

'Abi!' Veronica bellowed, sticking her head through the hole trying to see where she'd gotten to.

Her sister reappeared a minute later.

'Where did you disappear to?'

'More wine, to deal with the shock. I'm here now.'

'Right, well can you take this? There's three of them. It shouldn't be too heavy.' She passed the box down awkwardly seeing Abi stagger under its weight.

'It is so bloody well heavy.' She put it down and pushed it down the hall with her legs into the living room before coming back to repeat the process.

They managed to get the three boxes onto the ground without mishap and Veronica climbed down dusting herself off at the bottom. 'There's no point putting it away, I'll only have to get it down again in an hour or so,' she said to herself, eyeing the ladder before following Abi through to the front room. Scruffy-bum was poised precariously on the back of the sofa, leg cocked as he industriously licked his bum. Abi had drawn the curtains and kicked the worst of her mess over into the corner of the room by the television, clearing some space for them to sit down and begin going through whatever flotsam and jetsam their mother had been unable to part with.

'I'll fetch some scissors, and then give you a hand moving the coffee table out the way,' Veronica said, disappearing into the kitchen and returning a moment later with the weapon needed to slide down the join in the masking tape. She and Abi took an end each of the coffee table, careful not to tilt it and send the various cups and bowls Abi had neglected to return to the kitchen over as they lifted it, putting it down so it rested flat against the sofa.

'Right then,' Veronica said, rubbing her hands together. 'We are good to go. 'I'll start on this one, you can start on that.'

She was sitting cross legged on the floor with a pile of birthday and Christmas cards she'd glanced through next to her along with old address books and ring-binder folders filled with household bills and receipts. She didn't know why her mum had thought she needed to keep hold of these. She'd turf them, she decided, given the five or was it seven years you were supposed to hang on to this sort of thing was just about up. She'd no need of any of it now.

She'd drawn the short straw, she thought, seeing Abi sipping her third wine in between smiling over old photographs in the album she was pouring over. Sauvignon Blanc and denial were obviously her sister's coping mechanisms. The next item in her box was a green, hardback notebook and picking it up she already knew what she'd find inside. She was right, she saw, opening it to a random page and eyeing the neat columns handwritten in biro. It was her mother's weekly household budget. Flicking through it she saw page after page of carefully itemised spending. She could remember her mum sitting at their kitchen table working out what they had and where it had to go, writing in this very book or at least one just like it. Her eyes rested on an entry for new pointe shoes for Veronica and she bit her bottom lip.

She'd never gone without, not once, but she was certain her mother had to make sure her girls had everything they needed.

'I had such a fat face. Look.' Abi turned the red, leather-bound album to show the Polaroid shot of herself striking a ballet pose for the camera.

Veronica managed a grin at her sister as a three or four year old. 'Chipmunk cheeks.'

'I wanted to be just like you,' Abi said. 'But I knew I was never going to be as good as you were at dancing so I didn't even try.'

'Did you?' Veronica put the notebook down. She was surprised; she'd never had a sense of adoration from her sister. Yes, she'd follow her about but all her friends who had younger sisters would also bemoan the fact they never got any peace from them.

'I idolised you. All my friends thought you were amazing when I was growing up. This gorgeous ballerina who was going to be famous. I was super proud of you.'

'You never said. I always thought you thought I was pain.'

'Well that too, obviously.'

They looked at one another and this time Veronica laughed.

'You took so much of Mum's attention. I was always relegated to the background and I resented it. Not so much you but the ballet.'

'At least Mum left you alone to get on with things. I could feel the weight of her expectations on my shoulders right from that very first class.'

'But you loved it and you were a natural. She could see that, she just wanted you to fulfil your potential.'

'I think she wanted me to fulfil *her* potential too. You've heard her sing; she should have been on the stage. And I did love it but I probably would've loved it more if I didn't have to keep proving myself.' She remembered the way Abi had seemed to have their parents wrapped around her finger when she was small. 'I was always envious of you.'

'Why? What was there to be jealous of?'

'All you had to do was flash those baby blues of yours and you'd get your own way with Mum and Dad.'

'Well, it didn't do me any good where Dad was concerned, did it? Because he left anyway.'

'I suppose. Abi, I'm sorry I wasn't a better big sister back then.'

'We were both dealing with the Dad shit in our own way.'

'AD,' Veronica said softly.

'What?'

'It's how I always think of the time after he left, After Dad.'

Abi nodded.

They lapsed into silence as they went back to their respective tasks. Veronica pulled out a wodge of letters secured by a rubber band, feeling a jolt of excitement. There was bound to be something in this lot, she thought, taking off the band and sorting through them. She was right, she thought, holding the envelope addressed to her mother in her father's handwriting up to the light. 'Oh my God, Abi. Jackpot! Look,' she waved the envelope at her. 'It's from Dad.' She turned it over in her hands and saw the address. 'He sent it from an address in Bridgwater.'

'Where's that?' Abi's skin was a mottled pink and white.

'Somerset.' Veronica had been there once with Jason. They'd stayed in a B&B and it made her shiver to think she'd been so close to her dad as they'd bumped the twins along in the pushchair wandering the historic old town's streets. What would she have done if she'd seen him?

Abi shuffled over and Veronica pulled the notepaper from the envelope angling it so as they could both read it.

The letter was short and to the point with no opening pleasantries.

Margo, I don't know how you found me but you're not to contact me again. I've drawn a line under that part of my life and moved on. I asked you for a divorce so I could marry Karen but you wouldn't agree to it and in the end I decided to take matters into my own hands. She knows nothing about you or the girls and I want it to stay that way. Me and her, we've a baby on the way and I'm stretched tight so if it's money you're looking for, there is none. I've made a fresh start and that's what you and the girls need to do too. It would be better all round for all of us if you pretended I was dead.

Phil

IT WAS A COLD LETTER and Veronica shivered as she dropped it watching it flutter to the floor. Abi gave a choked sob and her own throat tightened as her eyes began to sting as the memory of the father she'd always held in a haloed light began to fade.

'How could he just wipe us away?' Abi asked.

Veronica pulled her close and rested her chin on her sister's soft hair. 'Who knows, Abi. Maybe he had a breakdown. They weren't happy for a long time, him and Mum but I do know we've cried enough tears over him.' Even as she said it her own cheeks were wet. She hugged Abi tight just as she had when their mother had given them the news their dad, was dead. Now, she wished he could have stayed that way.

'What about Mum? Does this change things with Mum?'

'Only if we let it.'

'She did it for us didn't she? She thought it would be easier for us to accept he was dead than to know he'd decided to scratch us from his life.'

'Yes, I suppose she did, and what a thing to have carried around with her for so many years.'

'What do we do, Ronnie?'

'We drive to Bridgwater tomorrow and see him for ourselves.'

'Confront him you mean?'

'I don't know.'

'Poor Mum.' Abi sniffed.

'Poor all of us,' Veronica added, thinking how so many paths taken led back to their father.

Chapter 38
Isabel

ISABEL PUSHED OPEN the doors to The Rum Den stepping inside the pub. The darkened interior and low beamed ceiling gave the feeling of lives and stories having played out over a pint or two through the years. The pub was heaving tonight with Ryde's vying pub quiz teams shouting their orders over the bar. Brenda was stalking about behind the counter in her element and Tilly, poor girl, looked flustered as she pulled pint after pint. Isabel remembered what it was like and although she missed the banter with the punters it was nice to be on the other side of the bar.

She hung back, waiting for the crowd to thin, and spied the quizmaster sitting on his stool in the corner of the pub. He was flicking through a sheaf of papers and she realised he was new. Although, as she took in his pork pie hat and dicky-bow tie, she surmised he was clearly as eccentric as the old one had been. Gerry had been quizmaster when she worked the bar and he'd insisted on donning a top hat which had always made Isabel feel he should be doing magic tricks not asking questions. She wondered if odd hats and wardrobe choices were part of the quizmaster job criteria.

She'd been meaning to call in to say hello to her old boss one evening after work and tonight, with Rhodri heading out for a pottery class at Nico's, was as good a time as any. He was going to meet her here for a drink afterwards. She was pleased he'd gone to his class. He'd been on the fence about going, saying he wasn't in the right mood. She'd talked him into it, telling him it would be a distraction, something to immerse himself in other than worrying over how things were going to work out with Sally where Austin was concerned. Isabel lifted her hand in greeting at the two women pulling the beer pumps and called out a hello to a few of the familiar faces as the regulars moseyed back to their tables with drinks in hand. She found a spare stool and perched on the edge of it.

'Hello.' She greeted the publican and barmaid when the crowd vying for drinks had dispersed. 'Busy night?'

'Hi, Isabel, sure is.' Tilly smiled, her cheeks pink from the last mad ten minutes of service. She only just caught the cloth Brenda tossed at her. 'You'd think they'd been running a marathon, that lot, with the thirst on them, not sat on their arses doing a quiz.'

Isabel laughed.

'Thirsty punters are who pays your wages. Give the bar a wipe, Tilly, luv,' Brenda instructed, turning her attention to Isabel. 'And what can I get you? It's on the 'ouse.' She was dressed in a tight black, low-cut top and black jeans leaving nothing to the imagination. Her feet, Isabel saw as she peered over the bar to check out Brenda's legendary footwear were squeezed into red stilettos.

'Those heels must be killers on your feet, Brenda, and thanks, I'll have one of those lovely local ciders please.'

'I can't be doing with flat soles, Isabel, you know that, they hurt my back and I can hardly see over the bar.'

It was true, Isabel mused, as Brenda went to retrieve a bottle of the locally brewed apple drink from the fridge; Brenda lost a foot when she took her shoes off.

The chilled cider and a glass were put down in front of her and she smiled her thanks.

'What type of animal is Skippy?' The quizmaster boomed into his microphone.

'A kangaroo,' Isabel informed Brenda in a hushed voice before pouring the fizzy golden liquid into her glass. She enjoyed the fruity aroma for a moment and then took a sip, the bubbles popping on her tongue.

The pub was quiet now, apart from the conspiratorial whispers as to what the answer was.

'You should join one of the teams. You're good at trivia. Sandra's Septuagenarians could do with some help, they're a player down tonight.' Brenda pointed a red, bejewelled talon in the direction of a table of women, silver heads bent together.

'No, I go blank when I'm under pressure. Besides, I called in to see how you're getting on.'

'My bunions haven't been too bad this week, since you asked.'

Isabel hadn't asked but since she'd been informed as to the state of the bane of her old boss's life, she replied. 'No thanks to those shoes, Brenda. But I'm glad to hear it. How's Russell?' She'd expected to find Brenda's son, who was a dead ringer for an East End thug but who had a heart of gold, behind the bar helping out.

'He's in London seeing his bruver and dad for a few days. It's giving me a break from picking up after him. E' always was a lazy sod.' The affection in her voice didn't escape Isabel and she laughed as Brenda leaned forward, giving her an eyeful of impressive cleavage as she lowered her voice, 'I'll swing for 'im leaving that loo seat up like he does, one of these days. You just wait and see.'

'It's a man thing, Brenda.'

'Don't I know it. How did it go having Rhodri's young fella to stay? Spit of his dad 'e is. Lovely little chap.'

'Yes, he is, and we got off to a rocky start but then things fell in to place. I miss him already and it's hard for Rhodri not knowing when he'll see him next but he rings him every night after he's had his tea and we both have a quick chat with him about his day.' The first thing he always asked was how his fish were. If anything, Rhodri was more antsy after these phone calls. He'd flick through the television channels or get up to make yet another cup of tea of an evening and he was keeping her awake at night with his tossing and turning. 'He's been to see his lawyer about getting a permanent arrangement in place. It'll be better for everyone, especially Austin, if it's set out clearly what's happening and regular visits with his dad and me has to be a good thing.'

Brenda nodded. 'Kids need routine and to know where they're at. And 'ave you 'eard from Constance?'

Isabel smiled over the rim of her glass. 'I have. She's having such a wonderful time.'

'Glad to 'ear it.'

'So, are you going to tell me what's on your mind now we're all caught up on everybody else?' Brenda scrutinised her beneath two identically pencilled eyebrow arches.

'I don't know what you mean?'

'I can read you like a book, young lady. What's got your knickers all twisted?'

Tilly was busy herself emptying the dishwasher and the quizmaster was asking which two body parts continue to grow throughout your entire life.

'I told you, I'm adopted,' Isabel said, staring into her glass.

'You did.'

'Well, I asked Mum for my birth records a while back and didn't do anything with them, but then after everything that happened with Constance finding Edward and Rhodri meeting Austin, I decided to reach out to my birth mother to see if she'd like to meet me. I wrote her a letter.' There was no point saying she'd written loads of them before finally settling on the one still tucked away in her bag.

Brenda was nodding as she listened. 'Go on.'

'I wrote it weeks ago but I've still not sent it. I'm scared, I suppose. What if she doesn't want to know anything about me? Or, what if she does want to meet and I think she's horrible? And what if—'

'I bet you've been driving your Rhodri mad with your what ifs, Isabel. I've never known anyone like it. What if she's a lovely lady who's been waiting her whole life to hear from you?'

Isabel rustled up a smile because there was no reason for that not to be the case. She'd send it tomorrow, she definitely would she resolved, jumping all over those pesky self-doubts.

'You're right.' She took a swig of her apple fizz.

'I always am.'

Isabel grinned. 'Not when it comes to wearing high stilettos and bunions.'

She chattered amicably and munched her way through a bag of crisps while sipping on her drink for the next half hour or so, occasionally telling Brenda and Tilly the answers to the questions being shot across the pub, then with perfect serendipity, just as she drained her glass, Rhodri appeared.

He exchanged pleasantries with Brenda and ordered another cider for her and a pint before settling himself on the stool next to Isabel.

His hair was starting to look on the shaggy side; she'd remind him to get a trim this week she thought, asking, 'Did you finish your mug?' Brenda slid his pint in front of him. When Rhodri had asked what his next pottery project should be, Isabel had told him to make a mug.

'Yes, I'm firing it next week.' He took a sip of his ale and looked wholeheartedly satisfied by the brown brew. 'That's hit the spot.'

'So, you'll leave my priceless, family heirloom alone when you bring it home?' Isabel took the bottle from Brenda with a smile. She was having him on about the Princess Anne mug she'd commandeered from her mum. She'd moved in to Pier View House as a lodger initially but as Rhodri's partner she'd wanted to put her mark on the place and to have something of her own on display. The problem was she didn't have anything, not with having been backpacking for the last couple of years. She'd travelled light and put extra cash towards moving on not mementos. In the end she'd asked her mum on a visit home if she could have a family heirloom to put on the sideboard. Babs Stark had been aghast, 'You don't mean my Princess Di mug?'

'No, Mum, you can keep Princess Di. I meant something of sentimental value.'

'My Princess Di mug is of great sentimental value,' Babs had sniffed, opening the china cabinet. 'Here, you can have this.' She produced a bowl like mug with Princess Anne's face emblazoned on the side. 'Your Nana Stark bought me this for my fiftieth birthday so it's of great sentimental value.'

Her dad's mum, a hard-faced woman with a helmet of died brown hair and a tendency to shout, given her refusal to wear her hearing aid, had sprung to mind. Isabel didn't know where sentimental value came into it—given her mum's none too fond memories of her late mother-in-law, she was probably glad to be rid of it. Still, it was something from home and she'd taken it to her new home, Pier View House to put in pride of place on the sideboard only Rhodri had decided it was the perfect size for a mug of tea.

'I will,' he said grinning over the top of his glass and Isabel smiled back. This was her Rhodri. She'd missed him since they'd said goodbye to Austin.

'I had a call while I was at Nico's, from Sally.'

The cider suddenly sat heavy and flat in Isabel's stomach. 'What was she wanting?' Her voice was waspish and it didn't escape Rhodri's notice. He straightened on his stool.

'She wants to meet up to see if we could come to a suitable arrangement for Austin's visits between ourselves. She doesn't see the point in me involving my lawyer and wasting my money.'

'Well, no she wouldn't, would she, because it's all about what suits Sally. I don't see why you need to meet up. What's wrong with the telephone for talking?' It slipped out but now she'd said it Isabel needed to get the rest of it off her chest. 'Isn't it better to have the arrangements for Austin laid out clearly so she can't mess you, *us*, around because this is about me too, you know. It seems to me the ball has been entirely in her court from the start.' She banged her glass down, earning her a sidelong glance from Tilly.

'Isabel, stop.' Rhodri put his own glass down and took her hands in his.

She pulled them free. 'No. I'm sorry, Rhodri, but I think she's playing you. She clicks her fingers and you go running and it's not fair on Austin or me.' She felt the tears of frustration and fear she'd kept a lid on since Sally had first come back into their lives threaten to spill over.

'Listen to me, would you?'

She sniffed.

'I told Sally I thought it was better for us to take the legal route. I want to contribute financially for Austin as well and have the visitation agreement set down on paper in a binding document. There won't be any mucking about because she's not going to use Austin as leverage, Isabel. Do you understand?'

'Really?'

He nodded and this time when he went to take her hands she let him. 'I'm sorry. I shut you out and then I expected you to go along with whatever happened next with Austin.'

'I don't want you to be hurt.' Her mother had said the same thing to her regarding her contacting Veronica. 'And I want Austin in our lives. I just don't want Sally coming between us. You loved her enough to marry her once.'

'Once, a long time ago, and I don't feel much of anything where she's concerned now. She's not a threat to us Isabel. I love you and watching you and Austin together made me feel like I had everything in the world except maybe one day another baby.' He leaned over and kissed her firmly on the mouth.

'Oi, we'll have none of that in 'ere, thank you,' Brenda said with a wink as she filled a glass with a shot.

They broke apart grinning. 'I haven't even checked in with you about your letter to Veronica, have you sent it?' He shook his head. 'I'm sorry I've been totally preoccupied with myself.'

'Understandably,' Isabel said. 'And no, it's still in my bag.'

'Send it, Isabel. We'll do it on the way home, aye? You've nothing to be scared of because no matter what, you've got your mum and dad and me and Austin. Anything else is just extra icing on the cake.'

It was true, Isabel thought, and not just them, she had Constance and Brenda, Delwyn and Nico. She had people who loved her in her life, constants who were there for her and nothing was going to change that. She downed her glass and urged Rhodri to do the same. 'Come on, let's post it now and then I think an early night could be in order.'

'Promise me you'll leave your mobile downstairs.'

Isabel giggled. The last time they'd been in the throes of love making her mum had decided to ring, and ring, and ring.

They said goodnight to Brenda and Tilly and Rhodri draped his arm around her shoulder as they wandered around the corner to where the post box was illuminated by the orange misty glow of a street lamp. Isabel opened her bag and pulled the letter out, glancing at the address one last time before she slid it through the slot, hearing it land with a plunk. It was gone. She'd done it, and now she'd have to wait to see what happened next.

Chapter 39
Veronica

VERONICA AND ABI REACHED Bridgwater by late morning. Abi had insisted they make the journey in her Range Rover, adamant her vehicle would make for a far more comfortable road trip than Ronnie's red rust bucket. Veronica hadn't put up any argument; she was right. The drive had taken them three hours in total with two stops en route. The first was a brief visit with Margo. She'd been animated, with the drama of yesterday washed clean from her mind. The second stop had been for coffee and a pastry. Today was very much a chocolate Danish day, or at least it was for Veronica. Abi was doing keto, she'd stated sanctimoniously and couldn't possibly indulge because it would throw her out of ketosis. It sounded like a horrible disease, Veronica had thought, munching into the flaky deliciousness.

They wound their way around the quiet Sunday morning streets of the town's suburbia that held none of the charm of the historic centre Veronica remembered from her previous visit. At last the GPS announced they'd reached their destination, the address their father had scrawled on the back of the envelope.

Abi indicated, and pulled over on the opposite side of the street a few doors up from number eight, their dad's house. A man pottered back and forth with his lawnmower on the grass verge two doors down from where they planned on doing surveillance. Other than that, the neighbourhood was quiet.

'I feel like we're undercover detectives,' Abi said, slouching low in the driving seat. She had a baseball cap on with her blonde hair pulled through the back. She was clad head to toe in black and hadn't heeded Veronica's advice to wear flat shoes behind the wheel insisting she was a far better driver in heels. 'I wish we had binoculars.'

'You could cross the street in three strides, even in those ridiculous sandals, you don't need binoculars and I don't know why you're slouching, there's nobody there,' Veronica pointed out. She was disappointed as she peered past her sister to get a better view of the house—a non-descript bungalow. 'At least it's not a mansion, that would be a bitter pill to swallow.'

Abi agreed with her and then reached for the packet of gum next to the two empty takeaway cups of coffee. She tapped a piece into the palm of her hand popping it into her mouth before offering the pack to Veronica.

'No, thanks. You'll get wind you know. It's a fact. It says so on the pack.'

Abi pulled a face. 'It says excessive consumption. This is only my second piece.' She eyed the crumbs on her sister's lap. 'I told you that Danish would make a mess.'

Veronica opened the door, got out and shook herself off.

'Get back inside, you'll draw attention to us.' Abi hissed.

Veronica clambered back in. 'For a slob you're very finicky about your car,' she said. 'And I think the curtains are twitching at number eleven.'

Abi glanced over to the house they were parked outside. It wasn't dissimilar to the one they were keeping an eye on. The last thing they needed was someone coming out and asking what they were doing.

'I was teasing, relax,' Veronica said, seeing her alarmed expression.

'Dumb thing to say, Ronnie. How can I?'

It was true. It was hard not to be sitting like a pair of coiled springs given what they'd driven here to do. 'Well, let's talk about something else other than Dad.'

'Alright, but how long are we going to sit here? I mean we didn't think things through properly, did we, because we can hardly play knock on the door and runaway,' Abi said recalling the childhood game.

She was right, Veronica thought, absorbing the trivial fact the garden outside their father's house erred toward being unkempt. There were flowers that needed to be deadheaded in order for fresh blooms to be allowed to burst forth. The grass too was a tad too long. They hadn't come to confront him and they certainly hadn't driven down to inform him his garden needed doing. Come to that, neither sister wanted to *actually* speak to him but they both agreed there was a need to see him for themselves. It was time they pushed him off the pedestal they'd had him perched on. They needed to move on where Philip Kelly was concerned.

What if he didn't come out? Or worse, what if he no longer lived there? What then? It would have been a wasted journey and, Veronica admitted silently, she'd be disappointed. She wanted to clear her slate of him the way he had them because he didn't deserve her, definitely not her sons, or Abi in his life. She needed to see him for closure, it was as simple as that and fate couldn't be so unkind for him to have died twice. She crossed her fingers and silently muttered, 'Let him be there.'

'He was a creature of habit from memory, Abi,' she said out loud. 'He always went to the pub around midday on a Sunday.' It was a gamble to think he still did so, given it had been well over thirty years since Veronica had sat with her nose pressed to the glass watching him set off down the road for a Sunday session but they were here now.

Abi pulled her phone from her pocket and began scrolling through her Instagram feed. 'Did I show you the video of me demonstrating how to do a smoky eye with this new spring colours palette I was sent to trial.'

Veronica leaned in for a look. 'Very nice, but shouldn't it be a spring eye. You know, soft springy colours, yellows, greens that sort of thing. I'd have thought smoky was more a winter look.'

Abi gave her a withering look. 'Yellows, greens? I'd look like I had a black eye.'

They sat in silence for a few minutes until Abi spoke up. 'Do you want to know why I took off for London as soon as I was old enough?'

'Because you thought you were Patsy Kensit and you were looking for Liam?'

'Oh shut up, Ronnie I'm being serious.'

'Sorry. Why?'

'Because nothing was the same at home again after you came home from Paris. You were moody and closed off and there was this awful atmosphere of stuff being unsaid. As for Mum, you know what a fighter she'd always been where we were concerned but when you stopped dancing it knocked the stuffing out of her. She didn't see me, Ronnie. I tried so hard to impress her in so many different ways but I couldn't make up for the dreams she'd had for you. I couldn't take it anymore, so I left.'

Veronica remained silent. It was a shock to her to realise how much what had unfolded back then had impacted her sister too. There was guilt milling about in the mix too as she registered the repercussions her actions had clearly had, not just for herself, but her mother and sister too.

'I'm sorry, Abs.'

'If we'd known why you'd come home it might have made a difference.'

So many might haves and what ifs. 'I'd do things differently if I could go back but I can't'

'Do you wonder what she's like?'

'Isabel?'

Abi nodded, turning her gaze to her sister.

'Every single day.'

Abi reached over and put her hand on her sister's arm.

Veronica was no longer paying her any attention though. 'Look, oh my God, Abi, is that him?'

They both gazed over to where an older man was walking down the front path of the bungalow across the street. This wasn't the dad Veronica remembered, the handsome man with the swaggering confidence that she'd watched wither as his and their mother's relationship deteriorated. He'd stopped in her memory in his late twenties and this man she was looking at now was nearing the pension age.

'He's bald.' Abi stated the obvious. 'And he's got a paunch.'

'It's him, though, Abi.'

She nodded, unable to tear her gaze away. 'How do you feel?'

'Honestly?' Veronica asked, watching him.

'Yes.'

'He could be anyone. I don't feel a thing.' It was true. She was looking at a man she didn't know and had never known.

'Me neither.' Abi turned back to her sister, her eyes bloodshot from her outburst moments earlier. 'But I do feel a little shaky.'

'That's probably your ketosis.' A weak joke but it raised a small smile from her little sister. 'Shall we go?' Veronica couldn't see the point in hanging around. They'd done what they came to do. The spectre of the father they'd known had been laid to rest because this man here, walking down the street oblivious to the children he'd left behind watching him was a stranger.

'Yes.'

Abi started the car and as they pulled away from the kerb the man looked towards the vehicle which was too big for the street. The engine was an intrusive noise on a quiet lunchtime he thought, frowning at the two women inside it. For a moment Veronica locked eyes with him; she held her gaze and fancied she saw his eyes widen as they drove away.

The journey home was a silent one and Veronica stared out the window at the unfurling greens and golds, unable to stop the voice whispering inside her head that perhaps Isabel would feel nothing if she were to meet her. The thought of that was terrifying.

Chapter 40
Isabel

ISABEL OPENED HER EYES and patted about the bed. Rhodri's side was empty but still warm which she deduced meant he hadn't been up long. She lay there luxuriating in waking up slowly as she star-fished her legs back and forth a couple of times. It was Sunday, there was nowhere she had to be this morning unlike Rhodri who'd be opening the gallery at ten. She could hear him moving about downstairs and upon detecting the clatter of pots her nose twitched. He was doing a Sunday fry-up! The perfect start to the day. She reached over and grabbed her phone, turning it on to see a text from her mum asking her to ring when she was up and about. It was followed by a GIF of a dog in workout gear, including a pink headband, doing weights. She shook her head and pulled herself up to sitting, hearing Rhodri pounding up the stairs.

'Morning, beautiful.'

'Morning, yourself.'

'Breakfast will be ready in ten minutes.'

She smiled at the sight of him, hair still wet from the shower, clad in jeans and a T-shirt and the frilly, floral pinny her mother had gifted her with in the hopes she might show more interest in the kitchen tied around his waist. 'Looking good.'

He grinned. 'I don't want bacon fat on the jeans.' He leaned in to give her a kiss before heading to the door. 'Ten minutes, alright?'

'Ten minutes.' She nodded picking up her phone again and waving it at him. 'I'll just give Mum a quick call.'

He raised a brow. 'There's no such thing as a quick call where Babs is concerned.'

'There is if it means my bacon's getting cold.' He left her to it and she pushed her mum's number settling back against the pillow as she relished being a lady of leisure.

'Morning, Isabel. Are you up and about?'

'I'm still in bed but Rhodri's cooking me breakfast as we speak.' She was dreading when her mother got the hang of FaceTiming. Nothing would be sacred then.

'He's a keeper that Rhodri and you're not getting any younger you know, Isabel. I was well and truly married by your age. You two want to seal the deal.'

'Right, thanks for the advice, Mum. I shall tell Rhodri you think we need to get married because I'm getting long in the tooth.'

The sarcasm sailed over the top of her mother's head as Isabel had known it would and Babs carried on blithely. 'Well, you're virtually married as it is. What skin off either of your noses is it if you make it legal and make your old mum and dad happy?'

'Mum, enough.'

'I'm just saying, Isabel.'

'What are you and Dad up to today then?' A change of subject was required.

'The day's not off to a good start. Prince Charles peed on the kitchen floor and your dad nearly slipped over in it first thing this morning. He was in his socks and morning glory.'

Isabel refused to let the image of her starkers father, barring a pair of the argyle socks he favoured, doing the splits in the kitchen spoil her appetite. 'I don't need the gory details, Mum, just the basic facts will do, thanks.'

'It was before he'd had his cup of tea and you want to have heard his language, Isabel. I tell you, if his mum was still alive, she'd have had the soap in his mouth faster than you could say Jack Robinson. Luckily, he managed to stay upright thanks to some nifty footwork because the last thing I need, now he's finally coming to salsa classes with me, is a hip injury or the like. The upshot of all this carry-on is Prince Charles is in disgrace in his basket and your dad's sulking in the front room with the weekend papers.'

'Ah well, Mum, things can only get better.' Isabel studied the duvet for a moment, debating whether she should say what was hovering on the tip of her tongue. She decided to just come out with it. 'Mum, I've written to Veronica asking her if she'd like to meet me. I posted it in the week.'

There was nothing but the sound of breathing for a moment or two and Isabel wondered if she'd stuck Prince Charles on but then Babs spoke. 'I'm pleased you've taken that step, Isabel. No matter what happens next me and your dad are here for you.'

'I know that, Mum, thanks. I love you.

'Love you too.'

She hung up and tossing her dressing gown on skipped down the stairs ready to tuck into a fry-up.

ISABEL DECIDED SHE'D make good on her long overdue promise to Bev Barrett and whip up a brew of the healing tea she'd promised her. Rosemary was good for increasing blood circulation and liver function, improving the memory and aiding digestion, and Bev happened to have a bushy plant of the herb growing in a pot on her balcony. Of course, by the time she'd extricated herself from Bev's chatty presence as her daughter manned the shop for her, the morning had gone. She'd come home with a generous cutting of the rosemary which she planned on potting herself and, fetching Molly's journal, she'd looked up the recipe she had in mind.

She could have made a stock standard tea by seeping the sprigs in boiling water but Molly's had the addition of a few secret extra ingredients she'd brought home with her from The Natural Way. It made it that little bit more interesting in Isabel's opinion and hopefully this boost to its anti-inflammatory properties would help Bev's aching joints. She put the mixture in a container and sealing it took it round to her grateful, almost, neighbour. She'd whiled away the middle part of the afternoon in a sunny nook near the window of their living area with a book she'd been meaning to get stuck into for ages.

'What's that smell?' Rhodri asked, appearing at the top of the stairs, the gallery now closed for the day. 'It smells like you've brought the sea and forest in here. I like it.'

'A Molly brew for Bev down the road,' she answered, snapping her book closed. She'd lost track of the time.

Rhodri pointed to where the sun was still streaming in through the window. 'Do you think you could rouse yourself for a stroll out along the pier? I don't want to waste what's left of a day like this inside.'

'Will you buy me an ice cream while we're at it?'

'If you're good.'

'I'm always good.'

They set off ten minutes later, Isabel figuring Rhodri wanted to stretch his legs and feel the sun on his face. They licked their respective cones and weaved their way around the other Sunday afternoon strollers. She realised Rhodri had come to a halt and she turned to see what he was up to. It registered that he was down on one knee with a box in his hand and that a small huddle of curious passers-by were dawdling and gawping waiting to see what was going to happen next.

'Rhodri, what are you doing?' Isabel's face had grown hot and her heart was threatening to jump out of her T-shirt.

'Isabel Stark. This is the very spot where you were standing when I knew I'd fallen in love with you.'

'The mermaid painting.'

He nodded. 'Will you do me the honour of becoming my wife?' He opened the box and she stared, overcome with the swell of emotion rising inside her at the sight of the round aquamarine stone encircled with a beading of diamonds.

'We can always change it if you don't like it. But aquamarine's your birthstone and when I saw it, I thought it looked like you.'

The people around them faded into the background and at the moment it was just Isabel and Rhodri on Ryde Pier.

'I love it, Rhodri! And I would love to be your wife.' A great big lips-stuck-to-gums grin spread across Isabel's face and a cheer went up as Rhodri slid the ring on her finger, his own smile a mirror image of hers. They embraced and rocked back and forth with the excitement of it all and then spent the next five minutes receiving pats on the back of congratulations from complete strangers. When the crowd of well-wishers had moved on and they'd shared a long, lingering kiss, Isabel dug her phone out. It was her turn to send her mum a photo and so she took a selfie of her and Rhodri, him kissing her on the cheek, her holding her hand up so the ring was the star of the show and hit send.

'What do you reckon?' Rhodri asked. 'One minute before she calls?'

'I'll give her thirty seconds.'

It was ten.

Chapter 41
Veronica

THE HOUSE WAS SILENT when Veronica got home from work. She stood in the doorway and called out hello, knowing if the boys were upstairs it was likely they wouldn't hear her anyway, not if they had those expensive ear pod thing-a-me-bobs in. Jason had bought them a pair each in a fit of fatherly guilt over missing something or other he'd promised to be at. She hated the ear pods because she'd stood issuing instructions many a time from the bottom of the stairs which had literally fallen on deaf ears. She had a hard enough time as it was getting them to listen.

Abi wasn't home, she saw, upon checking the front room. Perhaps she was finally meeting up with Brandon. 'Please let them sort things out,' she muttered, shutting the door on the mess. She loved her sister, she really did, she just loved her more when her crap wasn't cluttering her living space. She heard a soft thump and it was followed by a mewl from the top of the stairs. She could always count on Scruffy-bum she thought, cheered by the sight of the tabby padding down the stairs.

'Hello, you. Come and have a cuddle.' She picked him up, snuggling him close enjoying his gratifying purr. 'It's your teatime, isn't it? We better go and see what we can find.' She carried him through to the kitchen which smelt of stale cooking oil. The boys had fried chips for afternoon tea she deduced, opening the back door to let the cool evening air flow through. She noticed the laundry she hadn't had time to put on this morning was still piled in the basket waiting to go into the machine. Would it have been too much to have asked for one of them to put it on before they went out? On a positive note, at least the boys were putting their dirty gear in the basket these days and not stepping out of it and leaving it where it lay on their bedroom floor which was more than could be said for Abi.

'Right, Veronica, first things first, feed the cat, put the washing on, then start dinner. She set about the tasks. She'd had a middling day for a Monday. Suit-man had appeared wanting to buy the matching Tom Ford deodorant to go with his aftershave which had proved a great distraction from revisiting the weekend that had just been for the hundredth time. She'd noticed he was wearing the same linen suit as last time. Unfortunately, he was out of luck with the Beau de Jour deodorant but he'd bought Mr Ford's Neroli Portofino stick version instead.

He'd looked as though there was something he wanted to say but whatever it was he hadn't, taking his Tom Ford bag and leaving without incident. She'd ignored Tyrone who'd wrapped his arms around himself turning his back on her pretending he was kissing someone. Her buoyant mood deflated half an hour after Suit-man's visit to her counter when Heidi pranced past saying, 'Smile, Veronica, you're in sales not the funeral business.' It had cheered her marginally and she had indeed cracked a smile, seeing Tyrone flick his middle finger at her retreating, sanctimonious back.

Her mobile bleeped a message and she turned the washing machine on before checking it. It was a text from Saskia. *I haven't heard from you. What shall I tell Luis? Is it a yes to dinner? Go on live dangerously.*

Veronica frowned at the phone before punching out a reply. *No. I prefer an uneventful life. I mean it.* God, her life had been anything but uneventful of late, she thought, hitting send. There was definitely no room in it for some strange man called Luis even if he was an architectural whatever it was Saskia had said he was. She hit send.

She was about to put dinner on, a frozen lasagne, when she saw the plain white envelope. She didn't know how she could have missed it earlier. It was leaning up against the salt and pepper shakers on the kitchen table and she stared at the handwritten address. It had a proper stamp on it too and hadn't been franked like a bill or put in a prepaid envelope. This was an anomaly in a day and age where the only thing that came through her letterbox of a morning were the electric and telephone bills. Christmas being the exception to the rule because she had a handful of elderly relatives who could always be counted on for a card.

She put the lasagne down on the worktop and picked it up, turning it over to see who'd sent it. The neatly printed name on the back made her heart pound. The blood rushed to her head in a roar and she knew she'd better sit down or risk falling down. She pulled out a seat and sank down on it staring at the name she'd never thought she'd see. Isabel.

Chapter 42
Isabel

THE LETTER HAD ARRIVED with Saturday's post and Rhodri handed it to Isabel as she breezed in from work without ceremony. The gallery had one customer down the far end looking at the postcards and Isabel was grateful as she stared at the unfamiliar handwriting and then back at Rhodri.

'Do you want me to close early and come upstairs with you?'

She loved him for offering and told him so, adding, 'I'd like to read it on my own if you don't mind.' Her stomach was tying itself in anxious knots and she didn't want Rhodri to see her face crumple if it wasn't the news she was hoping for. If Veronica had written to say she didn't think it was a good idea for them to meet and she didn't want her to be part of her life or for Isabel to get to know her sons, she knew she'd be crushed. Holding the envelope in her hand now it was clear to her how badly she wanted to be welcomed by this woman and she wasn't sure how she'd handle rejection.

'Of course I don't mind,' Rhodri said, pulling her to him for a quick hug before she disappeared out the back and up the stairs.

Isabel sat down at the dining table. Her heart was pounding and she took a few calming gulps of air. *Rip it open, Isabel, like you rip a plaster off.* Her hand wouldn't obey her though. She'd always been a coward when it came to plunging in. Instead, she eked things out peeling it open bit by bit before, finally, pulling out the piece of lilac writing paper and unfolding it. She held it to her face and inhaled. She could smell a soft, sweet fragrance and it gave her a modicum of confidence. Her eyes scanned the text and it took her brain a moment to catch up with what she'd read. Veronica wanted to meet her. This time she re-read the letter slowly allowing each word to sink in.

Dear Isabel

I've waited such a long time to hear from you and never gave up hope that one day I would. There're so many things I want to tell you. Firstly, you were such a loved baby but the timing was all wrong. I desperately wanted to keep you but I wasn't with your father and I couldn't do it on my own. Reading that you've had a lovely upbringing by your parents made me very happy. It's the not knowing and the imagining that's the hardest, Isabel. You put my mind at rest.

I've never been to the Isle of Wight but have always wanted to visit there. I'd like more than anything to meet you and for you to meet your brothers, Haydn and Hunter. I hadn't told them about you because I never knew how to and what would I have told them anyway? That I didn't know where you were or what sort of a life you'd had? I decided to bite the bullet and explain to them about you. The funny thing was, when I sat them down and finally opened up they looked at me and said, 'Is that it, Mum? Can we meet her?' I don't know what I'd expected, accusations of how could you, maybe. It was something I'd wondered myself many times. They told me they'd always known about you because they'd found the box where I keep your birth certificate and the most precious item I have, the baby blanket I wrapped you in. For the longest time I used to take that blanket out of the box and hold it to my face hoping to smell your new baby smell. When it faded, I convinced myself it was still there. I should have known the boys would find the box, nothing gets past them.

Haydn and Hunter are from my marriage to Jason Stanley. We separated a few years ago and are on good terms. The boys are a handful, teenagers who grunt, eat and spend far too much time on their phones but they're also funny, loving and kind and they're desperate to meet you.

I grew up here in St Rebus where I still live and have one sister, Abigail, who is five years younger than me. She lives in London, or at least she's supposed to, she's been staying with me since she fell out with her boyfriend. She can't wait to meet you too. My mum, her name's Margo, is in a care home not far from where we live as she has Alzheimer's. She's only in her early sixties, it's very unfair. It's a cruel disease and it's been a painful time for us all watching her illness progress. I'd dearly love for you to meet her.

I work on a perfume counter in St Rebus's only department store, Blakeley's. I like my job because I love perfume but I wish there were more hours in the day sometimes. It was wonderful to read you are on track to a career you're passionate about. When I was younger, I did ballet. I was passionate about that too and I was good at it but it fizzled out. I've wondered whether you inherited my love of it. My mum was musical, she loves classical music and has a voice like an angel, perhaps you take after her?

Giving you up was the hardest thing I've done in my life. You were wanted and you were loved, Isabel, I want you to know that. I also want you to know your letter has helped to heal my heart, which broke the day you were taken away.

I've one hundred and one questions for you as I'm sure you have me. I know you want to know more about your father. It's not something I felt able to write about but I will tell you when we meet. If you'd prefer to meet me on my own initially without the boys I understand. Tell me where and when and I'll be there.

Love your birth mum, Ronnie. xx

'ISABEL, ARE YOU OKAY?' Rhodri called up the stairs.

'Yes.' Her voice was choked.

She heard his tread as he ran upstairs. 'The gallery's empty,' he said, coming up behind her and resting his hands on her shoulders. 'What does it say?'

'She wants to meet.' She held out the letter for him to read.

When he'd finished, he looked misty-eyed himself. 'It's a good letter.'

She nodded.

'Will you phone her?'

'Yes. Now she's written back I don't want to mess about waiting for the post. I'd like to go to her and see where she lives and meet Haydn and Hunter and Abi and their mother. Will you come with me?'

'Of course.'

Isabel leaned her head back against his belly, it was hard but had a hint of softness. 'I love you, Rhodri.'

'I love you too.'

Chapter 43
Veronica

VERONICA HAD TAKEN the morning off work, enlisting Sophie to cover for her. She'd bitten her nails down in the hours since she'd rolled out of bed, a habit she'd broken once out of her teens. What would Isabel think of her? What would she think of the boys—their home? She knew despite Haydn and Hunter playing it cool as they threw down their cereal and toast earlier, they were excited. She eyed their breakfast debris already knowing she wouldn't be shouting for them to come back downstairs and clear up their mess not when any distraction even clearing dishes was a welcome one this morning.

She went through the motions, stifling a yawn as she waited for the kettle to boil. She'd set the alarm an hour earlier so she could get stuck into the dusting and hoovering as well as put the chicken she was slow cooking for dinner à la the BBC Good Food website on. She'd decided to do a smoky flavoured pulled chicken which could be served with the enormous coleslaw she'd picked up from the supermarket along with the fresh rolls, bottles of good wine and craft beers, in case that was Rhodri's preference, on her way home from work last night.

Haydn and Hunter hadn't been impressed when she'd bustled into their rooms at the crack of dawn wielding the vacuum cleaner, but the alternative she'd told them breezily was they do it themselves. That had quietened them down. All that was left for her to do was clean up in here and then the house would be the straightest it had been in a long while. Abi had finally gone back to London last week after Brandon had sent an enormous bouquet of roses in a flamboyant very un-Brandon-like gesture to woo her back. Flamboyant had worked. Her jammy sister had walked straight into a new temp position too. She'd telephoned Veronica, her voice sparkling with the thrill of being off the sofa and back in the honeymoon period with Brandon, as she told her who she was working for. It was an advertising company with an unpronounceable name which didn't smack of smart marketing to Veronica.

She poured boiling water on the teabag wondering what time Abi would arrive. She'd tried to put her off coming for this initial meeting, worrying it would be too much for Isabel but when Veronica had gushed to her sister, 'I'm finally going to meet her. I'm going to get to see how she turned out and the boys will meet their sister.' Abi had snapped straight back.

'*We're* finally going to meet her.'

'Listen, Abi,' Veronica had said. 'You've only just patched things up with Brandon. You're away this weekend and if you come down again next Saturday, there's another day you could have been spending with him. There'll be another time. I think it might be best to keep meeting Isabel for the first time to just me and the boys.'

Abi had tried to frown but the vehemence behind her words conveyed exactly how she was feeling. 'Don't you dare do that, Ronnie. You're not putting me off, so don't bother trying. We're family which means Isabel is part of my family too. She's my niece.'

Veronica had conceded she was right and they'd both frantically trolled through Isabel's social media posts. They weren't up to date but they were something and Veronica had stared at the face that had beamed out of her screen in wonder. She'd been hopping on and off Isabel's Facebook obsessively since calling out to the boys now and again to come take a look. Abi said she looked like her.

She abandoned her tea on the table letting Scruffy-bum, who'd made himself scarce when the vacuum had revved into life, in through the back door. She scooped him up and cuddled him close. He purred happiness and she sat down at the table with him but he'd had enough, springing off her lap in order to find a sunny spot to curl up in. She was betting he'd head for the sofa. He'd been spending his days languishing on that, now Abi was gone, happy to be king of his castle once more. Her phone, beside the fruit bowl began to ring. Speak of the devil.

'Hi, Abi, everything okay?' Veronica asked, adding quickly, 'You're not driving are you?'

'No, I'll leave around eleven, if I'm still allowed to come.'

'What do you mean?' Veronica picked up an apple from the bowl inspecting it.

'I've got a confession to make. Are you sitting down?'

'I am, what is it?' *What had she done now?*

'Gabe's on his way to your place.'

'What did you say?'

'I said—'

'I know what you said but I can't have heard you right, can I?'

'Erm, yes you did. Listen, Ronnie, I wrote to him after you came home from Paris a handful of times and I've always kept tabs on where he is and what he's doing, sent him Christmas card updates as to what we're all up to, that sort of thing.'

'What? But why?' She must be dreaming this conversation she thought.

'Because he was like a brother to me and I missed him. I'd lost Dad and then I felt like I was losing you and Mum too.'

'Jesus, Abi, who made you God!' The room seemed to tilt and she was suddenly very glad she was sitting down. What was it with the women in her family?

'Ronnie, please don't be mad, I just didn't want to lose him too.'

'I don't believe this. I just don't believe it. Abi, how could you?' What gave you the right to step in and tell him that Isabel reached out? I haven't even met her yet and now you're telling me Gabe's on his way here.'

Veronica knew under normal circumstances she'd yell at Abi and tell her she had no right to do what she'd done but the words wouldn't come. Shouting, she knew first hand as the mother of teenagers, got you nowhere. The wheels were in motion and it was dawning on her slowly that just as her choices with how things had played out had been influenced by Mrs Darby-Hazleton so too had Gabe's. In their own ways they'd neither of them had any real say in what happened to Isabel. Why meeting him had to happen now she didn't know. Surely, they could have eked things out. Taken things slowly with each other and Isabel but then again maybe it was better this way. Like a cold pool it could prove easier to jump straight in rather than dip a toe.

She only hoped Isabel could handle meeting her crazy rainbow birth family. It seemed however she wasn't going to get the opportunity to mull over facing the music with Gabe, dealing with her sister, or ponder how Isabel would manage walking into the chaos that was her life because it was too late now, someone was knocking at the door.

Chapter 44
Isabel

RHODRI RECKONED THEY'D arrive in the town of St Rebus by three o'clock at the latest and it had been arranged they'd stay for the afternoon and have dinner at Veronica's house. The address was written on a piece of paper in her bag and she'd checked and rechecked she still had it, not trusting it to her phone alone. She chewed her bottom lip, hardly able to believe it was going to happen, as the patchwork fields outside her window changed from the brilliant yellow of rapeseed to soft green grazing grass.

The traffic was moving at a steady flow which was just as well because if they'd struck gridlock she'd have had a melt-down. Her emotions were veering between nerves, anxiety and excitement and it was making for a volatile mix because in a few hours she would meet the woman who gave birth to her, along with the brothers she'd only recently found out she had not to mention a new aunt called Abi.

Rhodri rested his hand on her leg and reassured her yet again it would all be fine. She did what she'd always done when an impending new situation she'd no prior experience of loomed. She closed her eyes and moved herself forward in time, telling herself, she'd done it, she'd met them all and it had been great. She was still assailed with the nerves which had seen her pass on the breakfast Rhodri had stopped for an hour down the road. He'd booked them into a B&B in the area and they'd head home to the island in the morning.

She'd spoken to her mum last night and told her of today's plans. She didn't want her parents thinking she was keeping secrets from them. Babs had taken it in her stride but Isabel knew by the way she was talking extra fast and in a higher pitch than normal that she was nervous for her. She'd made her promise to ring that evening to tell her how it had gone.

They'd done today's journey in one hit leaving early, with Isabel having made Delwyn promise she and Nico would take a nice long break sometime soon so she wouldn't feel so guilty about her and Rhodri's comings and goings. Delwyn wouldn't take her up on it over the busy summer months, Isabel knew, but she might head away come autumn. She hoped so. Nico had waved her apologies away saying the extra money she was earning from manning the fort at A Leap of Faith was all that was stopping her from becoming a starving artist.

'Forty minutes and we'll be there,' Rhodri said as they drove past a motorway sign. He glanced across at Isabel. 'Breathe, it's going to—'

'If you say, it's going to be fine one more time, I'll, I'll, oh, I can't think straight.' She shook her head.

He grinned. 'Don't worry they're going to love you. How could they not?'

Chapter 45
Veronica

VERONICA COULD SEE the outline of him through the glass panel in the door and her breath caught in her throat. Gabe, here now after all this time. She hung back, trying to compose herself but knew it was a fruitless task and so she opened the door.

There he was and she whirled back in time to the hundreds of times he'd stood on her doorstep waiting for her. 'Gabe—' she couldn't speak. There were no words only tears.

'Don't cry, Ronnie. Please don't cry.' He thrust a bunch of flowers at her. I know they'll give you hay fever but I didn't know what else to bring.'

Insecurity flashed across his face and for a moment he was the old Gabe, despite the years giving his familiar handsome features a more etched appearance.

'They're lovely.' She tried to pull herself together knowing Mrs Doyle next door would be peering through the nets at what was going on. 'Come on inside.'

'Mum, who is it?' Haydn shouted down as she closed the door behind Gabe.

'An old friend of mine. I'll call you when Isabel arrives.'

She cocked her ear for the familiar sounds which meant he was on his way to see for himself but there were none and she was relieved. She needed to be alone with Gabe for a few minutes at least.

'You've twin boys, Abi told me.'

That sister of hers. 'Yes, they keep me on my toes.'

'You've a lovely home,' he said, following her down to the kitchen.

'It's ours. Mine and the boys, Haydn and Hunter, they're fourteen. I'm divorced but Abi probably told you that too,' she said, trying to equate the formality between them with the boy she'd known.

He nodded. 'I was sorry to hear that.'

Veronica shrugged. 'It's life. We've both moved on and we get on. It's important, you know for the boys.'

He nodded. 'Are they like you?'

'A bit.' She managed a small smile. 'They're calmer than I was at their age and they haven't found their 'thing' yet, but they will.'

He was standing awkwardly in the doorway and Veronica busied herself finding a vase and going through the motions of putting the flowers in water. She felt her eyes itch and begin to water and a loud sneeze exploded a moment later.

'Sorry, I should have known better.' He shrugged apologetically.

'They're very pretty but I might put them in the living room. Why don't you sit down?' She gestured to the table before carrying the vase to the living room. She placed it on the coffee table glad of the few seconds reprieve from Gabe. She had no idea how to be around him or where to start.

He was still standing where she'd left him, she saw, as she ventured back to the kitchen. 'I like your hair.'

'I wanted to stand out.'

'You always stood out,' Gabe said softly, and she looked up sharply. 'It's me, Ronnie, Gabe,' he said holding his arms out to her. The years fell away as she moved into them resting her head against the denim of his jacket to breathe in the essence of him like she used to. He smelled the same.

'I'm so sorry.' She was crying again now.

He stroked her hair. 'I'm sorry too. We were kids though, Ronnie.'

She nodded and pulled away to look at him properly. 'Is my mascara down to my chin?' She sniffed. 'I don't want Isabel to take fright when she sees me.' He took her hands and held them up. 'You still wear our ring?'

'It makes me feel close to Isabel and you. Don't you dare cry, Gabe,' she ordered, looking up at him. 'I won't be able to stop if you do.'

He cleared his throat and shut his eyes for a second, opening them to say, 'You're beautiful. You haven't changed.'

'Neither have you.'

They both managed watery grins at the blatant fib.

'What's it like?'

Gabe knew what she meant. 'It's everything we thought it would be, only harder. You never got your chance because of me.'

'No, Gabe, after Isabel I didn't want it anymore. I didn't want to dance at all and because I left the ballet I have my sons and now we're going to meet Isabel.'

'Isabel.' There was a note of amazement in his voice. 'It's such a lovely name.'

'I chose it for her and her parents kept it. She's had a good life she said in her letter.'

'Abi filled me in. She lives on the Isle of Wight with an artist she's engaged to.'

'He runs a gallery there, yes, and she's studying to be a naturopath.'

'We have a daughter,' Gabe said, shaking his hair so his fringe, still a tad too long, fell into his brown eyes.

'We do. And what about you, do you have a partner?'

He hesitated and she reached up and touched his face. 'I want to know if you're happy?'

'It took me a long time to fully accept myself for who I am but yes, I have a partner, Jacques. We live in Paris together and yes, I'm happy. Are you?'

Was she? Right here, right now, smelling him, being held by him and knowing their daughter was going to be here soon, she knew the answer. 'I am.'

'Abi told me about Margo. I was sorry to hear she's unwell.'

'It's a cruel disease but she's in a lovely home and well looked after.' They were platitudes but it was what it was. Veronica couldn't bring herself to ask after his mother.

He read her face just like he used to. 'My mother died a few years ago. We were estranged.'

Veronica nodded, not feeling much of anything at this news. She didn't want to waste her time dwelling on unhappy memories either. There was so much to catch up on she thought, trying to arrange the questions vying for attention into order of importance. 'Where are you staying?'

'I'm at the George in town.'

Veronica had never been inside the old Victorian hotel. It had been refurbished and she'd heard it was nice.

'It's fine. Comfortable and clean. I've booked for three nights and then I have to be back in Paris for a performance. I was hoping we could spend some time together while I'm here.'

'I'd love that.'

I love you, Ronnie. I always have.

'I love you too.' They let go of one another's hands long enough to sit down at the table, only to reach out to one another once more. Veronica found strength in knowing whatever happened next, Gabe would remain a part of her life. She would not lose him twice because he was her soulmate.

Chapter 46
Isabel and Veronica

RHODRI WAS SHAKING hands with Gabe. Abi was milling about, putting holes in the lino with the spiked heels of her boots and Veronica and Isabel were hugging. Tears streamed down Veronica's face. She couldn't believe the moment had come. She was holding the baby girl she'd given birth to twenty-seven years ago in her arms and she'd grown up into a beautiful young woman. Isabel too was sniffing as she clutched hold of this woman who she didn't know but instantly felt she did know. She'd looked into eyes that matched her own when she'd walked into the kitchen. Veronica released her and they grinned at each other before Veronica remembered her unexpected visitor. 'Isabel, this is Gabe. Your birth-father. I would have told you he was coming today but I only found out—'

'An hour ago.' Gabe stepped forward. He had such presence and a lovely smile, Isabel thought, as she was hugged once more. 'And I'm sorry to spring myself on you but I had to come.'

Veronica opened her mouth to explain but Gabe shook his head gently. There'd be time for that later; for now it was all about marvelling over similarities and finding common ground.

Veronica introduced herself to Rhodri whom she liked instantly; he had kind eyes. You could always judge a person's make by their eyes, she thought. He complimented her on the delicious smells coming from the crockpot and, hearing his melodious Welsh accent, she liked him even more.

Abi was watching the scene unfold as she leaned against the kitchen sink with a smile on her face.

There was a commotion on the stairs as the boys decided to make their presence known. They herded themselves into the kitchen and it was standing room only as they eyed Rhodri and Gabe curiously before turning their attention to Isabel.

It was Haydn who spoke up, 'So, I've got a mum with blue hair and a sister with pink hair.'

Everybody laughed.

Chapter 47
Veronica

TWO BOTTLES OF PARIS, check, two bottles of Opium; Veronica was working her way through the order that had not long arrived from Yves Saint Laurent. Two weeks had passed since she'd met Isabel and gotten to know the adult Gabe. She'd been walking around in a bubble of happiness ever since. Gabe had gone back to Paris but would be back to stay with Jacques in a few weeks. They were all going to travel to the Isle of Wight to see where Isabel and Rhodri lived and worked. She'd spoken to her on the telephone too and little by little was getting to know her. Isabel had even given her a remedy to try to clear the eczema she'd noticed on the side of her neck. It had worked a treat. They'd all spent a wonderful evening squeezed into her kitchen, drinking, talking, and laughing; the only person missing was Margo. She'd even turned a blind eye to the beer the boys had helped themselves to.

The next day she and Isabel had arranged to meet and travel to Holly Grange so Isabel could meet Margo. Margo had stared at her and said. 'You're a beautiful dancer.' Isabel and Margo had sat quietly together, with Isabel holding her hand as she talked quietly about what her life had been like. Margo had listened and Veronica liked to think she'd understood. It had given her a sense of peace to watch them together and she hoped that her mother was at peace somewhere too.

'Erm, hello.' A voice intruded on her thoughts.

'Oh, hello.' Veronica jumped and her eyes widened as she looked up from the order she'd been checking off until she'd gotten distracted and begun reliving her time with Isabel, yet again. It was Suit-man! She hadn't seen him approaching. It seemed Tyrone had however, because he was making kissy faces while he paused in his dusting of his already gleaming cosmetic display unit. She tried to ignore him, focusing on her customer as she'd been taught.

Today's suit was a deep green, worn with a white T-shirt underneath it. The fabric an airy cotton, linen and she couldn't see over the counter to check but she was guessing he'd have brown loafers on his feet. He'd be perfectly at home swanning around Milan or New York for the day, she concluded.

'Hi, it's Veronica isn't it?'

She glanced down at her name badge. 'Yes, that's me.' She hadn't thought she'd see him again unless it was in passing on the street. St Rebus was busy these days but it was still a small town. There'd be no reason for him to come to her counter again, not unless he had a new girlfriend he wanted to woo and he couldn't be out of his Beau de Jour already either.

He'd tracked her gaze. 'That's not how I know your name. I'm Luis by the way.'

Why did his name ring a bell? Veronica's smile faltered and if it wasn't because of her name badge, how did he know her name? *Please don't let him be a weirdo. It would be such a waste.*

'Sorry. I'm not coming across very well, am I?' He appeared shy, almost vulnerable as his skin coloured and Veronica relaxed.

'I know Saskia that's how I knew your name.'

'You do?' How could Saskia not have introduced her to him?

'Yes. I've been mates with David, her partner, since uni and I saw you two out together a few weeks ago.'

The wave, when she'd been off to the wine bar with Saskia, it had been meant for Saskia not her.

'I thought about calling into Harry's where you'd gone for a drink but you looked like you were having a great laugh and I didn't want to barge in on your night.'

'You wouldn't have been barging in.'

He smiled then and she saw his shoulders loosen inside his jacket. 'They'd been trying to set me up on a blind date you see. Dave's got it in his head I need to get back out there.' He gestured to the street beyond the department store. 'But it's scary.' His grin softened his words.

Veronica smiled back. 'I know where you're coming from because Saskia's the same. She's always on at me to sign up to this new dating app or trying to set me up on a blind date.' Slight exaggeration there, she'd only tried to do the blind date thing the once. 'I just can't imagine myself meeting someone online and then going for a drink with them. It's, well, I can't wrap my head around it to be honest. Life's too busy and complicated as it is.'

'Millions do.'

'They do, and it can work out great. Look at Saskia and David.'

'Yes. I'm with you, although personally I prefer the old-fashioned way of meeting someone you like and asking them out. That's why I'm here.'

Veronica held her breath; the conversation had taken a turn she had not expected.

'First though, I've a confession to make.'

Veronica reminded herself to breathe.

'When Dave told me Saskia had a friend who he thought I'd get on well with, I was dubious. I got it out of her as to where you worked and well, as you know I came to see you. I've had a few dating disasters and it makes you cagey.' His smile was rueful. 'The thing is, the blind date Saskia was trying to get you on wouldn't have been a blind date for me which gave me an unfair advantage. As it happened it didn't matter anyway because she told me you were adamant it was a no.' He shrugged. 'The Beau de Jour was for me and Mum got treated to a nice bottle of perfume when I came back a second time to see if I could summon the courage to ask you out.'

'The Chloe was for your mum?'

'Yes. She loved it by the way, although she's a bit heavy handed with it to be honest. It enters the room before she does and stays long after she's left.'

Veronica giggled.

'Have I told you I like your hair. It suits you.'

'Thank you.' She flushed, wishing she found compliments easier to accept.

Anyway, that's why I'm here today. I've come to ask you the old-fashioned way, in person, if you'd like to go out for dinner with me? Oh, and I bought you something.' He fumbled around in his jacket pocket and produced a small gift-wrapped box which he placed in front of her. 'Saskia told me you'd like it.'

Saskia had a lot of explaining to do Veronica thought, not quite believing what was unfolding.

She unwrapped the box, vaguely aware Tyrone was now leaning on the glass counter in a manner that would give Heidi conniptions; his chin was cupped in his hands as he observed the drama playing out on the opposite stand.

Veronica gasped as she peeled the pretty gold paper away and a box containing a bottle of Quelques Fleurs by Houbigant was revealed. She held it in her hands reverently. She'd dreamed of this perfume.

Taking it out of the box, Veronica placed the bevelled glass bottle with its clear stopper on the counter. It was elegant, understated, and divine. It was the fragrance Princess Diana had worn on her wedding day and the story went she'd spilled perfume on her dress moments before the ceremony. In an image seen by millions around the world, she'd walked down the aisle holding her dress to conceal the mishap. Then, she remembered herself. 'I can't accept this.' It was the one fragrance Blakeley's didn't stock. This was a fragrance that belonged on the Fifth Avenues of the world. According to its makers, the historic house of Houbigant, around fifteen thousand flowers were curated per ounce, making it the height of luxury. She placed it back in the box and put the lid down.

'Please, I want you to have it. You told me how much you love the stories behind all these.' He made a sweeping gesture of the shelves behind her. 'Well, this one has a helluva story.'

Veronica nodded. 'I know. It's the most renowned classic fragrance of all time. A genuine multi-floral bouquet modernised for the discerning woman,' she recited.

'See, a woman who knows all that deserves to have a bottle of it. Please keep it and don't feel obligated to go out with me. I want you to have it.' He turned then as if to go and Veronica reached out touching his arm.

'Wait, Luis.' There were things in her forty-four and three-quarter years she regretted, choices that had been taken away from her and there were wonderful things that had happened as a result. She was being offered a choice this time that was hers alone to make and she intended to make the right one.

'I'd love to go out for dinner with you and thank you.'

Chapter 48
One Year Later
Isabel and Veronica

THE LIGHT TRULY WAS different in Tuscany, Isabel thought. It was clearer, sharper somehow like a camera that had been bought into focus. She was sitting on the picnic blanket nursing a glass of wine and thinking about popping another of the juicy plump black olives marinating in herb-flavoured olive oil into her mouth. They'd been to a market earlier in the afternoon and put together a picnic of local produce. Rhodri was sitting next to her, his long legs stretched out in front of him. He was munching on crusty bread he'd spread with tapenade. His lap was a mess of crumbs. Her husband. She kept saying it to herself when she wasn't twisting her glistening rings around to admire them that was. She was Mrs Rees-Stark. She'd wanted to keep her surname because there was no one else to carry the Stark family name on. Her mum and dad had been pleased. Her mum especially because she thought it sounded gentrified.

The wedding was wonderful. A simple affair by the Solent, on a day that had been a scorcher, followed by a pub lunch and drinks at The Rum Den where the Angels of Wight had performed. Constance had been escorted onto the sand, in a queen's chair, by Rhodri and her dad, who'd lifted her down to where a seat at the front of the gathering was waiting. She'd sat in between Babs and Rhodri's parents. Her dad had walked her down the flower-strewn sand with Austin bringing up the rear as her pageboy. Rhodri's brother, who was a slightly shorter, louder version of his brother had been his best man.

Veronica, Luis, Gabe and Jacques had all been there and they were now occupying various corners of the picnic mat. Isabel still cringed every time she thought about how macho her dad behaved around Gabe and Jacques.

She'd elbowed him and told him he didn't have to worry about them fancying him, they weren't Bruce Springsteen fans. It had been strange introducing her mum to Veronica but they'd been very grown up about it all. Her mum had told her later, Veronica had said to her, 'You're Isabel's mother but I'm hoping I can be her friend.' Abi and Brandon, who'd looked like they'd stepped off a Rolling Stones cover added a touch of glamour and Isabel would never forget looking at the people she loved most in the world as she and Rhodri parted from their kiss, officially married, to see Margo sitting there. She had a teddy bear she was cradling and she was smiling at her. Isabel smiled back at her and that was the moment she began to sing *Can you Feel the Love Tonight* oblivious to those around her. It had been perfect.

The sun dipped low and a Chinese whisper whipped through the crowd, all eagerly waiting for the man himself to appear on the stage in front of them.

Her brothers, Haydn and Hunter, along with Austin were all at the villa they'd rented. The pool held more appeal than a world-famous opera singer. Abi was looking after them. She was on a break from Brandon who'd been mean apparently. She'd jumped at the chance to be the babysitter if it meant a week under the Tuscan sun. The twins and Austin got on great which was lovely to see. Austin had told her they were almost as cool as his fish.

Isabel's gaze flicked to the urn next to Veronica. Margo. She'd passed away. Her heart had stopped the doctor said. It was Margo's dream to hear *Andréa Bocelli* sing at the Teatro de Silencio, and when Isabel heard this she'd been dumbfounded by the coincidence. So, they'd decided to come. This was Veronica and Abi's goodbye to their mother. It was also Isabel and Rhodri's honeymoon. Unconventional but perfect, she thought.

A roar went up and the lights on the stage angled in, spotlighting the man himself. Isabel held her breath, leaning forward waiting to hear what he would say.

'This is for you, Mum,' Veronica said.

The End

THIS BOOK REALLY IS a story close to my own heart as my family knows dementia and adoption intimately. It isn't our story though it belongs to Veronica, Isabel and Margo. I hope it touched you and made you smile and if it did then I've done my job. I wrote the first draft but the help of Helen Falconer in advising me as to what was working and what wasn't was invaluable. I can't thank her enough. I'd also like to thank Ségolène Breugnot of the Opéra national de Paris for the information she provided me about the Paris ballet. Thanks to Melanie Underwood for her final edit which always gives me the confidence to send my book into the world. Thank you Amanda Horan of Let's Get Booked for her beautiful cover design. Thanks to our dear family friend, Fiona Mills for casting her eyes over the story. Thank you to my husband Paul who picks up the slack so I can write and to our boys. Finally, thank you to each of you who chose to read my story x

If you enjoyed The Dancer then taking the time to say so by leaving a review would be wonderful. A book review is the best present you can give an author.

Also by Michelle

When We Say Goodbye is available from your favourite e-book store by clicking on this link: https://books2read.com/u/47EX5q

'heart-warming...When We Say Goodbye is an ideal novel to curl up with as the autumn evenings draw in.' NetGalley Review

Can you love when all seems lost?

Ellie Perkins life was right on track until her boyfriend Sam suffers a near-fatal car accident, leaving him in a coma and all their future plans in limbo.

Desperately in need of something to fix, Ellie has to find a project and when her grandparents old house is put up for sale, she jumps at the chance. Because, like Ellie, the house is broken. And if she can fix the house, then surely, it's just a matter of time before she and Sam are back on their path to happily-ever-after...

In life, when the worst happens how do you pick up the pieces?

A heart-breaking story of love, loss and the path to forgiveness, perfect for fans of Faith Hogan and Amanda Prowse. To be read with tissues.

Come and Stay at O'Mara's
O'Mara's—The Guesthouse on the Green, Book 1

A JILTED BRIDE TO BE, a woman with a secret past and a pesky red fox...

Take a break you'll never forget at O'Mara's Manor House—the Georgian Guesthouse in the heart of Dublin's Fair City. Its cozy and elegant setting is where you'll fall in love with a cast of characters who'll stay with you long after you finish the book. Oh, and a full Irish breakfast is included.

If Aisling O'Mara hadn't winged her way home to the Emerald Isle to take over the running of the family guesthouse, she'd never have met Finn, and her heart wouldn't have been broken. She's been trying to put her life back together since he left, but now he's back and says he's sorry. Can she trust him again?

Una Brennan's booked into the guesthouse she used to walk past each morning when she was a girl full of hopes and dreams for her happy ever after. She left Dublin more than fifty years ago vowing she'd never set foot in the city again. Why did she leave and what's brought her back?

Meanwhile, the little red fox who raids the bins outside O'Mara's basement kitchen door at night would like to know why the woman in Room 1, cries herself to sleep each night.

Witty, sad, and insightful with a touch of romance. Come and stay at O'Mara's.

https://books2read.com/u/bwq7ny

Printed in Great Britain
by Amazon